WHEN COMES THE SPRING

JANETTE OKE

BETHANY HOUSE PUBLISHERS

MINNEAPOLIS, MINNESOTA 55438

A Division of Bethany Fellowship, Inc.

Published by Bethany House Publishers
A Division of Bethany Fellowship, Inc.
6820 Auto Club Road, Minneapolis, MN 55438

Printed in the United States of America

Library of Congress Cataloging in Publication Data

Oke, Janette, 1935-
    When comes the spring.

    I. Title.
PR9199.3.038W34   1985   813'.54   85-11261
ISBN 0-87123-795-4 (pbk.)
ISBN 0-87123-884-5 (large print edition)

Dedicated with love to
my patient and peace-loving
fourth sister,
Margie L. Wiens,
and to her equally easygoing
husband, Wilf.
I love you both.

JANETTE OKE was born in Champion, Alberta, during the depression years, to a Canadian prairie farmer and his wife. She is a graduate of Mountain View Bible College in Didsbury, Alberta, where she met her husband, Edward. They were married in May of 1957, and went on to pastor churches in Indiana as well as Calgary and Edmonton, Canada.

Janette's husband is professor at Bethel College, Mishawaka, Indiana. As well as maintaining the family home for their four children, three boys and one girl, she is active in the Women's Missionary Society. She also serves as a Sunday school teacher in her local church.

Contents

Synopsis—*When Calls the Heart*

When well-bred, sophisticated Elizabeth Thatcher, a city girl from Toronto, agreed to a term of teaching in the newly formed province of Alberta, it was more to please her mother and to become reacquainted with her half-brother Jonathan than from a sense of adventure on her own part. Elizabeth was more than a bit hesitant to leave the comfort and security of her father's house to mix with the rough and uncultured people of the new frontier.

But upon arrival in the West, Elizabeth soon learned to love her big brother and his wife Mary and their four small children. She also was captivated by families and students of the small, one-room school and by the West itself.

Then into Elizabeth's life came Wynn, the tall, handsome and dedicated member to the Royal North West Mounted Police. Elizabeth, previously determined never to marry a Westerner, began to have second thoughts. Wynn was the one who now resisted. He was adamant in his belief that the rigors of the Mountie's life were too demanding to be shared by a wife, particularly a woman as lovely and cultured as Elizabeth.

Elizabeth, feeling rejected and hurt by Wynn's apparent lack of feeling for her, decided to return to Toronto where she belonged. But Wynn knew he could not let her go—at least not without expressing to her his deep feelings of love and giving her the opportunity to respond. A proposal at the train depot brought Elizabeth into Wynn's arms with her assurance that she was more than willing to face whatever the future held— for them together.

Characters

ELIZABETH THATCHER—young, Eastern schoolteacher who loved her God, her family and her pupils. Pretty, sheltered, yet with a mind of her own, Elizabeth was quick to respond to the promptings of her God and the needs of others.

JONATHAN, MARY, WILLIAM, SARAH, KATHLEEN, BABY ELIZABETH—Elizabeth's Western family. Jonathan was a half-brother from her mother's first marriage. The West had drawn him from Toronto as a young man. There he met and married the red-haired Mary, and their home was blessed with one son and three daughters. Little Kathleen was especially fond of her Aunt Beth.

JULIE—the attractive, rather flighty, but much-loved younger sister of Elizabeth.

MATTHEW—Elizabeth's younger brother. Matthew was the youngest, rather pampered member of the Thatcher family.

Elizabeth's Toronto family also included two older married sisters, Margaret and Ruthie.

WYNN DELANEY—nicknamed "Dee" by Jon's children. Wynn was a dedicated, competent member of the Royal North West Mounted Police. He had already spent some time at a northern Post and knew the difficulties and loneliness that such a Post presented.

Chapter One

Days of Preparation

"Is it done yet?"

It must have been at least the tenth time that my young niece, Kathleen, had asked the question in the last few days.

"No," I answered patiently, "not yet."

She stood silently beside me, her favorite doll dangling lopsidedly from her arms.

"How come it takes so many times to make a wedding dress?" she asked again.

Much time, the schoolteacher in me silently corrected her. Aloud I said without lifting my eyes from the needle moving smoothly in and out of the creamy white satin, "Because a wedding dress must be perfect."

"Per-fect?" queried Kathleen.

"Um-hum. That means 'just right'—for the man I'm going to marry."

"Dee's not gonna wear it." Her voice boded no argument.

I lifted my head and chuckled softly at Kathleen's perplexed look. It sounded as if Wynn's nickname was still firmly in place.

"No, *he* won't wear it. But he is going to see *me* wear it, and I want it to be just right."

Kathleen stood there stubbornly, now a look of frustration on her pixie face.

"He won't care," she said with feeling. "Daddy said that Mama would'a looked beau'ful in an old 'tata sack."

I laughed and drew Kathleen to me. "Maybe you're right," I said, pushing back a soft curl from her forehead. Her eyes told me that something else was troubling her. I decided the dress could wait for a few minutes. Checking to see that I had left the sewing machine foot in proper position and the precious folds of satin material carefully placed on the tissue paper spread beneath them, I rose from the chair. My back ached and my shoulders felt cramped. I needed a break. Perhaps I should have done as Mother had suggested and arranged for Madam Tanier to sew my dress after all. I had wanted to sew my wedding gown myself, but I had had no idea what a big job it was going to be. I took Kathleen's tiny, somewhat sticky, hand in mine and led her to the door.

"Why don't we take a little walk around the garden?" I asked her.

The shine in her eyes was her answer. She wedged her flopping doll under one arm and skipped along beside me.

We walked through the garden together. The early flowers were already in bloom. As I looked at them, I found my mind rushing ahead to the wedding planned for the first part of September, and I wondered what flowers would be available. That was another decision that had to be made. Oh, my! Was there no end to them? It seemed that ever since Wynn had asked me to become his wife, I had been making one decision after the other—some big and some not-so-big. As my thoughts turned to Wynn, I smiled to myself. How fortunate I was to be engaged to marry such a man. He was everything a girl could ever desire—his height, his bearing, his smile, his quiet self-assurance, his caring. And he loved *me*! I would have gone on and on daydreaming but Kathleen interrupted me.

"Mama's gonna make my dress."

I nodded.

"Have you seen the color?"

I nodded again, remembering the hours Mary and I had spent poring over materials and styles, debating and deciding. Both Kathleen and Sarah were to be in my wedding party.

"*It's* gonna be perfect, too," insisted Kathleen.

"Yes," I agreed. "With your mama doing the sewing, it's going to be perfect, too."

"Mama is already done Sarah's dress."

There was silence while I studied the soft shades of a garden rose. *These colors would be just right,* I was thinking, *but will they still be blooming in September? I must ask Mary*. But again Kathleen interrupted my thoughts.

"How come I'm last?"

"Pardon?" My busy mind had not followed Kathleen's line of wondering.

"How come I'm last? Sarah's dress is already made, but Mama has just started mine."

I looked at her anxious face. It was an honest question but, for such a small girl, a troubling one.

"Well," I stammered, reaching for some satisfactory explanation. "Well ... your dress will be ready in no time. Your mama is a very good seamstress and a very efficient one. It doesn't take her long at all to sew a dress—even a fancy dress like she will be making for you. Your dress will be ready long, long before September gets here. In fact, your dress will be ready long before mine will, I'm sure. So yours won't be last ... mine will."

Kathleen's eyes had not left my face as I spoke. She seemed to relax with my final words. Her breath escaped in a soft little sigh.

"You're slow, all right," she agreed solemnly. "I'm glad Mama's fast."

Then her thoughts turned in another direction.

"Why is Mama making the dresses so quick?"

"So soon? Because your mama has so many things that she wants to do, and the dresses are one thing that she can do now."

"What things?"

"Well, she is planning the reception dinner. And she wants lots of time to get ready for Grandma and Grandpa. And she has some redecorating she wants to do. And she plans to give the house a thorough cleaning ..."

I continued thinking of poor Mary and all of the work that my coming wedding was causing her. How I loved her! It wasn't one bit necessary for her to fuss so, but she insisted. After all, it would be the first time her in-laws would be in her home and she, too, wanted everything to be perfect.

"Is Grandma fuzzy?" asked Kathleen seriously.

"Fussy?" I smiled but did not let Kathleen know her word had come out wrong. "Well, yes and no. Grandma likes nice things, and when she is in charge she tries very hard to see that everything is just right. But she does not judge other people by the same rules she uses on herself."

"What's that mean?"

"It means that Grandma loves people as they are. She doesn't ask for everyone to be perfect or to live in perfect houses."

"It's gonna be fun to see Grandma," Kathleen enthused.

My eyes misted and I swallowed the lump in my throat. "Yes, it will," I said softly. "It will be just wonderful."

But it still seemed such a long way off. The folks would not be arriving in Calgary until just before our September tenth wedding, and this was only the middle of July.

"Would you like to swing for a minute?" I asked the now quiet Kathleen, to get my thoughts back to safer ground.

She grinned at me, and I took that for her answer. Kathleen loved the swing.

"The tree swing or the porch swing?" I asked her.

"The porch swing," she quickly decided. "Then you can sit by me."

We settled on the porch swing and set it in motion with the rhythm of our bodies. Kathleen cuddled up closely against me and rearranged the dangling doll into a more baby-like position. I realized then that she had been missing personal attention. With my thoughts all concentrated on the upcoming wedding, and even Mary wildly involved in the preparations, we had both subconsciously pushed the youngsters aside. I determined that in the days ahead I would be more sensitive and considerate. I pulled Kathleen closer to me and held her—such a precious little thing. We swung in silence for many minutes. My mind went to the other children. Were they feeling the strain of the busy household as well?

"Where is Sarah?" I asked Kathleen.

"She went to Molly's house. Molly's mama is letting them make doll dresses out of the scraps from Sarah's new dress."

Good for Molly's mama, I thought, *but no wonder Kathleen has been wandering around feeling left out.*

"And where's William?"

"Daddy took him down to the store. He's gonna help pile things. He even gets money for it." Kathleen squirmed to look at me, her envy showing on her face. "William thinks he's *big,*" she said with some disgust. "He's gonna save the money and buy a gun that shoots little roun' things."

Kathleen curled up her short fingers to demonstrate the little round things. Then she ventured some more information. "An' Baby 'Lisbeth is sleepin'. She sleeps most all the time. An' Mama is sewing. Not for me—for Baby 'Lisbeth. An' Stacy said that the cookie jar is already full, so we can't bake any more cookies."

My arm tightened about her. *Poor little dear,* I thought, but I didn't say it. Instead I said, "How would you like to take the streetcar uptown and stop at the ice cream parlor?"

The shine was back. "Could we?" she cried. "Could we, Aunt Beth?"

"I'll ask your mama."

Kathleen clapped her hands in her excitement and then threw her arms around my neck. I felt the combs holding my hair in place being pushed all askew.

"Let's go check," I said. Kathleen jumped down and quickly ran ahead of me to find Mary.

By the time I had entered Mary's sewing room, Kathleen was already there and had excitedly posed the question. Could she go with Aunt Beth uptown for ice cream? Mary looked at me with a question in her eyes.

"Have you finished your dress?" she asked pointedly.

"No. I have quite a ways to go yet," I answered honestly, "but a rest will do me good." I didn't add that I thought Kathleen needed some special attention, too.

Mary nodded. "A little break would do me good, too," she said, pushing back from the machine. "Come, Kathleen, I will clean you up." Mary rubbed her tired neck and led Kathleen from the room.

I went back to my own room to change my dress and repair my hair. My eyes wandered to the pile of lustrous satin. Part of me ached to be there at the machine. I was so anxious to see the final product of all my labors. But I pushed the dress from my mind. Kathleen was more important. Besides, I had been so busy with details of the wedding that I had felt myself becoming tense and edgy. I had not even been able to relax and enjoy Wynn's company, and he would be coming to call in the evening. An afternoon in the pleasant company of Kathleen might be just the thing to put me in a more relaxed frame of mind. I picked up my small brocaded purse and left the room, shutting my door on all the satin and lace. I took a deep breath and smiled as I went to meet my excited niece.

Chapter Two

Good News and Bad News

Wynn arrived a little earlier than I had expected. I was still in my room making last-minute preparations, so it was Sarah who let him in. All afternoon she had been looking for people who would admire her doll all dressed up in the finery of her new hand-stitched dress, a shimmery pale blue. Wynn gave it a proper inspection and complimented the young seamstress on her fine work. Sarah beamed and deserted Wynn to wait on the steps for the return home of her father. She was most anxious to show him the new dress as well.

Kathleen took over entertaining Wynn, regaling him with all our afternoon adventures. I'm sure Wynn must have been surprised that I had found *time* in my rushed schedule to spend a rather leisurely afternoon with my niece. All he had heard from me recently was about the plans and work and preparation and diligence I was giving to every detail of the coming wedding. Kathleen had succeeded in bringing me up short. *People are more important than fussing over preparations. Why, I haven't even been good company for Wynn,* I realized, looking back in humiliation over some of our last evenings spent together. Well, I would change that. After all, a *marriage* was of far more importance than a *wedding*.

I hummed to myself as I walked slowly to the parlor. I had intended to be in the parlor waiting for Wynn when he arrived, instead of entering rushed and harried after he had already come . . . like I had done on so many previous evenings.

Wynn was listening attentively to the chattering Kathleen, and I couldn't help but smile at the homey picture they made.

"An' after that, we went an' looked in the store windows— just for fun," explained Kathleen. "An' then we took a ride on the streetcar just as far as it would go—just to see where it went—an' then we took it back *all the way home again*!" Kathleen waved her small hand to show Wynn just how far all the way home really was.

Wynn smiled at the little girl. Clearly he was enjoying their conversation.

"Was it fun?" he asked, not because he needed the answer but because he sensed Kathleen needed to be able to express it.

"It was *lots* of fun!" exclaimed Kathleen. "We ate *two* kinds of ice cream. Even Aunt Beth ate two kinds. An' we brought home lemon drops for Sarah and William.—Baby 'Lisbeth might choke on lemon drops," she explained seriously, so Wynn would understand why Baby 'Lisbeth had been left out. "Then we walked all the way up the hill, right from the bottom, 'stead of ridin' the streetcar—'cause Aunt Beth said she needed the ex'cise." She giggled. "To work off the ice cream," she added. "And we sang songs when we walked."

It *had* been a fun day. I realized it even more as I listened to Kathleen share it with Wynn.

"Next time will you take me, too?" Wynn asked seriously and Kathleen nodded, suddenly feeling sorry that Wynn had missed out on so much.

"Maybe we can go again tamora," she said thoughtfully. "I'll go ask Aunt Beth."

Kathleen bounded from the couch to run to my room and then noticed me standing by the door. Wynn's eyes looked up, too. Surprise, then pleasure, showed on his face as he stood to his feet and held out a hand to me. Neither of us spoke, but I could read questions coming my way.

"We had a wonderful day," I confirmed Kathleen's story.

"You *look* like you've had a wonderful day," Wynn said, taking my hand and drawing me closer to him. "Your cheeks are glowing and your eyes are shining—even more beautifully than usual."

I pulled back a little as Wynn tried to draw me close, thinking of the curious eyes of young Kathleen. Wynn must have read my thoughts.

"Kathleen," he said, turning to the wee girl, "why don't you go out on the step and wait with Sarah for your daddy and

William to come home. They'll want to hear all about your big day, too."

Kathleen ran from the room, and Wynn smiled at me and pulled me close. I did not resist him. The strength of his arms about me and his gentle kiss reminded me again of how much I had missed really spending time with him during the previous distracting days. I would be so glad when the long weeks ahead had finally passed by and I would be *Mrs. Wynn Delaney*. Right now it seemed forever. I forgot about all I had to do in the next few weeks and thought instead of this man I loved.

When he stopped kissing me, he whispered against my hair, "I love you, Elizabeth. Have I told you that?"

I looked up at his face. His eyes were teasing, but his voice was serious.

"Not often enough, or recently enough," I teased back.

"I must remedy that," he said. "How about a walk in the moonlight tonight?"

I laughed, thinking of how late the Alberta night would be before the moon was shining.

"Well," I said, "I'd kind of like to hear it before that. You know it doesn't even start to get dark until after ten o'clock. That's an awful long time to wait."

Wynn laughed too. "Let's not wait for the moon then," he agreed. "I'd still like to go for a walk."

"We'll walk," I promised, "and just talk. We have so much to talk about, Wynn."

"More wedding decisions?" He sounded almost apprehensive.

"Not tonight. That can wait. Tonight we will talk—just about us. There is still much I want to know about the man I'm going to marry, you know."

Wynn kissed me again.

The sound of the front door told us that Jonathan had arrived home. He entered the house to encounter his two young daughters talking excitedly. Jonathan tried to listen to them both, attempting to share in the excitement and the enthusiasm they felt. And William had tales of his own he was bursting to tell. He had worked just like a man at his father's business and was making great plans for all the money he was sure to make over the summer.

Mary joined the happy commotion in the hall and was greeted by her husband with a warm hug and a kiss. Jonathan did not agree with the tradition of parents hiding their affection from their children's seeing eyes.

"Who needs to know more than they, that I love you?" he often told Mary; and the children grew up in a household where loving was an accepted and expected part of life.

At the sound of the family moving our way, I drew back reluctantly from Wynn. Perhaps now wasn't quite the time for me to openly show my feeling for Wynn in front of Jonathan's children, though I knew it was not in the least hidden. How could I hide it, feeling as I did?

The pleasant supper hour seemed to pass very quickly. All around the table was shared laughter and chatter. The children were allowed and even encouraged to be a part of it. Baby Elizabeth, who now insisted on feeding herself, was the reason for much of the merriment. Her intentions were good, but not all of the food got to its intended location. She ended up adorned with almost as much as she devoured. The children laughed, and Elizabeth put on even more of a show.

Wynn enthusiastically entered into the gaiety of the evening. Now and then he reached beneath the damask white tablecloth to give my hand a gentle squeeze. From all outward appearances, he was his usual amenable self; but, for some reason, the meal had not progressed very far until I sensed that something about him was different. There seemed to be an underlying tension about him. I looked around the table to see if any of the others had noticed it. Jonathan and Wynn were talking about some of the new businesses that had recently been established in our very young city. They were pleased for the growth and what it meant to the residents of the town. Jonathan seemed to sense no difference in Wynn. My eyes passed on to Mary. Though busy with the struggling Elizabeth who was refusing her proffered help, Mary seemed to be her usual relaxed self. I decided that maybe I had imagined the undercurrent and concentrated on what was being said.

But, no. I was sure it was there. The way Wynn looked at me, the way he pressed my hand at every given opportunity, the way he leaned slightly my way so his arm brushed against my shoulder—all sent unspoken little messages to me. I found myself anxious for the meal to end so I might be alone with this man I was to marry.

I had no appetite for dessert. I begged off with the excuse that I had already eaten two cones of town ice cream with Kathleen. I sat there, impatiently twisting my coffee cup back and forth in my hands as I waited for the rest of the family to finish the meal. I had determined to be completely relaxed tonight—completely relaxed and a pleasant companion for Wynn. I had determined to push aside all of the plans and decisions concerning the coming wedding so I might concentrate only on him—and here I was, tensing up inside again. And for no reason I could explain.

"Why don't we take that walk?" I asked Wynn when the meal was finally over. I was rewarded with a broad smile.

"Why, there is nothing I would rather do, Miss Thatcher," he teased. But I saw a certain seriousness in his eyes, and a funny little chill of fear went tingling through my body.

We left the house and strolled up the familiar street. We had not gone far when I turned impulsively to him and asked, "Would you mind very much if, instead of walking, we went for a drive? I'd love to drive up to where we could see the mountains."

He smiled. "That's a wonderful idea," he agreed. "Perhaps we can stay and watch the sunset."

The sun would not be setting for several hours. I smiled back at Wynn. It sounded good to me—all of that time to sit and talk.

We walked back to the house and were about to enter Wynn's car, when he suggested, "Perhaps you should have a shawl or coat, Elizabeth. It may be cool before we get back. Can I get you one?"

"I left a light coat in the back hall. It will do."

Wynn helped me into the car and went for the coat. I imagined that while inside he also told Jon and Mary of our change of plans. When we were on our way, Wynn chatted easily. We left the city and drove up the familiar hill to the place we could look out at the mountains to the west. Still I could sense something, though I did not question him.

When we reached the summit, we left the car and walked

to a fallen log. It was a perfect spot from which to look out at the mountain grandeur before us. I sighed as I settled myself. In just about seven weeks' time, I would be visiting those mountains—visiting them as Mrs. Wynn Delaney. I wished instead that our wedding would be next week—no, I wished that it were tomorrow!

Wynn sat down beside me and his arm pulled me close. He kissed me and then we fell into silence, both of us gazing out toward the mountains. His arm tightened. He must have been thinking of the coming honeymoon, too, for he broke into my thoughts with a question.

"You aren't going to change your mind, are you, Elizabeth?"

"Me?" I said, astonished.

"Well, I wondered with all the work and preparations if you might decide that it wasn't worth it after all."

I sighed again, but this time for a different reason. "I've been a bore, haven't I? All the talk and all the fretting and all the frustrations showing. I'm afraid I haven't been much fun to be with recently, but I—"

Wynn stopped me with a gentle kiss. "I haven't been very supportive, have I?" he confessed. "The truth is, I would like to be, but I just don't know how. I had no idea that along with a wedding came so much planning and . . . and . . . frustration," he ended weakly. "I'm sometimes afraid it will all be too much for you and for Mary. You both look tired and pale."

"Oh, Wynn," I almost wailed. "It's awfully silly. Today I saw just how silly. I'm going to talk to Mary tomorrow. We can do things much more simply. There is no need to wear oneself out before beginning life together. Why, if I put half as much effort into making a marriage work as I have put into trying to prepare for a wedding—"

I left the sentence dangling. Wynn's arm tightened about me again.

"Is that what is bothering you?" I finally asked.

I felt the tension in Wynn's arm.

"Did I say something was bothering me?" he asked.

"No. You didn't say it," I said slowly, "but I could sense it somehow. I'm not sure just how, but—"

Wynn stood up, drawing me with him. He looked deeply into my eyes.

"I love you, Elizabeth," he said quietly. "I love you so very much. How foolish I was to ever think I could live without you."

He pressed my head against his chest, and I could hear the low, steady beating of his heart.

"There is something, isn't there?" I asked, without looking up, afraid of what I might find in Wynn's eyes.

Wynn took a deep breath and lifted my chin so he might look into my eyes.

"My posting came today."

His posting! My mind raced. It must be a terrible place to make Wynn look so serious. Well, it didn't matter. I could take it. I could take anything as long as we were together.

"It doesn't matter," I said evenly, willing him to believe me. "It doesn't matter, Wynn. Really. I don't mind where we go. I've told you that, and I really mean it. I can do it—really I can."

He pulled me against him again and pressed his lips against my hair.

"Oh, Elizabeth," he said, and his words were a soft moan. "It's not *where,* it's *when,*" he continued.

"When?" I pulled back and searched his face. "When? What do you mean?"

"I'm to be at my new post by the first of August."

My head refused to put everything into focus. I tried hard to get it all to make sense, but for some reason nothing seemed to fit.

"But you can't," I stammered. "Our wedding isn't until September the tenth."

"But I must. When one is sent, one goes."

"But did you tell them?"

"Certainly."

"Can't they change it? I mean—"

"No, Elizabeth, they expect *me* to do the changing."

"But where are you posted? Is it up north as you had hoped?"

"Yes, it's up north."

"But that's such a long way to travel to come back for the wedding. It really doesn't make sense to . . . It would be such a long trip back and forth and would waste so much of your time—"

"Elizabeth," said Wynn gently. "The Police Force does not

allow men to come out of the North until their tour of duty is finished."

"What do you mean?"

"I mean that once I go to my posting, I will be there—probably for three or four years without returning. It depends on—"

But I cut in, my eyes wide and questioning. "What are you saying?"

"I'm saying that there can't be a September wedding."

I felt the strength leave my body. I was glad Wynn was holding me—I'm afraid I could not have stood on my own. For a moment I was dazed, and then my foggy brain began to work again. No September wedding. The Police Force would not let Wynn travel back from the north country once he had set up residence there. Wynn was to be at his posting in only two short weeks. That didn't leave much time.

I willed the strength back into my legs and lifted my head to look at Wynn again. I had never seen his face so full of anguish.

"How long does it take to get there?"

He looked confused at my question, but he answered, "They said to allow six days for travel."

"Six days," I mused. "That leaves us only nine."

Wynn looked puzzled. "Nine?"

"My folks can be here in three or four days," I hurried on. "By then I should have my dress ready. That will make it about right for a Saturday wedding. That leaves us four days in the mountains and one day to pack to get ready to go. Can we do it, Wynn?"

Wynn was dumbstruck.

"Can we do it?" I repeated. "Can we pack in a day?"

"Oh, Elizabeth," Wynn said, crushing me against him. "Would you—would you—?"

I moved back and looked deeply into Wynn's eyes. The tears were burning my own.

"I couldn't let you go without me, Wynn. I couldn't," I stammered. "The wedding might not be just as we planned, but it's the marriage that counts. And we will have our family and friends there. It will still be beautiful."

There were tears in Wynn's eyes as he kissed me. I finally

pulled away and looked out at the mountains. So it wouldn't be seven weeks before I would be visiting there as Mrs. Wynn Delaney. It would be less than a week. It seemed unreal, almost heady. Wynn must have thought so, too. "Bless the Police Force," he murmured in almost a whisper.

"Bless the Police Force?" I repeated, wondering at his sudden change of emotion.

He grinned at me.

"September always seemed such a long, long ways off."

I gave him a playful push, though the color rose in my cheeks. I could feel the glow. "Well, September might have been an awful long ways off," I agreed, "but this Saturday is awfully close. We have so much to do, Wynn, that it's absolutely frightening."

I suddenly realized the full impact of the statement I had just made.

"We'd better get back to Mary. My, she will be just frantic."

"Hold it," said Wynn, not letting me go. "Didn't you promise me this whole evening?"

"But that was before I knew that—"

Wynn stopped me. "Okay," he said, "I won't hold you to your original promise. I will admit that things have changed somewhat in the last five minutes. However, I am going to insist on at least half an hour of your undivided attention. Then we will go to the house and Mary."

I smiled at him and settled back into his arms.

"I think I'd like that," I answered shyly.

Chapter Three

Stepped-Up Plans

The house was full of commotion in the next few days. Mary seemed to be running in every direction at once. Surprisingly, it was I, Elizabeth, who took things rather calmly—I who had always dreamed of the perfect wedding. I who had pictured myself many times coming down the aisle of a large stained-glass cathedral on the arms of my father, the altar banded with delicate bouquets of orange blossoms or gardenias, my exquisite arrangement of orchids trailing from my satin-covered arm. I had envisioned masses of attendants with shimmering gowns designed by the best seamstress in England or Paris. I had listened wistfully to strains from the magnificent pipes of the organ, as the wedding march was played.

And now I was to be married in a very simple, tiny, rough-constructed church. There would be no stained-glass windows to let in the summer light. There would be no magnificent sounds from the throat of a pipe organ. There would be few attendants, and their gowns would be unnoteworthy by the fashion world's standards. And yet it would be sheer heaven, for I would be standing at the altar with the man I loved. That was all that mattered, I suddenly realized. And so it was I who slowed Mary down and calmed her with words of assurance that everything would be just lovely. Everything would be just right.

The telegram was sent home, and Mother and Father and Julie and Matthew would be arriving on Friday's train. My one regret was that I wouldn't have more time to see them before the Saturday wedding. Well, it was far more important that I be ready to go north with Wynn.

I hurriedly finished my wedding dress, and it was ready on time—in fact, I had a whole day to spare; so I turned my attention to other things. I went quickly through my wardrobe, selecting the few things that would be suitable for life in the North. I packed all the clothing I had used in the classroom and then took the streetcar uptown to make some more purchases. Wynn had assumed all the responsibility for purchasing and arranging the household items we would need. I felt a bit of misgiving but realized that Wynn—having lived in the North—would have a much better understanding of what would be needed than I would. Still, I found it difficult not to be involved. My womanly instincts told me that Wynn might be a little short on home comforts and concentrate instead on survival. I tried to push the anxious thoughts from me whenever they invaded my mind and told myself that I could trust Wynn completely.

Thursday fled all too quickly. I lengthened the day by staying up half the night. I continued to sort and pack and try to think ahead of what a woman would need to survive the rigors of the north country for three or four years without a return to civilization. My mind seemed to go blank. How would I know? I had never been farther than a few short miles from the city shops.

Wynn had been every bit as busy as I—sorting, crating, and labeling the items and supplies we would need for our household. It would not be fancy, he kept reminding me; and I kept assuring him that I did not care. I gave him the few items I had purchased last year for my housekeeping chores in the teacherage, hoping they would help curtail our expenses. He seemed pleased with them and told me that with all I had, plus the few essential items which would already be in stock in our northern cabin, there were few things further he would need to add.

I thought much about our home in the wilderness. I did want to make it a home, not just a bare and functional place that Wynn came to at the end of a long, hard day. But how did one go about converting log walls and wooden floors into a cozy homelike place? Curtains and cushions and rugs seemed to be the answer. I had no time for such things now. I had all I could do just to get packed and ready. I decided to purchase some materials for these things to take with me. So, early Friday morning, I boarded the streetcar for uptown. I did not buy thin, flimsy muslins. Instead, I spent my time poring over heavier, more masculine materials. They seemed far more suited to a northern cabin than the lighter, frillier furnishings would be. In the heavier materials I chose bolder, brighter prints than I normally would have purchased and then added a few finer fabrics just in case I should be sewing for a new member of the family before we got back from the North. My cheeks flushed slightly at that thought, and I hoped no one I knew was observing my shopping for pastel flannels. I had almost neglected to even think of such a possibility in my lastest rush, but three or four years was a long time.

With all my purchases weighing me down, I took the streetcar back to Jon's and tried to rearrange my trunks to crowd in the additional items. I had to leave behind a few dresses, but I decided I would do very well without them. The sewing material was much more important. After pushing and straining and shoving things as tightly into place as I could, I did manage to get the lid of the trunk down and latched.

I sat back on the floor, perspiration dampening my forehead. *I must look a mess,* I mused. I could feel my coppery curls beginning to slip from their combs. My face felt flushed and warm, my dress was crumpled, and my hands . . . I looked at my hands. They were trembling—trembling as though I had had an awful fright or just plain overexerted myself. Well, it mattered not. I had done it. I was packed and ready. Ready to go with Wynn to his north country. All that remained to be done were the final preparations for our wedding; then we would be off for a very brief honeymoon. And then, after a hurried day of final preparations, we would be on our way to the little cabin we would call home.

I pushed the hair off my forehead with my shaky hand and, with the help of my nearby bed, pulled myself to a standing position. It was twenty minutes until the noon meal would be served. I still had time for a quick bath and a hair repair job. I mustn't stand around brooding. I must hurry. Friday morning was gone and there was still much to be done for my wedding. And my family would be arriving on the four o'clock train.

"Beth!"

Julie's cry made many heads turn in time to see the pretty,

well-dressed Easterner drop whatever was in her arms and rush headlong for me.

I wanted to cry her name and run just as headlong to her, but I checked myself. I did run to meet her though, and the two of us fell into each other's arms. I had not known until that very minute just how intensely I had missed her. We both wept as we held one another. It was several minutes before we could speak.

"Let me look at you," Julie said, pushing herself back from me.

I just wanted to cling to her. I knew how short our time together would be.

She had changed. She was still just as attractive. She was still just as bubbly. But there was a certain maturity about her. How I loved her! I had missed her more than I could describe.

She threw her arms wildly about me again, dislodging my hat. "Oh, I've missed you so!" she cried. "How could you, Beth? How could you come out here and decide to marry some man who will take you off from me forever?" But there was teasing in Julie's voice.

"You just wait until you *see* the man," I teased back.

"Ah," said Julie, pushing back again and reaching up one hand to help my wayward hat. It didn't seem any more secure after Julie was done with it. "Ah," she said again. "Beth, the practical one, has met her match."

We laughed together, and then I was claimed by other arms. Mother arrived not in a whirlwind as had Julie but in her usual, quiet, dignified way.

"Elizabeth," she said very softly. "How are you, dear?"

My tears came again, rushing down my cheeks and threatening to soak everyone near me. Mother was weeping, too, but softly—like gently falling rain, not in wild torrents.

We held each other close for a long time. "You look beautiful, dear," she whispered in my ear. "Methinks that love becomes you."

"Oh, Mother!" I exclaimed, "just wait until you meet him. I can hardly wait—"

"Nor can I, dear." Wynn, on duty till 5:30, could not be with us to meet the train.

Jon claimed Mother then. It was touching to see mother and son greet one another after the many years they had been separated. After Jon had held her and allowed her to again regain her composure, he proudly introduced his Mary. The two of them seemed to fall in love immediately. The children crowded around. I could hear them as they took their turns being hugged by their grandma and Aunt Julie. But I was busy getting some hugs of my own. Father held me. I had often been held in my father's arms, but this time it was different. I think we both sensed it. For this time, I was no longer his little girl. I was now about to leave his care and be turned over to the arms of another man. He brushed a kiss against my hair just above my ear and whispered to me. "I'm happy for you, Elizabeth. Happy— and sad—all at one time. Can you understand that?"

I nodded my head against his shoulder. Yes, I understood, for that was the way I felt. I hated to leave my family. It would be so wonderful if I could have just packed them all up too— like I had done my simple dresses and the yards of material— and taken them along with me into the northland. But, no. I honestly wouldn't have wanted that. I didn't even need that. Not really. Wynn was all I really needed now. Things had changed. And, though I still loved my family, I was not dependent on them anymore. I was cutting the ties. I was binding myself to another. The solemn words would be spoken on the morrow, but my heart knew it had already made its commitment. Already, in thinking and feeling, I was Wynn's—his alone for all time and eternity. He would be my family, my protector, my spiritual head, my lover, my friend.

"I love you, Daddy," I said softly. "Thank you for everything. Thank you for raising me to be ready for a home of my own. I didn't realize it until—until—now. But you did. You prepared me for this—for Wynn—and I thank you."

Suddenly I felt calm. Very calm and sure of myself. I had been too busy to even think of just what a difference the morrow would make in my life. I had been too in love to even consider that there might be problems to face and adjustments to be made, but I saw it now. The arms of the man who held me made me think clearly of all that was ahead, and I suddenly realized that I was indeed ready for it. This was not just a whim, not just a schoolgirl romance. This was a love. A love deep and lasting, and I would be a wife and a helpmeet for the man I loved. My father had showed me how. Unconsciously, in all of those years of my growing up, he had been showing me the way to a good marriage relationship—with his kindness, consideration, and strong loyalty to those he loved. I held him more tightly. I loved him very much.

When Father released me, I was facing a tall young man with gangly arms and a lopsided grin. At first I just stared at him, unable to believe my eyes. But it was, it really was, my dear Matthew. He wasn't quite sure of himself, nor of just how he should handle all this emotional greeting of his family members; so he stood back a pace somewhat as an onlooker. I blinked away tears and looked at him again. How he had grown in the short year I had been away. I wasn't quite sure how to greet him either.

"Matthew," I said, barely above a whisper. "Matthew, my—you've—you've grown up—so tall."

He took one step toward me as I moved to him, and then I was hugging him just as I had done so often when he was a little boy. His arms tightened around me, holding me tightly.

"Oh, Matt, I can't believe it! You're taller than Father." I tried not to weep, but it was impossible to stop all the tears from falling.

Matthew swallowed hard. He was almost a man, and weeping was not to be considered. Instead, he rather awkwardly patted my back, much as one would greet an old school chum. Jonathan was there then. It was the first time my younger brother had met my older brother, and they sized each other up man to man. They must have liked what they saw; for, moving almost as one, they changed from the handshake to a warm embrace. I could see Matthew's eyes, for he was facing me. They shone with admiration. I knew then that this trip west was going to have a lifelong effect on young Matt.

We finally collected ourselves and all of our belongings, piling into the two cars waiting for us. Jonathan had engaged the services of a friend to help transport us all back to the house. Wynn was invited to join the family for supper. I could hardly wait to show him off to my family and to introduce my family to him. I was so proud of them all. I loved them all so very much!

It was a noisy group that arrived at Jonathan's. We had so much catching up to do. And then there were the children. Each one of them was in a terrible hurry to make up for lost time and get to know their grandma and grandfather and this new aunt and uncle as quickly as possible. As usual, we all seemed to talk at once.

Jon and Mary showed each of the family members to their respective rooms, Mary apologizing that the intended cleaning and redecorating had not been done because of the earlier wedding date. Mother declared that everything was just lovely as it was; and I think Mary felt that Mother meant every word of it.

Julie, as exuberant as ever, exclaimed over everything. She and Baby Elizabeth, who was now taking a few shaky steps on her own, seemed to be kindred spirits. The other children all loved Julie immediately, too, but I noticed that Kathleen still clung to me.

Matthew soon found an admirer in the young William. He looked up to Matthew with the same devotion showing in his eyes that Matthew had for Jonathan.

Julie was going to share my room with me, so with both of us loaded down with her suitcases and hat boxes, we climbed the stairs.

"Oh, that old train," lamented Julie. "It was so stuffy and so warm! And there was this fat little man with foul cigars who sat right in front of me. And there was this party of four who sat down the aisle and kept talking and laughing in such a crude manner that—"

Julie would have gone on, but I stopped her with a laugh. She looked at me, bewildered, but I reached over and gave her another hug.

"You've changed," I told her. "A few years ago, you would have been seeing each one of those men as a possible suitor."

Julie's eyes twinkled. "Oh, I did that too," she admitted. "The only difference is that I'm a bit more selective now. There were some very fine-looking specimens on that train. I just haven't gotten to that yet."

"Oh, Julie. You little goose," I teased.

"I still can't believe it. My big, cautious sister marrying a frontiersman!"

"He's not a frontiersman. He's a Royal North West Mounted Policeman," I corrected her.

She shrugged and threw her hat on my bed. A few years back, I would have reminded her that was not where it was to go. Instead, I picked it up myself and laid it carefully on the closet shelf.

"You wait until you see him," I reminded Julie. "You'll be jealous of me."

Julie laughed. "Well, I sort of figured that where there is one good catch, there should be more of the same. Right, Beth? How about introducing me to a few of Wynn's friends on the Police Force? There are other unmarried ones, I expect."

"Certainly. A number of them. But don't expect to find another one like Wynn."

"He's that special, is he?" Julie's eyes shone. "Perhaps, Elizabeth Marie Thatcher, you're a wee bit prejudiced."

"We'll see," I told her, willing away the minutes until Wynn would arrive and Julie could see for herself.

"I must go help Mary," I finally told Julie, reluctant to leave her even for a minute. "You make yourself at home. The bath is just down the hall and the laundry room is down the steps to the right if you need to press anything."

It is so good to have them all here, my heart sang as I went down the stairs. *I just wish I had more time to visit with them.* But tomorrow was our wedding day, and after that Wynn and I would be leaving. And yet I did not wish, for one moment, that I could push my wedding into the future—not even for the chance to visit with my family. I started to hum as I entered the kitchen. The tune sounded something like "Here Comes the Bride."

Chapter Four

Preparing

"Is everything ready?" Wynn asked as we took a little walk alone later that night. We needed this solitude. Inside, the house was still buzzing. My family had taken an immediate liking to the man I was to marry, and it seemed to me that each one of them enjoyed monopolizing his time. Julie especially was awestruck. I could see it in her eyes. It was difficult for her to believe that her big sister, who had so many times expressed her disgust with the male side of the species, was so fortunate to be blessed with a union to one as marvelous as this.

How did you do it, Beth? her expression seemed to ask across the room. *Where did you ever find him?*

To which my eyes silently answered, *I told you so.*

But now Wynn and I were finally alone, and things were quiet enough so we could actually have a decent conversation.

I was momentarily checked by Wynn's question. Not sure that it had registered properly, I repeated it. "Is everything ready? I—I honestly don't know. My thoughts are all in a whirl. But does it matter? I mean, does it *really* matter? You have the license and the ring; I have my dress; the family is here. We're ready enough to go ahead with the wedding. So what if some of the details—"

Wynn laughed and reached for me. "You are unbelievable, Elizabeth," he said. "Who would ever have expected my stylish Eastern miss to be making such statements!"

He kissed me. It was still light and we were walking on a Calgary sidewalk with many homes nearby. Someone was bound to see us. His "stylish Eastern miss" pushed back from him without really wanting to.

Wynn laughed again. "I'm sorry, Elizabeth," he said. "I just couldn't resist. But I'll be good, I promise. Until tomorrow." His eyes twinkled.

I flushed slightly and resumed walking.

"Your family is wonderful," Wynn said, suddenly changing the subject and our moods.

"And they all love you!" I exclaimed. "I knew they would. Oh, Wynn, I'm so happy."

Wynn reached for my hand and squeezed it. I did not try to withdraw it. Let the neighbors watch and frown if they cared. This was the eve of my wedding day, to the man I loved.

"Are *you* all ready?" I asked.

"Everything's all set and crated. I had an awful time finding enough of the medical supplies I need. Had to have some sent down from Edmonton, but I finally got it all together."

"Medical supplies?" I queried, surprised.

"We need to take everything, Elizabeth," he reminded me. "Not just for ourselves but for the whole settlement."

I had forgotten Wynn had such a big task. "They have a Hudson's Bay Post there," he went on, "and shipments of supplies coming in. But one never counts on them for such important things as medicine. Blankets, flour, salt, traps—now, those things we will be able to get there with no problem."

Traps. I thought of this strange world to which I was going. It fascinated me. There was so much to learn. I was eager to get there, to get involved in Wynn's life.

"I'm all packed, too," I proudly informed him. "I got everything shoved into the one trunk. Mind you, it took some doing! I had to leave behind those books I had wanted, and that one hat I was going to take, and two pairs of shoes and two dresses, but I got all the rest in. I won't really need all those things anyway."

"You should have some of your books, Elizabeth. They might be a—"

But I cut in, "Oh, I did take a few of my favorites. The ones I left were mostly those I thought I might use if the Indian children would like to have a school."

"You still haven't given up on that idea, have you?"

"Well—" I hesitated. "No."

He pressed my hand again. "I'm glad," he said. "It would be

wonderful if you could teach some of them to read." I smiled, appreciative of Wynn's understanding and encouragement.

"I think I might be able to find some little corner to stick more of your books in if you'd like, Elizabeth."

I wanted to throw my arms about his neck and hug him, but we were still on the Calgary streets and it was still daylight; instead, I squeezed his hand and gave him another smile. "Oh, thank you. I would so much like to take them. There really aren't very many and they don't make a very big stack, but I just couldn't get one more thing into my trunk."

We walked on, talking of our new life together and many other things. There was something very special about this night before we would become husband and wife. We hated to see it end.

When we did return to the house, the western sun had just dipped behind the distant hills. A soft light glowed from each of the windows along the lazy sidewalk. The air was becoming cooler but was still pleasant. Wynn slowed his steps as we went up the walk.

"I don't think I will come in, Elizabeth. You need this last evening with your family. I'm going to have you for the rest of our lives."

Wynn stepped from the walk to the warm shadows of the big elm tree. I knew I would not protest this time when he took me in his arms.

"I won't see you until tomorrow at the church," he whispered. "Now don't you go and change your mind."

"There's not a chance," I assured him, my arms locked tightly about his neck.

"I still can't believe it—tomorrow! And tomorrow is finally almost here. You'll never know what a fright it gave me when I got that early posting."

"Fright?"

"I thought I would have to leave you behind. I knew it would be unfair to ask you to wait for three or four or even five years. I was almost beside myself. I thought of quitting the Force, but I didn't have the money to start out some place else."

"Oh, Wynn."

"I never dreamed you would ever be able, and willing, to

rush into a wedding like this. I hope you never feel that you've been 'cheated,' Elizabeth."

"Cheated?"

"Cheated out of the kind of wedding you've always dreamed of."

I laughed. "The fact is, Wynn," I said, "I spent very little time dreaming about weddings until I met you. *Then* I dreamed—I dreamed a lot. But the wedding wouldn't be much without you there by my side, now would it? So, if there's a choice between the trimmings or you—then it's easy to leave out the trimmings."

Wynn kissed me again.

"I must go," he said after several moments. "My bride must be fresh and glowing on her wedding day; and if I don't let you get your beauty sleep, it will be my fault if you aren't."

He saw me to the door and left. I went in to join the family. Father and Mother were ready to retire for the night. It had been a long, hard day for them. At Father's suggestion, we gathered in the living room for a time of Scripture reading and prayer. Tears squeezed out from under our eyelids as we prayed together. Even Matthew, somewhat shyly, prayed aloud. I was touched at his earnest petition that God would bless his big sister Beth and her Wynn as they started out life together. It was a time I shall always remember. Never had I felt closer to my family than when we sat, hands intertwined, praying together as our tears flowed unheeded.

I did not really get the rest Wynn had suggested, for Julie and I could not refrain from catching up on a whole year in the next few short hours. We talked on and on. Each time the downstairs cuckoo sounded out the hour, I would determine that I must stop talking and get some sleep; but each time one or the other of us would think of something we just had to share or had to ask the other.

Julie insisted on knowing all about Wynn—where I had met him, how I had won him. She would have loved to hear each detail of our romance; and, if I had been like Julie, I might have wished to share it all. I was not like Julie and therefore kept many of the details to myself. They were treasured things and not to be shared with any other than Wynn himself.

"When did he first tell you he loved you?" asked nosey Julie.

"Hey," I said sleepily, "isn't that a bit personal?"

"Oh, come on, Beth. It must have taken your breath away. Tell me about it."

"Not a chance," I countered. "It took my breath away, yes. But it is for me alone."

I thought back to the scene at the railway station when I was all set to head back east. That was the first time Wynn had confessed that he loved me. I still tingled as I thought of it.

"How long did it take before he proposed?" Julie persisted.

"Forever," I said with meaning, and Julie laughed.

"Oh, Beth. Get serious."

"I'm serious."

"Did you love him first?"

"I thought I did. I thought so for a long time. Wynn has told me since that he did love me. He was just so sure it wouldn't work that he wouldn't admit he loved me."

" 'Wouldn't work'?"

"Because of his job. He didn't think I was the kind of woman who could endure the North."

"Oh, pshaw!" exploded Julie, then covered her mouth guiltily in case she had disturbed the sleeping household.

"My feelings exactly," I returned in a loud whisper; and we both giggled, bringing the blankets up to our faces to muffle the sound like we used to when we were kids and had been told to go to sleep but talked instead.

"How did you finally convince him?" Julie asked.

"Well, I—I—I'm not sure," I stammered. "I left."

"Left?"

"On the train—for home."

"But you're still here."

"Well, yes. I never really went. But I was going to leave. I was all set to go. I had even shipped my trunks. I was all ready to board the train."

Julie, sensing an exciting romantic adventure, squealed and then jerked up the cover to smother it.

"Look, Julie," I said firmly. "That's all that I'm going to tell you. I was leaving; Wynn came to get me. He asked me to stay;

he asked me to marry him. I stayed. Now, let's talk about something else."

"We really should go to sleep." Julie tried to hide the disappointment in her voice.

"Well, we have only tonight to talk. Or do you want to go to sleep? You must be tired after all that time on the train."

"Oh, no. I'm not tired. Not at all. I want to talk. I haven't even told you yet—"

For several hours, I lay and listened to Julie recount her romances of the last several months. There were thrills and there were heartbreaks. There were fantastic fellows and there were bores. There were ups and there were downs. I wondered whom Julie would have to share all her secrets with once I was gone.

"Is there anyone special?" I finally asked.

Julie thought deeply. "You know, that's a funny thing, Bethie. Even as I lie here and think of them all, not a one of them is really what I want. Isn't that silly?"

"I don't think so."

"Then why do I pay any attention to them?"

"You just haven't found the right one yet," I assured her. I could have also added, *and you just haven't matured enough to know what it is that you do want,* but I didn't.

"You know what I think?" said Julie slowly, deliberately, as though a new and astonishing truth had suddenly been revealed to her. "I think I've been going at this whole thing all wrong. I've been out looking for the fellow—oh, not particularly the right one, just anyone—and I should have been like you and let him come looking for me."

"But Wynn wasn't looking for me, either," I confessed.

"Well, it happened, didn't it? You did get together. Somebody *must* have been looking for *someone!*"

We lay quietly for a few minutes.

"Beth," Julie whispered. "Did you ever pray about the man you were to marry?"

"Sometimes. I prayed that God would keep me from making a wrong decision."

"And Mother prayed. I know that. She prays all the time. She doesn't say much about it, but I'm always finding her praying. And Father prays. In our family prayer time, he always prays that God will guide each of his children in every decision of life."

"What are you getting at?" I had to ask her.

"Maybe it wasn't you—and maybe it wasn't Wynn. Maybe it was God who saw to it that you got together."

"I've always felt that," I answered simply.

"Well, I've never seen it that way before. Guess I sort of thought if I left it to God, He would pick out some sour-faced, serious older man with a kind, fatherly attitude—and poor looks. I'm not sure I was willing to trust Him to choose my future husband."

I laughed in spite of myself, but Julie was very serious.

"No, Beth, I mean it," she continued. "God didn't pick that kind of man for you. Wynn is just—is just—"

She hesitated. I wasn't sure if she couldn't come up with the right word or was afraid I would object to her "swooning" over my husband-to-be.

"Perfect." I finished for her.

"Perfect," she repeated. "Tall, muscular, strong—yet gentle, understanding, and so very *good-looking*!" she finished with an exaggerated sigh.

I laughed again.

"Do you think God could really find me one like that?"

"Oh, Julie. There is only one just like Wynn."

"I s'pose," Julie sighed again. "Well, what about second best?"

"Look, Julie, when God finds you the right one, you won't think he is second best—not to anyone in the world."

"Really? Do you truly think God could direct in *this*, too, Beth?" Julie was serious again.

"Why don't you leave it with Him and see?" I prompted her.

"Why is it so much easier to trust God for some things than for others?" she wondered.

"I really don't know. We should be wise enough to know we can trust Him with everything, but it seems as if He is forever needing to remind us—one thing at a time. Maybe it's because we just hang onto some things too tightly, wanting our own way too much."

"It's hard to let go of some things."

"I know."

"I wasn't going to tell you this, Beth; but, after you left home, I cried. I cried every night for two weeks, and then I finally realized I had to let go. I prayed about it—and really meant what I prayed—and God took away the sorrow from my heart and gave me a new love and respect for my older sister. I can be happy with you now, Beth, even though it means I really am going to lose you."

I reached out a hand in the darkness and placed it on Julie's cheek. It was damp with tears, but her voice did not break.

"I missed you, too," I said honestly. "I missed you, too; and, Julie, my deepest desire for you is that someday God truly might bring someone into your life—oh, not another Wynn, but someone you can love just as much, be just as proud of. I'm sure that somewhere there is someone—just for you. Be ready for him, Julie. Be ready to be the kind of wife he needs, the kind of woman he can love deeply, can be proud of—not just of her outer beauty but of her inner beauty as well. I love you, Julie."

Chapter Five

The Wedding Day

In spite of the fact I had not slept much the night before, I awoke the next morning with excitement bringing me quickly and easily from my bed. Julie still slept, one hand tucked beneath her pretty face. She looked more like a beautiful child than an attractive young woman, still oblivious to the world and all the duties of this important day.

I tiptoed about as I dressed and left the room. The wedding ceremony had been set for eleven o'clock. Following that would be the reception dinner with family and close friends. Mary, bless her heart, had insisted she would be responsible for that and had engaged some caterers to help her with the preparations and serving.

After the reception, we would open the wedding gifts and spend some time with family and friends before boarding the four o'clock train for Banff.

Our honeymoon would not be nearly as long as we had once planned it. Four days in the beautiful mountains did not seem nearly enough. We would not travel leisurely. We would not be taking a cabin in some remote area where we could hike and climb and just rest and relax in the grandeur of those magnificent mountains. Instead, we would take the train; Wynn had booked a room at the hotel, and from there we would make our little excursions into privacy.

The day we would be returning from Banff would be the day before we headed north, so all of our time then would be taken with last-minute preparations and final packing.

My friends from Pine Springs had been so disappointed we would not have time to visit them before leaving. They had planned a community shower to follow our wedding, if it had occurred in September as originally planned.

"Ve can't let you yust go off—like dat," wailed Anna. "Ve need to gif you our vishes, too!"

"Can't you come to the wedding?" I pleaded over the sputtering lines of the telephone system.

"Ve'll try. Ve'll try so hard. Da little ones vould hurt so to miss," said Anna. "Dey haf talked 'bout not'ing else for veeks."

"Perhaps Phillip would have room to bring you," I suggested. But I was afraid Phillip's car might be full.

"Ve'll see," promised Anna. "Ve'll see."

But I shoved all of that from my mind and tried to concentrate instead on what needed to be done in the few brief hours before my wedding.

Mary, already in the kitchen, motioned me to a chair beside her and nodded her head toward the coffeepot on the back of the stove.

"Pour yourself a cup, Beth, and join me. Always best to organize one's thoughts before plowing on ahead. Saves time that way."

I agreed and went for a cup. The next several minutes were spent "organizing."

Mary held a pencil in her slim fingers and jotted down as we discussed.

"The flowers!" she squealed suddenly. "Beth, did you order the flowers?"

My hand shot to my forehead. I had not. I had thought of it a number of times but never did get it done.

Mary looked nervous. "What ever will we do?" she asked me, not nearly as composed as when we began.

For a moment I was stunned; then suddenly I remembered those beautiful roses growing in Mary's backyard.

"Do you mind sharing your roses?"

"My roses?"

"The ones out back. They are beautiful. I noticed them a few days ago. They would work—"

"But we have no one to arrange them," Mary interrupted me.

"You can arrange them. You do a beautiful job. I'd like two bouquets—one on each side of the altar."

"But your bridal bouquet—"

"I'll carry roses, too."

"But—" Mary was going to protest again.

"I'll just carry a loose bouquet. Just a few long-stemmed flowers. They'll be beautiful."

"They are all thorns," Mary argued.

"We'll cut the thorns off. Matthew or William will be glad to do that."

Mary smiled. Then she nodded her head and took another swallow of coffee.

"So we have the flowers settled. Where do we go from here?"

We went over everything again. My dress was ready. Julie was to stand beside me. Her dress would need pressing after its long train ride, but Julie would take care of that. The dresses were all ready for Sarah and Kathleen. The cake had been done by a lady friend of Mary's. It was simpler than it would have been had she been given more time; but I was finding more and more beauty in simplicity. Phillip, Wynn's brother, was to stand up with Wynn; and Phillip, Jr., was to bear the rings.

"We have no pillow for the rings!" I cried suddenly when we came to that item.

"That's no problem," a soft voice said behind me. "I've been feeling bad that I have had nothing to do with getting ready for my daughter's wedding. Just give me some pretty scraps and I'll have a pillow in no time."

It was Mother. I jumped from my chair to hug her. She held me for a moment.

"Do you have any suitable pieces?" she asked at last.

"I have some nice bits left from my wedding dress."

"That will do just fine. And lace?"

"I've some of that, too, though I'm not sure it's enough."

Mary had been pouring another cup of coffee. She set it on the table and pulled up another chair for Mother.

"I've lots of ribbon and lace," she assured us. "I sew most of the girls' things, and they always insist upon 'fancies' on all of their dresses."

We drank our coffee and continued to cover all the details of the coming wedding. Here and there we had to improvise and make other arrangements. For some reason, it did not panic me. The "organized Elizabeth" of old would have been horrified to do up a wedding so—so *haphazardly*. Instead, I went through the activities of the morning in a comfortable daze. In just a few short hours, all the fussing would be behind me; and I would be Mrs. Wynn Delaney.

Chapter Six

Marriage

Our wedding day was gloriously sunshiny. I had not even thought to check the weather until I was actually in Jonathan's car and on my way to the church. It could have been pouring and I would never have noticed in my state of excitement. I stopped long enough to breathe a very short prayer of thanks to God for arranging such a beautiful day and then turned my thoughts back to my wedding again.

There had been some moments when I thought I would never make the eleven o'clock date with Wynn. In spite of our "organizing," there was much last-minute commotion, and the whole house seemed to be in a frenzy. Even Jonathan and Father were enlisted for tying little girls' bows and putting on slippers.

After I had slipped into the soft, creamy folds of my satin gown, I began to work on my hair. The locks that normally fell into place with little coaxing refused to go right. I tried again with similar results. I noticed then that my hands were shaking in my excitement. Julie came to my rescue and, with a few deft turns and skillful motions, she had my hair smartly and firmly in place, ready for the veil. I thanked her and went to slip into my wedding shoes.

By the time Julie and I came downstairs, one carload had already left for the church. Mother and Father waited in the hall looking serene and composed in spite of the last-minute flurries of the household. Mother's eyes misted slightly as she looked at me.

"You look beautiful, my dear," she whispered. "Your dress is lovely."

Father remarked, "It's a shame to spend so much time on

something that will scarcely be noticed."

I looked at him, puzzled.

"With your cheeks glowing and your eyes shining so, Elizabeth, no one will be able to take their eyes from your face."

Understanding, I smiled at Father as he stepped closer, and I reached up to kiss him on the cheek.

We formed a close circle, the four of us—Father, Mother, Julie and I—our arms intertwined as we stood together for one last time in the hallway of brother Jon's lovely Calgary home. Father led in prayer, asking that the Lord would make my home, wherever it might be, a place of love. "Might there always be harmony and commitment, love and happiness. Might there be strength for the hard times, humor to ease the tense times, and shoulders always available for the times of tears," he prayed. I found it difficult to keep the tears from falling now, but I did not want to reach the church with swollen eyes and a smudged face, so I refused to allow myself to cry. Mother blew her nose softly and wiped at her eyes, and then we hastened to the car.

As I stood waiting at the entrance of the church, my eyes on the back of the man whom I would soon be joining at the altar, my heart pounded wildly. Father must have sensed it, for he reached a reassuring hand out to me and held my hand tightly. I watched Julie slowly make her way down the aisle with proper and graceful steps, her soft skirts swirling out gently as she went. For a moment it had a dizzying effect on me, and I closed my eyes. It was my turn next, and I must be ready.

I was still standing with my eyes tightly closed when Father took his first step. Startled, my eyes quickly opened and Father hesitated, to let me get in step with him. It was time—time for me to walk down the aisle to meet Wynn.

I was completely oblivious to all the people in the pews. I don't even remember seeing the preacher who stood directly at the end of the aisle. All I remember is Wynn's face as he turned to watch me make that long, long, short walk to him. In a few minutes, I would be his wife! *My husband, Wynn*, was the refrain in my thoughts as I moved toward him. *Lord, make me a worthy wife to this man.*

With a gentle pressure on my arm, my father stopped me. Had he not checked me, I'm sure, I would have kept right on walking until I could take Wynn's hand. My thoughts began to sort themselves out, and I hurriedly went over the ceremony in my mind. I was to wait here with my father until he responded to "Who giveth this woman to be married to this man?" Then I could step forward to be at Wynn's side.

From then on, I concentrated very hard on the ceremony and was able to make the right responses at the right times. I was very, very conscious of Wynn by my side, of the significance of the words we were saying. As the soloist sang "The Wedding Prayer," we looked deeply into one another's eyes, secret messages passing between us. Wynn was saying, *Are you absolutely sure?* And I answered without a moment's hesitation, *I've never been so sure of anything in my life*. We had time for each to add, *I love you so very, very much*, and Wynn gently squeezed my hand.

The ceremony was over, and we walked back down the aisle together. Husband and wife. From now on, I would be with Wynn always. There would be no separation. Nothing would ever come between us.

The entry of the church was packed with well-wishers. Anna and her entire family were there. I did not even have opportunity to ask them how they had come. We hugged one another and she kissed my cheek, telling me how beautiful I looked. I greeted the children. Lars had grown noticeably, even since I had last seen him. Olga grinned and whispered a few well-rehearsed phrases about my future happiness, but Else stopped and cautiously reached out a small hand to caress my dress.

"It's beautiful. Did you make it?"

"Yes, I did," I answered her.

"It's beautiful," she said again. "So soft and smooth. You're a good sewer, Miss Thatcher."

I did not notice the familiar title, but Wynn did. "Whoa now, Else," he laughed. "It's not 'Miss Thatcher' anymore."

Else flushed slightly but laughed with Wynn. She put a small hand to her mouth and giggled, "I mean 'Mrs. Wynn,'" she corrected herself.

We let that go. Mrs. Wynn. It sounded rather homey. I wouldn't mind being called Mrs. Wynn at all.

After we had been greeted by those who had shared our day,

we returned to Jon and Mary's house for the reception. I don't remember much about the reception. I guess I was just too excited. I'm sure the lunch was delicious, but only because I heard other people say so.

The meal was cleared away and we opened our gifts. We received so many lovely things, it kept me busy imagining how much they would add to our little wilderness home. There would be no problem in making it cozy and homelike. I also reminded myself of the last busy day we would have when we returned from our honeymoon—all of these additional things would have to be carefully packed. I was too excited to give it further thought now. I must take one thing at a time.

It was finally time for us to change for our train trip to Banff. I went to the room I had shared the night before with Julie and eased the satin gown carefully over my head to keep from disarranging my hair. I stepped out of the brand-new shoes that pinched slightly and kicked them from me. It would be nice to wear something more comfortable.

I decided to take a quick bath before dressing for the train. It would take only a few minutes and would help me to be relaxed and fresh.

Afterward I donned a summery-looking suit of teal blue that Mother had brought with her from Madame Tanier's shop. I loved being so stylish way out here in the West! Father had chosen the hat, they said; I carefully put it in place, pleased at how well it suited me. I then picked up my bag and, with one last glance in the mirror, went to join Wynn.

Jon was driving us to the station, so it would mean saying goodbye to my family before we left. I would have hated leaving them had not the future held so much promise. To enter the new life meant to say goodbye to the old. There was no way to hang onto both. Even I knew that.

But it was hard to leave all those I loved. Our goodbyes were rather long and tearful, and repeated a number of times. Yet I was eager to be off, and finally we were able to pull ourselves away. Jon's car left the drive at a bit faster pace than normal. It would never do for the Banff train to leave without us.

We reached the station just in time and, with a flurry of bags, managed to board the train.

At first I was still in a whirl. Though my body had ceased to rush about, my mind still raced back and forth. Part of it was back with my family; part of it was reliving the wonderful, the harried, the tense, the busy moments of the wedding. Part of it was busy imagining my new life with Wynn. I tried to ease myself into the cushiony seat of the Pullman; but neither my body nor my mind would cooperate.

Wynn seemed perfectly relaxed. He stretched out his long legs and smiled contentedly. He looked at me, and his eyes told me he would like to sweep me into his arms. Respecting my reserve in front of an "audience," he refrained because of the many other passengers on the train. Instead, he gave me a wink that made my heart leap. He reached for my hand and I clung to him. He must have felt the tenseness in me, for he began to stroke my fingers, talking softly as he did so.

"It was a lovely wedding, Elizabeth. I don't see how it could have been nicer even if you had had all the time in the world."

My whirling thoughts went over a few things I had over-looked or mixed up or that were not as I would have planned them.

"Your gown was beautiful; did I tell you that?"

I managed a little smile. "Father said no one would notice," I murmured.

"I almost didn't," Wynn admitted. "Then I remembered a note of advice from brother Phillip. 'Be sure to take a good look at the dress,' he told me. 'She will expect you to know every detail, each row of lace, and the number of buttons.' Well, I will admit, Elizabeth, I didn't count the buttons, nor even the rows of lace, but I did take a good look at the lovely silk dress."

"Satin," I corrected.

"Satin," Wynn repeated, still rubbing a big finger softly up and down the back of my hand. "How would I know silk from satin? All I know for sure is that it wasn't serge or denim."

In spite of my preoccupation, I laughed. It eased my tense-ness some. I thought of Father's prayer about humor for the tense times! I hadn't realized before how important a bit of laughter could be. Wynn's pressure on my hand increased.

"What will you remember about today, Elizabeth?" I knew he was trying to help me relax, and I appreciated it. I tried again to let my body snuggle against the back of the seat, but it was still stiff and resistant. I turned slightly to Wynn, making my voice even and light.

"The rush. The last-minute flurry. The fear that I would never make it on time and that you would be waiting at the church, furious with me for being so late—and maybe even change your mind about getting married," I teased.

Wynn smiled. "Oh, I wouldn't have changed my mind. There were at least three other single ladies there—I checked, just in case."

I pulled my hand away in a mock pout. Wynn retrieved it.

"What else?" he prompted.

I became more serious then. "Father's prayer. He always prays with us before any big event in our lives. I remember when Margaret was married. I was her bridesmaid, so I was there for Father's prayer. It was so beautiful. I remember thinking, 'If I don't ever get married, I'll miss that.' Still, I wasn't convinced that the prayer was sufficient reason to risk a marriage."

"You're serious?"

"At the time I was. Honest! I didn't really think I would ever feel inclined to marry."

"Here I was taught to believe that every young girl is just waiting for the chance to lead some man—any man—to the altar."

"I guess some are."

"Then why not you?"

"I don't know, really. I guess it wasn't because I was so against marriage. I just didn't like the insinuation that it was all a sensible girl thought about—that women were just for the marrying, that if I didn't marry, I was nothing. I didn't like that—that *bigotry*."

I wasn't exactly calming down as Wynn had intended. The thoughts from my past and the ridiculous beliefs of some of the people I had known were stirring me up instead. I pulled slightly away from Wynn and was about to expound further on the subject.

"Women are quite capable—" I began but was interrupted.

"Hey, take it easy, Mrs. Delaney. You don't need to convince me. I believe you. I watched you in the teacherage, remember; and I'm sure that you, as a single woman, could handle anything. But I'm glad you didn't decide you must prove your point for an entire lifetime. *You* might not need a man—but I need you. That's why women marry, Elizabeth—to give their inner strength to some weak man."

His face was serious, but I knew there was a certain amount of teasing there, too. I slumped back against him and let the intensity die quickly from my eyes.

Wynn reached over and lifted my chin, tipping my face slightly so he could look into my eyes.

"Your inner strength—and your outer beauty, Elizabeth—I need both."

I wanted to lean over and kiss him, but my upbringing forbade it. Instead, I looked back at him with my love in my eyes and then leaned against him, my body finally relaxed enough to comfortably fit the seat. After a few moments of silence, I took up Wynn's little game.

"What will *you* remember about today, Wynn?"

There was no hesitation. "The look on your face when we said our vows. The way your eyes said that you meant every word of them."

"I did," I whispered. "I do."

"The dimple in your cheek when you smiled at me."

Self-consciously, I put a hand up to my cheek.

"The way your hair glistened when the sun came through the window."

I waited for more.

"The softness of your hand when I held it." He caressed the hand now, looking down at it as he did so.

"The beautiful color of your eyes, so deep and glowing."

I looked at him teasingly and added one for him. "And my 'silk' dress."

He laughed. We were both completely relaxed now. The long, beautiful, tiring, tense day was over. Our wedding had been lovely, but it now was in the past. Our whole future lay before us. Our marriage. I think that at that moment, as never before, I determined in my heart to make my marriage a thing even more beautiful than my wedding had been.

Perhaps Wynn felt it too, for he whispered softly against my hair, "This is just the beginning, Elizabeth. We have today as a memory, but we have all of the tomorrows as exciting possibilities. We can shape them with hands of love to fulfill our fondest dreams. I wasn't much for marrying either, Elizabeth, but I am so glad you came into my life to change my mind. I've never been happier—and with God's help, I plan to make you happy, too."

Chapter Seven

Banff

Banff was beautiful. There are no words to adequately describe the beauty of those mountains. I wanted to look and look at them—to carry them always in my heart.

The next morning we arose to another glorious day of sunshine. We enjoyed a leisurely breakfast in the hotel's terraced dining room and watched the sun turn the valley rose and gold as its fingers reached into the depths. After some inquiring, Wynn discovered a church, and we took hotel transportation into the sleepy little town of Banff to attend the morning services. Afterward, we found an inconspicuous little cafe where we enjoyed our lunch of mountain trout and then spent a lazy afternoon walking through the town, enjoying the sights and feel of the mountains and the enjoyable companionship of one another.

"Tell me about Banff," I said rather dreamily as we walked along in the sunshine.

"As far as the white man is concerned, this is a very young town," responded Wynn. "Of course, the Indian people have known the area for many years. Explorers came through the area first. They came and went and didn't pay too much attention, except to admire the beauty, until in the 1880s when the railroad arrived and the small town of Banff was born."

"And people loved it and just couldn't stay away," I ventured.

"Well, what really brought the visitors was the discovery of the mineral hot springs in 1883. And then, those who knew people and knew investment built and opened the Banff Springs Hotel to care for the trade. The hotel was billed as 'The Finest on the North American Continent' and was visited by tourists from all over the world."

"And here I get to spend my honeymoon in this famous hotel," I interrupted, excited by the thought.

"People have always been fascinated with mountains; and all the unclimbed, unconquered, and uncharted mountains have brought many climbers to see if they could be the first ones to the summits. They brought in experienced Swiss guides to help attract mountaineers, and the area was soon famous."

"I think it's still rather—" I paused for the right word. "Rustic," I finally decided.

Wynn smiled at my choice. "Yes," he agreed. "I guess that's part of its charm. The ruggedness, the trail guides, the fur traders—they all mingle on the streets with the wealthy from around the world. While we've walked, have you noticed all the different languages around us?"

I had noticed. It was rather exhilarating, like being in a foreign country.

I sighed deeply. "There are so many things I would like to see that I don't know where to begin," I told Wynn. "We have such a short time."

"We'll plan carefully," he assured me. "Right now, let's start with some place to eat."

As we ate our evening meal in the luxurious hotel restaurant, I heard the people at the table next to ours discussing a hike they had taken that day and the sights they had seen.

"Could we?—" I asked Wynn. "Could we go? Please? I would so love to really see the mountains, not just the town."

"Why not?" Wynn smiled. "It's a bit of a climb, but I'm sure we could do it. It will be very exhausting, especially at these heights, but worth it."

"When?"

"Let's do it tomorrow."

I clapped like an eager child, then quickly checked myself; it was too undignified for a married woman.

For the rest of the meal, we discussed our plans for the next morning. I planned to be up bright and early so we would get a good start.

When we went back to our room, Wynn said he had a few arrangements to make. He had mentioned having the kitchen prepare us a lunch to be taken along on the trail, so I nodded and set about looking over my long skirts to decide what I would be able to wear the next day. In spite of the rigors of the trail, I did want to look good for Wynn. No man wants a plain or shabby bride. I found a skirt I thought would do. It was stylish enough to be becoming but not too full to inhibit my walking. Then I selected my shoes. None of them were really made for a long hike, but I did have one pair with me that wasn't too uncomfortable or flimsy.

After I had made my selections, I ran a nice warm bath, humming to myself. I would take a leisurely bath while Wynn was gone. My thoughts were filled with anticipation for the coming day and the glorious climb we would have together. I prayed for good weather. I wanted to look out from some lofty peak at the beautiful, tree-covered valleys beneath me.

I soon heard Wynn return and stir about our room. I hurried then. I remembered I had left my clothes for the hike spread out on the room's most comfortable chair, the one Wynn might be wishing to use. Wrapped snuggly in my new white robe, I hurried out, intending to move the skirt and other articles of clothing. They were gone. Wynn now occupied the chair. One glance told me that Wynn had hung the clothing carefully back in the closet.

"Oh, thank you," I managed, but I was a bit embarrassed that he might think I was messy and careless. "I wasn't planning to leave it there," I hastened to explain. "I was just trying to smooth out some of the wrinkles for tomorrow."

"Tomorrow?" He looked questioningly at me. "I'm afraid by the time we have our hike tomorrow, there won't be time for anything else."

"That's what I mean. For the hike."

Wynn looked surprised.

"*That* outfit—for the *hike*?"

I was a bit taken aback, but stammered, "It's all I brought that was suitable, really. I thought the other dresses too fancy to be walking in."

"You're right. So is that one," he said, with a nod toward the skirt still visible through the open closet door.

"But it's all I've got," I argued.

"I got you something." Wynn sounded quite confident.

"You got me a dress?"

"Not a dress."

"Well—skirt, then?"

"No skirt. You can't climb a mountain with a skirt swishing about your legs, Elizabeth."

"Then—" I was puzzled and a bit apprehensive by this time.

"Pants."

"Pants?"

"That's right."

"I've never worn *pants* in my life," I blurted out, emphasizing the word with some disfavor.

"Then this will be a first," said Wynn, completely unflustered, nodding his head toward the bed.

I followed his gaze. There, tossed on our bed in a rather awkward and haphazard fashion, was a pair of men's pants. They were an ugly color and very wrinkled, and I almost collapsed in shock as I looked at them.

"Those?" I gasped.

Wynn was now catching on. He stood to his feet. His eyes sought my face. He must have read my honest horror, for his voice became soft.

"I'm sorry, Elizabeth," he apologized sincerely. "I guess I didn't think how they would look to you. They are rather a mess, aren't they?" I caught a glimpse of disappointment in his eyes as he crossed to the bed and picked up the pants he had just purchased. He awkwardly began to smooth out the wrinkles with his man-sized hands. I felt repentant. I reached to take them from him. "It's all right," I said, not wanting to hurt Wynn. "I could press the wrinkles out. It's not that. It's just that—that I couldn't go out—I couldn't be seen wearing something like that—in public and all—I—" I stammered to a stop.

Wynn said nothing but continued to stroke his hands across the coarse fabric of the pants. The wrinkles refused to give up possession.

"My skirt will be fine, Wynn; but thank you for thinking about—"

Wynn looked at me evenly and didn't allow me to go on. "You cannot climb a mountain in a skirt, Elizabeth. Those are not just hiking trails. They are steep. They are dangerous. You cannot possibly go without proper clothing."

Sudden anger flared within me. "And you call *that* 'proper clothing'?" I responded, jerking a thumb at the disgusting pants.

"For what we intend to do, yes."

"Well, I won't wear them," I said, a bit too quickly.

Wynn tossed them into a chair. "Very well," he said, and his voice was calm.

I had won. I wasn't sure if I should be happy or sad. It was our first little tiff and I had won. Now, as a wife, how was I to win graciously? I sought for words, for ways to show Wynn that I would not expect to win *every* battle. I didn't know what to say, so I crossed the room and began to take down my hair and brush it with long, easy strokes. The tension remained within me, even though Wynn seemed untroubled.

I stole a glance at him. He was reading a paper. He must have bought it, too, when he had gone out for the pants. I noticed a pair of brown boots sitting on the floor by the bed. I started to ask Wynn about them and then realized how small they were. They would never fit Wynn. What were they doing in our room? Then it dawned on me: Wynn had purchased them, not for himself but for me—*for me* to wear on my hike up the mountain! Not just the unsightly pants, but the mannish boots as well. How could he even have considered being seen with a woman in such outlandish attire?

I was stroking so hard with the hairbrush that I winced with the pain of it. I couldn't imagine a man even thinking such a ridiculous thing. Well, my skirt and shoes would be just fine. I wouldn't be caught traipsing around on my honeymoon looking so utterly unkempt and ridiculous.

Someone had to break the silence of the room.

"What time do we leave?" I asked innocently. We had already established a time, but I had to say something.

"Where?" said Wynn, lowering his paper.

"Up the mountain," I replied with some impatience.

Wynn was slow in answering. "Elizabeth, I'm afraid I'm guilty of not fully explaining our trip up the mountain." He laid the paper aside and rose to his full height. I felt dwarfed beside him.

"Parts of the trail are very steep. It's tough climbing. One doesn't need ropes, but one does need to be very careful. A fall could mean serious injury."

"You told me that. I'll be careful. I promise."

"Coming back down, there are parts of the trail where it is wise to sit down and ease yourself down over some of the steeper spots."

He looked at me to be sure I was understanding what he was saying. I nodded that I understood.

"There are places so steep that you need to use the branches of the nearby trees and the handgrips of the rocks to help boost yourself up."

I remembered that Wynn had told me that before, as well. I nodded again.

"It's a long way up to the mountain lake. It's a long, hard climb."

"Just what are you trying to say, Wynn?" I demanded. "Do you think I don't have the endurance to make the climb?"

"No," he said evenly. "I think you could make it. We wouldn't need to hurry. I could help you whenever you needed it—if you needed it. It would be my pleasure."

I thought of our much-talked-about trip up the mountain-side. I thought of Wynn's description of the beautiful mountain lake. I thought of sharing the sack lunch way up there in the isolation of the mountains. The thoughts stirred my emotions. I was more anxious than ever to go.

"So when should we leave?" I asked again.

Wynn took a deep breath and looked squarely at me. "I'm afraid we won't be going, Elizabeth."

My hand stopped midstroke. I stared at him incredulously. What was he doing? Punishing me for winning? But Wynn didn't seem the type to retaliate. Yet Mother had always said you don't know a person until you live with him. So this was Wynn? I couldn't believe it.

"Not going?" I finally choked out. "Why?"

"You can't climb a mountain in a dress, Elizabeth; and you have refused to wear the pants," he stated calmly and finally.

So I hadn't won. Wynn had agreed to the "no pants," but he hadn't agreed to the "no pants" *and* the mountain hike.

"That's silly," I almost hissed. "I've been in a dress all my life, and I've never been a casualty yet."

"You've never climbed a mountain yet," was his matter-of-fact response.

"And I guess I'm not about to now," I threw back at him. Even I was surprised at the intensity of my words.

"I'm sorry," was all he said. He turned and went back to his paper. I continued to briskly brush my hair. It didn't need it. I had brushed it quite enough already, but I didn't know what else to do with myself.

My thoughts whirled in a confused state. I had heard of first quarrels. I knew that Wynn was not one to be pushed around. But this was such a silly little thing to be fighting over. *Surely he doesn't expect me to give in and wear those ridiculous and unsightly pants!* No man who loved his wife would ask such a thing. I bristled even more. *Why, Mother would be ashamed to own me were she to see me in such an outfit!* Wynn understood nothing about women's dress and propriety.

Finally Wynn laid aside the paper. I knew he really hadn't been concentrating on it—just hiding behind it.

"You're angry with me, aren't you, Elizabeth?" His voice sounded so contrite that I prepared myself for his change of mind. I did not answer. I didn't yet trust my voice.

"Do you realize that we have been married for one whole day and we have already had a disagreement?" asked Wynn softly.

I still did not answer.

"I really wasn't prepared for this," stated Wynn. "Not yet, at any rate. I'm sorry, Elizabeth. I do love you—you know that. I love you very much and I do wish this hadn't happened." He spoke so sincerely that I laid aside the brush. Maybe he wasn't so stubborn after all. I was quite ready to make up and forgive and forget. Men didn't understand about women's concern for how they looked, that was all. Now that Wynn knew, there wouldn't be any future fusses on that score.

I crossed to him and put my arms around his neck. He pulled me down on his lap and held me close. I returned his kiss and ran my fingers through his thick, dark hair. I loved him. He was my husband and I loved him.

"I'm sorry," I whispered. "Truly I am. I acted like a spoiled child and I'm—I don't usually act so silly. I guess I was just terribly disappointed."

He kissed me again, holding me very close. I could scarcely breathe, but I didn't mind.

I traced the outline of his firm jaw with a finger. "What time would you like me to be ready?" I whispered.

"You won't be too embarrassed at being seen in men's pants?"

I started, then stood up, pushing away his arms.

"Wynn," I said firmly. "I am *not* wearing those pants!"

He stood up, too, and said just as firmly, "Elizabeth, if you are not wearing the pants, then we are not going up that mountain. Do I make myself clear? I will not take you over those dangerous trails, sweeping along a skirt behind you. You could fall and kill yourself. It's the pants, or not at all, Elizabeth. You decide."

I whirled from him. *How can he be so stubborn?* I couldn't believe the man.

"Then I guess we will have to find something else to do," I said defiantly. "I will not wear those pants. *Do I make myself clear?*" I stressed every one of the words. "I wouldn't be caught dead wearing those ugly men's pants or—those—those equally ugly heavy boots. Not even to climb a mountain on my honeymoon with the man I love."

I whirled again to leave him, but Wynn caught my arm.

"Don't fight dirty, Elizabeth," he said softly, but there was steel in his voice and a soft sadness, too.

The words jarred some sense into me. I couldn't believe how I was acting. This was not the way I had been raised. In our household, the man was always the one in charge; Mother had carefully schooled each one of her daughters to believe that was the right way for a Christian household to be run, and here I was—one day married—and fighting back like a bantam hen.

I bit my lip to stop its trembling and turned away from Wynn. He did not release me.

"We need to talk, Elizabeth," he said gently. "I don't think that either of us is quite ready for it now. I'm going to take a walk—get some air. I won't be long—and when I get back—if you are ready—" He left the sentence unfinished and let go of my arm. I heard the door close quietly behind him.

I really don't know how long Wynn was gone. I only know that I spent the time in tears and, finally, in prayer. Wynn was the head of the home—my home. Even though I did not agree with him, I still needed to submit to his authority if ours was to be a truly Christian home—a happy home. He had not been wrong. I had been wrong. Deep within myself I knew I would have been disappointed in Wynn if he had allowed me to be the victor when he felt so strongly about my safety. I needed to be able to lean on him, to know for sure that he was in charge. So then, why had I tried to take over? Why was mere fashion so important to me? I didn't know. I only know that by the time Wynn's footsteps sounded in the hall, I had worked it all out with prayer and tears of repentance.

I met him at the door. Considering my concern for how I looked, I must have looked a mess, but Wynn made no mention of it. He took me in his arms and began to kiss my tear-washed face. "I'm sorry," I sobbed. "I'm truly sorry. Not for hating pants—I don't expect that I'll ever like them, Wynn; but I'm sorry for getting angry with you for doing what you thought was right for me."

Wynn smoothed back my hair. "And I'm sorry, Elizabeth. Sorry to hurt you when I love you so. Sorry there isn't some other way I could show you that mountain lake. Sorry I had to insist on the pants if—"

"*Have* to insist," I corrected him.

He frowned slightly.

"Have to insist on the pants," I repeated. "I still want to see that lake, Wynn; and, if you will still take me, I'll wear the pants. Just pray that we won't meet anyone on the trail," I added quickly. "I wouldn't even want to meet a bear wearing those things."

Wynn looked surprised, then pleased, then amused. He hugged me closer and laughed. "Believe me, Elizabeth, if there was any other way—"

"It's all right," I assured him.

"I love you, Elizabeth. I love you. Trust me?"

I nodded my head up against his broad chest.

"There will be times, Elizabeth, when we won't agree about things. Times when I will need to make decisions in our future."

I knew that Wynn was thinking ahead to our life in the North.

"I might have to ask you to do things you will find difficult, things you can't understand or don't agree with. Do you understand that?"

I nodded again. I had just been through all that in my talk with my God.

"I love you, Elizabeth. I will try to never make decisions to satisfy my ego or to show my manly authority, but I must do what I think is right for you—to care for you and protect you. Can you understand that?"

I searched his face and nodded again.

"This time—the pants—it would be too dangerous on the trail in a skirt. I know the trail, Elizabeth. I would never expose you to the possibilities of a bad fall. I—"

I stopped him then by laying a finger gently on his lips. "It's all right. I understand now. I'm glad you love me enough to fight my foolish pride. I mean it, Wynn. Thanks for standing firm—for being strong. I needed that. I'm ready to let you be the head of the home. And I want you to remind me of that as often as necessary—until I really learn it well."

I had tears in my eyes. But then, so did Wynn. I reached up to brush one of them from his cheek. "I love you, Mrs. Delaney," he whispered.

"And I love you, Mr. Delaney," I countered.

His arms tightened about me. "I'm truly sorry this happened," he said.

I looked at him, deep into his eyes. "I'm not," I said slowly, sincerely. "I'm ready now—ready to be your real wife. Ready to go with you to the North—to the ends of the earth if need be. I need you, Wynn. I need you and love you."

Chapter Eight

Mountain Lake

We were up early the next morning. We had a quick breakfast and then went to prepare ourselves for the trip up the mountain. Wynn had gone to the kitchen to pick up our lunch, which he put in a backpack along with a good supply of water. I dressed while he was gone, not wanting even my husband to see me in the ugly pants.

I wasn't going to look at myself in the mirror. I didn't want to know what I looked like. I walked to the dresser to pick up a scarf and accidentally got a full look at myself. Later I was glad I did. The sight stopped me short and resulted in my doubling over with laughter. Wynn found me like this. He wasn't sure at first if I was really amused or just hysterical.

"Look at me!" I howled. "I look like an unsightly bag of lumpy potatoes." When Wynn discovered that I really was amused at how I looked, he laughed with me. The bulky pants bagged out at unlikely points, hiding my waist and any hint of a feminine shape. I had looped a belt around my waist and gathered the pants as tightly about myself as I could. This only made them bulge more.

"They are a bit big," Wynn confessed. "I guess I should have asked you about the size."

"I wouldn't have been able to tell you anyway, never having worn pants before. Oh, well, they'll do."

I stopped to roll up the legs and exposed the awkward boots on my feet.

"Are you about ready?" asked Wynn when we both stopped laughing at the spectacle I made.

"Ready," I answered, standing to my full height and saluting. We laughed again and headed for the door.

Wynn was kind enough to take me out the back way to avoid meeting other hotel guests. We circled around and followed the path to the mountain trail and began our long climb upward. We hadn't gone far when I realized what Wynn had meant. I had to grab for branches and roots in order to pull myself upward. Time after time, Wynn reached to assist me. We climbed slowly with frequent rests. I knew Wynn was setting an easy pace for me and I appreciated it. Every now and then, I would stop to gaze back over the trail we had just climbed. It was incredibly steep. I could catch a glimpse of one valley or another through the thickness of the trees. I could hardly wait to be above the timberline to view the lonely world beneath us.

By noon we had reached our goal. Sheer rock stretched up and up beyond us. Below us lay the valley with the little town of Banff nestled safely within its arms. It truly took my breath away. Here and there I could see the winding path we had just climbed, as it twisted in and out of the undergrowth beneath us.

"It's breathtaking," I whispered, still panting slightly from the climb. "Oh, Wynn, I'm so glad we came."

Wynn stepped over to wrap an arm securely about me. "Me, too," was all he said.

We found a place to have our lunch. By then I was ravenous. Wynn tossed his coat onto a slice of rock and motioned for me to be seated. I did, drinking in the sight before me.

"Where's the lake?" I asked him.

"See that ragged outcropping of rock there?" he pointed.

I nodded.

"It's just on the other side of that."

"Does it take long to get there?"

"Only about half an hour."

"Let's hurry," I prompted.

Wynn laughed at my impatience. "We have lots of time," he assured me. "It's faster going down than coming up."

He took my hand and we bowed together to thank God for the food provided. Wynn's prayer also included thanks for the sight that stretched out before us and our opportunity to share it together. I tightened my grip on his hand, thinking back on how close we had come to not making the climb. I looked down at the funny pants I was wearing. They no longer shocked me. They only brought a bubble of laughter.

We were almost finished with our lunch when we heard voices. Another group had also made the climb. They were getting very close, and I was looking about for a place to hide. I recognized one of the voices. It belonged to a very fashionable lady I had seen in the hotel lobby the day before. Oh, my goodness! Whatever would she think of me when she spied me in the insufferable pants? I could see no place to shield myself, and then I braced myself and began to chuckle. So what! I'd likely never see the woman again in my life. The pants had provided me with a very pleasant day with my new husband. They were nothing that I needed to be ashamed of. I took another bite of sandwich and flashed Wynn a grin. He had been watching me to see which way I would choose to run.

A man appeared. He was tall and dark, with very thin shoulders and a sallow face. He looked like he was more used to trolley cars and taxis than his own legs, and I wondered how he had managed to make the climb. He did seem to be enjoying it and turned to give his hand to the person who followed him. I was right. It was the attractive young woman. I wondered how she had managed to climb a mountain with her hair so perfectly in place. Her body came slowly up over the sharp rise and into view. I gasped. She, too, was dressed in ugly men's pants. Wynn and I looked at one another, trying hard to smother our laughter.

At that moment, she spotted us and called out from where she was hoisting herself up, "Isn't it absolutely glorious?" She had an accent of some kind. I couldn't place it at the moment. Around my bit of sandwich, I called back, "Yes, isn't it?"

They came over to where we were seated and flopped down on the rock perch beside us, both breathing heavily.

"I've never done anything like this before in my life," said the young man.

"I had a hard time talking him into it at first," informed the woman to my surprise.

"You've done it before?" I asked her.

"With my father—many times. He loved to climb." She

looked perfectly at home in her pants and stretched out her legs to rest them from the climb.

"This your first time?" she asked me, sensing that it must be.

"For me it is," I answered. "My husband has been here before."

She gave Wynn a fleeting smile. "Once you've been," she stated simply, "you want to come back and back and back. Me, I never tire of it."

"It's a sight all right," Wynn agreed.

I suddenly remembered my manners. I looked at our packed lunch. There were still some sandwiches left. "Here," I said, passing the package to them. "Won't you join us?"

"We brought our own," she quickly responded, and he lifted the pack from his back. "We just needed to catch our breath a bit."

We sat together enjoying the view and our lunch. We learned that they, too, were honeymooners. From Boston. She had pleaded for a mountain honeymoon and he had consented, rather reluctantly, he admitted; but he was so thankful now that he had. He was an accountant with a business firm, and she was the pampered daughter of a wealthy lawyer. Her father was now deceased and she was anxious to have another climbing mate. Her new husband hardly looked hardy enough to fill the bill, but he seemed to have more pluck than one would imagine. They were planning to take on another mountain or two before returning to Boston.

After chatting for some time, Wynn stated that we'd best be going if we wanted to see the lake before returning, and the young woman agreed. It was a steep climb back down the mountain, she stated, one that must be taken in good light.

We went on, bidding them farewell and wishing them the best in their new marriage, which they returned. I got to my feet, unembarrassed by my men's pants. If a wealthy girl from Boston could appear so clad, then I supposed that a fashion-conscious gal from Toronto could do likewise.

The trail around the mountain to the little lake was actually perilous in spots. I wondered how in the world any woman would ever have been able to make it in a skirt. She wouldn't. It was just that simple. I was glad for my unattractive pants that gave me easy movement. I was also glad for Wynn's hand which often supported me.

The lake was truly worth the trip. The blue was as deep as the cloudless sky above us, and the surface of the lake was as smooth as glass. It looked as though one should surely be able to step out and walk on it, so unrippled it was. Yet, when we got close and I leaned over carefully to get a good look into its depths, I was astonished to discover just how deep it was. Because of the clearness of the water, one could see every rock and every shadow. I stood up and carefully stepped back, feeling a bit dizzy with it all.

We did not linger long. The climb back down the mountain was a long one, so we knew we had to get on the trail. We met the other young couple. They still talked excitedly as they walked carefully over the sharp rocks and slippery places. I expected that their future would hold many such climbs. In a way, I envied them. The North held no such mountains—at least not in the place where Wynn had been presently stationed. Wynn had said the mountains did stretch way up to the north country as well; but they were for the most part uninhabited, so very few men were assigned to serve there. I was sorry for that. I would have liked to live in the mountains.

We felt our way slowly back down the trail. In a way, I found the climb down more difficult than the climb up had been. It seemed that one was forever having to put on the brakes, and it wasn't always easy to be sure just where one's brakes were. On more than one occasion, I started sliding forward much faster than I intended to. Wynn was right. One did need to sit down and attempt to ease down the steepest parts in a most undecorous fashion. *What if Mother could see me now?* I thought unruefully. I grasped for roots, branches, rocks—anything I could get my hands on to slow my descent. By the end of the day, my hands were scratched in spite of borrowing Wynn's leather gloves for the worst places; my men's pants were a sorry mess of mountain earth and forest clutter; and my hair was completely disheveled.

However, I still wore a happy smile. It had been some day, a memory I would always treasure.

We stopped at a gushing mountain stream. I knelt down and bent forward for a drink of the cold, clear water. It had come directly from an avalanche above, Wynn informed me; and I was willing to believe him. The water was so cold it made my fingers tingle and hurt my teeth as I drank it. We didn't really need the drink. Our backpack still held water we had carried with us, but Wynn felt that to make the day complete I must taste the mountain water. I agreed. I wiped the drips from my face and shook my hands free of the coldness and told Wynn how good it tasted. Wynn drank, too, as a reminder to himself that he had been right. No other water on earth tastes quite like that of a mountain stream.

Chapter Nine

Back to Calgary

The next day I ached all over. I wouldn't have believed that one had so many body parts to hurt. Wynn suggested a soak in a hot tub. It helped some, as long as I stayed there and sat very still. The minute I moved, I hurt again.

"I had no idea I had so many muscles," I complained.

Wynn offered to give me a rubdown, and I accepted it.

"I wonder how *he* feels," I mumbled into my pillow, as Wynn worked at sore muscles in my back.

"He? He who?"

"Her husband. That young couple yesterday. He didn't look exactly like he was built for climbing mountains."

Wynn chuckled at my comment. "Guess he didn't," he agreed.

"Come to think of it," I went on, "I wouldn't have picked her out as a climber either."

"Well," Wynn said seriously, "when I first saw a certain, beautiful young schoolteacher I know, I wouldn't have picked her out as a climber either."

I laughed in spite of my aches, and then I made a decision. "That's enough," I said to Wynn. "We have only one more day here in the mountains and I want to see as much as I can. Maybe my muscles will ease up some as I walk. Where can we go today?"

"You're sure?" Wynn asked, a bit doubtful.

"Positive," I answered.

"Climbing or walking?" asked Wynn.

"Just walking. Those old pants aren't fit to be worn anywhere till they are washed."

"Do you have proper shoes?" inquired my practical husband.

I pointed to the pair I had chosen for the day before. Wynn shook his head.

"Not good enough," he stated, and this time I didn't even argue.

"Okay," I said, "I'll wear the boots." I went for them, hoping with all my heart that my long skirt would hide them.

It almost did. I smiled to myself and announced to Wynn that I was ready to go.

We wasted no time. In the morning we went to Bow Falls. They were not high falls but were nevertheless lovely to watch. The water ran wildly between two uprisings of mountain rock which confined it on either side. As it pounded and boiled down the drop of several feet, the water turned from clear, bright translucent to a foaming milky white. One could hear the roar long before rounding the turn where one could look upstream and view the spectacle. It nearly took my breath away. I would have sat and watched the falls, mesmerized for the rest of the morning, had not Wynn roused me. "I hate to prod, but if we are going to fit in the Cave and Basin, we must be going. It's rather a long walk."

It *was* a long walk, and already my feet were tired from lifting the heavy boots step by step; so, as soon as we reached the area where public transportation was available, I agreed it would be wise to ride rather than try to hike all the way.

The guide at the Cave and Basin was a jolly Scot who seemed to be having the time of his life escorting visitors through what he treated as his private domain. When he saw Wynn, his face spread with a grin.

"Aye, an' how be ya, Delaney?" he cried, wringing Wynn's hand vigorously.

He didn't allow Wynn a chance for an answer. "An' shur now," he went on, "an' don't be a-tellin' me thet ye've found yerself a lass—an' a bonnie one she's bein'."

Wynn proudly introduced me. I hoped with all my heart that the jovial man would not look down and see my mannish boots peeking out from under my sweeping skirt. He didn't look down. Instead, he grabbed a lantern and hurried us off on our tour of *his* Cave and Basin.

"A sight like this ye'll never be seein', not anywhere in this world," he informed me, rolling his r's delightfully.

I shivered some as we followed the man into the cave and

along rocky uneven steps to deep within the earth. It got cooler and more mysterious as we advanced; and the old man talked in a spooky, confiding tone, pointing out strange shapes and shadows as he whispered eerie suspicions about what they might have been in some long ago yesteryear. I shivered more noticeably now, and Wynn reached to place a protective arm around me. "Don't pay any attention to his stories," he whispered in my ear. "He makes them up as he goes along."

"An' look there now," went on the Scot, leaning close and lowering his voice as though someone from the dead past might hear him and take offense. "See there by yonder wall—that there mysterious shape." His finger pointed it out, and the lantern swung back and forth, making the strange shadows dance.

"Right there," the man leaned even closer to me to make sure that my eyes were following his pointing finger. "Thet there is a skeleton. Thet of an Indian warrior caught here in the cave. He must have been wounded in battle—or else waitin' out a thunderstorm—and somehow he got caught and held here an' never did leave." He paused. " 'Course, I just tell thet to the young lasses thet I don't want to spook none," he added confidentially. "What really happened, I'm a-wagerin', is thet he was murdered right here." The r's rolled round and round on his tongue.

I shivered again and we moved on, the lantern bobbing and shivering, too. Again and again, we had things pointed out to us and then we descended a ladder to an underground pool steaming with heat.

"Kneel down careful like and put yer hand in."

I wasn't very brave and clung to Wynn's hand as I knelt to feel the water. It was, indeed, nice and warm.

"What heats it?" I asked in surprise.

"Aye," laughed the Scotsman. "Only the good Lord knows. He keeps a few secrets of His own. I'm a-guessin' we'll never know unless He decides to be tellin'."

We retraced our steps. I was looking forward to being back out in the warm sun again, though I wouldn't have missed the experience for anything. I was unprepared for the brightness as I stepped out from the cave. My eyes protested and I closed them tightly and turned away in the opposite direction so I might open them at my own choosing.

My eyes soon adjusted and I was able to turn back to the cheery guide with a smile of approval for his Cave and Basin. He seemed to feel it was very important that we had enjoyed our venture. I put out my hand.

"Thank you so much," I said, meaning every word of it. "I enjoyed that ever so much."

His eyes twinkled. He took the proffered hand and shook it heartily and then turned to Wynn.

"I always wondered why ye kept on a-waitin' and a-waitin' instead of takin' ye a wife, an' now I know. Ye were just a-waitin' fer the finest thet there be."

Wynn grinned.

"Well, the best to ye both now," said the Scot, and he gave Wynn a hearty slap on the back and turned to care for more of his tourists.

We were almost back to Calgary when my honeymoon reverie was broken and my thoughts went instead to all that needed to be done in one short day. I stirred rather uncomfortably and Wynn sensed my restlessness.

"Something wrong?" he asked, very sensitive to my changing moods.

"I was just thinking of all that needs to be done tomorrow," I admitted.

"It shouldn't be too bad," he tried to assure me. "Your trunk is all ready to go and most of the other things are all packed and waiting. There will just be a few last-minute things to be gathered together."

"But all those wedding gifts?"

"Julie and Mary volunteered, didn't I tell you?"

"I don't recall—"

"I'm sorry. I meant to tell you, so your mind would be at ease."

"That's fine," I said, feeling better about it. "I do hope they are careful and use lots of packing. Some of those porcelain things are very delicate."

"Packing?" echoed Wynn. "They won't need much packing.

Mary has volunteered to store them in her attic. They will be careful, I'm sure."

"Store them?"

Now it was Wynn's turn to show surprise. "Elizabeth, you weren't thinking we would be taking all these things with us, were you?"

"Well—yes—I—"

"We couldn't possibly. The Police Force allows so many pounds of baggage per person. We have already stretched our limit. Besides, such things would serve no purpose—have no function—in the North."

For a moment I wanted to argue. Their function would be to make a home—to make me feel more like a homemaker. Wasn't that function enough? I didn't argue though. I remembered well my prayer of three days before and my promise to my God to let Wynn be the head of the household. I waited for a moment until I was sure I had complete control and then I looked at Wynn and gave him one of my nicest smiles.

"I guess that is all taken care of then."

Wynn put an arm around me and drew me close, even though we were on a crowded train.

"Thank you, Elizabeth," he whispered against my hair, and I knew I had gained far more than I had lost in the exchange.

As expected, the next day was a busy one. My family was still with Jon and Mary. They would be staying for a few more days before heading back east. I was glad I still had this one brief day with them before I would be heading north.

However, there would be no more late-night chats with my sister Julie. Her things had been moved from the room I had used for so long at Jon's, and the room was now set up for Wynn's and my use. It seemed rather strange at first, but I quickly got used to the idea. Already, I didn't know how I had ever managed without Wynn, and I had been a married woman only four short days.

Wynn was gone a good share of the day, running here and there making final preparations. He had an appointment at the Royal North West Police Headquarters for last-minute instructions and took our last trunks and crates down to be weighed and checked in. We would be starting our journey by train, then switching to boat, and ending by ox cart or wagon. Had it been the winter months, we would have also used dog teams.

We did not retire early. There was no need to conserve our energy. We had all the next day to sleep on the train if we wished. It seemed far more important now to sit and chat with the family. Reluctantly, we finally went to bed.

I climbed the stairs to my room for one last time. Who knew when I might sleep here again? I had grown to love this room. I had always felt welcomed and loved in Jon's home. I would miss it. I would miss them. I would miss each one of the children. They might be nearly grown before I saw them again. And what of my dear mother and father? Would they still be in their Toronto home when I returned from the north country? What about Julie? Would she marry while I was gone? And Matthew? He would be a man.

I did not dread my future with Wynn in his North. The only thing that bothered me was that I would miss so much of what went on here. If only I could freeze everything in place until I came back again so I wouldn't need to miss so much. But that was impossible. One could only be at one place at one time. The world in Toronto and here in Calgary would continue to go on without Elizabeth Delaney, and I must accept the fact.

I felt a bit teary inside as I turned my face into my pillow. For a moment, I was afraid I was going to cry; and then Wynn reached for me and rubbed his cheek against mine.

"Are you ready for adventure, Elizabeth?" he whispered to me, and I could detect excitement in his voice.

"Um-hum," I murmured, reaching up my hand to feel the strength of his jawline. I smiled into the darkness, and Wynn could feel the pull of my facial muscles as they formed the smile. He kissed me on the temple.

"I've never been so excited about heading north, Elizabeth," he confided. "Always before, I've known how much I was really leaving behind. This time I can only think of what I am taking with me."

I stirred in his arms.

"I hope I never disappoint you, Wynn."

"I'm not worried about that." His voice was very serious now.

"I only hope and pray that you are never disappointed. The North can be cruel, Elizabeth. It's beautiful, but it can be cruel, too. The people—they are simple, needy people—like children in many ways. I guess it's the people who draw me there. I love them in some mysterious way. They trust you, lean on you, so simply, so completely. You sort of feel you have to be worthy of their trust."

"And I'm sure you are."

"I don't know. It seems as if I've never been able to do enough. What they really need are doctors, schools, and most of all missions. Missions where they can really learn the truth about God and His plan for man. They have it all so mixed up in their thinking."

A new desire stirred within me, a desire not just to teach Wynn's people how to read and write, but how to find and worship God as well. Funny. I had never met them—not any of them—yet I felt as if I already loved them.

Chapter Ten

The Journey Begins

After a teary last farewell, we were on our way. I felt sad and excited all at the same time. I couldn't really understand or sort out what was going on inside of me. Wynn sensed my feeling and allowed me some quiet thoughts. On occasion he did point out things of interest, but he didn't push me for enthusiasm. The first several miles of the trip I had seen many times, as it took us through Red Deer and Lacombe. As the train stopped in Lacombe, I looked closely for someone on the street whom I might know; I was about to conclude that there was no one when Phillip, Lydia, and young Phillip—Wynn's brother, sister-in-law, and nephew—came aboard, ushering Wynn's mother down the aisle.

"The conductor says they will be here for a few minutes, so he will give us warning when they are about to leave," Phillip informed us.

We soon became busily engaged in conversation, catching up on all of the area news. It was no time until the conductor came to tell us that the train would be ready to leave again in about five minutes. We hated to see them go but were so glad for the time we were able to spend together. It was the first I had been able to call Mrs. Delaney, Sr., *Mother,* and I took pleasure in doing so.

"God bless you, Elizabeth," she said. "It isn't as hard for me to let Wynn go this time, knowing he will be well looked after. You take care, though. From what Wynn has said in the past, the North can be a lonely place for a woman."

I tried to assure Mother Delaney that I would be fine and was quite prepared for all that lay ahead. I wasn't quite as sure of myself as I tried to sound. With every mile of the whirling train wheels, my stomach tied into a little tighter knot. Had it not been for Wynn beside me, I'm sure I would have panicked and bolted long before we had reached even Lacombe.

I tried to concentrate on the small settlements through which we passed. It was not easy. My mind was on other things. Even when Wynn spoke cheerily, pointing out this or that, I still couldn't get enthused—though I did try.

I finally decided I must be tired and what I needed was sleep, so I curled up beside Wynn with my head against his shoulder and tried to do just that. It didn't work. My mind was far too busy. Sleep would not come. I heard soft breathing coming from my husband and realized he had been successful. I was glad for him. He was even more tired than I, I was sure. I hoped he would rest well. I tried to sit very still so as not to disturb him. *I* might have been still, but the train was not. We made another jerky stop and then, with a hiss and a chug, we began shifting this way and that in an effort to disengage some of the cars.

Wynn quickly awoke and stirred slightly. I knew by the way he moved that he was afraid of waking me, so I sat up and smiled at him.

"It's all right," I assured him. "I'm already awake."

"Did you get any rest?" he inquired, concern in his voice.

"Rest, yes. Sleep, no," I answered.

"I'm sorry. Guess I dozed off there for a while."

"Not for long," I informed him. "You might have if the train didn't keep stopping at every little house and teepee."

Wynn chuckled. "That's the way it seems, doesn't it? Well, it isn't too much farther to Edmonton now."

"What happens at Edmonton?"

"We spend the night. I have a short meeting in the morning with some officials before we move on. You can sleep late if you like."

"When do we leave?"

"Not until about eleven."

"When do I need to be up?"

"I wouldn't think until about nine—unless you want to see a bit of the city."

"I think I'll pass," I said, smiling tiredly. "Even nine sounds way too early."

When I awoke the next morning, Wynn, as promised, had left me sleeping. I looked at the clock on the wall. It was already after nine, so I climbed quickly from my bed. I would need to hurry if I was to be ready when Wynn came back for me.

I had just finished doing my hair when Wynn's key turned in the lock.

"You're up," he greeted me. "I was afraid you might over-sleep."

"I did. A little," I admitted. "I really had to hurry to make up for lost time."

"I don't think your sleeping time was lost time," he assured me. "You needed that."

He crossed to kiss me. "You look more rested," he stated. "How do you feel?"

I smiled. "Fine," I returned, trying to hide any anxiety I might feel. "Ready to start the trip to your wilderness."

He gave me a big bear hug. "Then let's get going," he said. "You still need some breakfast before we start out."

We continued our trip by river barge, a new experience for me. At first I was rather apprehensive. The day was cloudy and overcast and I didn't feel too safe on the free-floating contraption. It was guided along the river with only the help of long poles held in the hands of the men in our crew.

Wynn said that in the earlier days we would have been able to make the same trip on the North Saskatchewan in the comfort of a sternwheeler cabin, but with the advent of the railroads the boats had lost business and had been retired. There was no railroad to take us where we wanted to go, and so now we traveled on the flat barge, allowing the river to carry us along as it flowed northeast. The men who owned and operated the boat did not believe in wasting fuel on the downriver trip. Coming back up-river, they would put a simple motor to work.

The sky looked like it might pour down rain. I wasn't sure how this odd boat would function if the waters started coming down from above. Would it still stay afloat?

The seats provided weren't all that comfortable, and I soon was aching for a chance to stand up and walk around a bit. There didn't seem to be any opportunity, as nearly every square foot of the barge was piled high with something. I couldn't believe the amount of cargo it had heaped within its bulging sides. I looked around for our trunks and crates and almost panicked when I didn't see them. Wynn must have read my thoughts.

"They're over there under the canvas," he stated simply, putting my mind at ease.

"Want to stretch?" he asked after many minutes had passed by.

"I'd love to," I responded quickly, "but where?"

"Come," he said, holding out a hand to me. "I think we can manage a few minutes of it."

It was difficult. We had to step over things, around things, duck under things, and hang on for dear life. The wind was up, and at times the river was rough. I tied my scarf more tightly under my chin and told Wynn that I would be fine for the time being. We returned to our uncomfortable seats.

In the early afternoon the rains came. There wasn't any place to go to avoid them. Wynn found some kind of slicker and wrapped it tightly around me. The wind kept whipping and tearing at it, making it difficult to keep all sides of me under it at any given moment. I could feel patches of wet spots grow bigger and bigger. I tried not to think about them, but it wasn't easy. The rainwater was cold and the increasing wind made it even colder. In a few hours' time, I was really miserable but I tried hard not to show it.

Wynn kept fussing over me—shifting the makeshift shelter this way and that, tightening it here, and tucking it in there. In the meantime, he, too, was getting wet. Those operating the barge seemed to take the storm for granted. They had likely been wet many times before while making this run.

As the day passed, the sky was getting darker and the rains heavier. I wondered if we would travel all night long. How far would we go on this river anyway? I had heard the word *Athabasca,* but I didn't think that was our destination.

Wynn came to tell me, "We're going to pull in early tonight. We'll try to dry out a bit. There's a little trading post ahead where we can take shelter. We should have gone farther tonight, but we'll wait for morning."

I shivered and nodded my head thankfully. It was good news to me.

It wasn't long until the shouting and straining of the barge crew told me that we were going ashore. There was a jolt and a thump as we hit some kind of dock in the darkness. Then Wynn was there to help me to solid ground. The wind and rain loosened my scarf, and soon my hair was tumbling crazily about my face. I tried to tuck it back again but I really didn't have a free hand. I gave up and decided to just let it blow.

We headed for a dark shape in the gathering gloom. Then I spotted a light in a misty window. Though faint, the light did signal humanity; and I breathed a prayer of thankfulness as I tried, with Wynn's help, to hurry toward it.

The smell of wood smoke reached my nose, and I thought of the wonderful warmth that would go with it. I hurried faster. In my eagerness to get to the house, I did not see the tree stump in my pathway.

"Watch out!" Wynn cried when he saw what was about to happen, but it was too late. I banged my shin hard against the tough wood, and let out a sharp little cry at the stinging pain.

Wynn kept me from falling, but from there to the house I stumbled along, limping painfully. Wynn asked to carry me but I stubbornly shook my head.

When we reached what I had thought to be a house and stumbled through the door, I was disappointed to see that it was no house at all. It was a shed—a shed for trade. Boxes and crates and heaps and piles were stacked all around the single room in a haphazard fashion. One dim lamp sat upon a make-shift counter, throwing out an anemic light. The single window was so stained and dirty I wondered how I had been able to see the light from outside at all.

In the corner of the room was what looked like a stack of furs. Upon closer observation, I discovered that it was, instead, a bed—of sorts. I shuddered to think of sleeping there.

"Howdy," a voice said, and I whirled to see an ill-kempt man sitting beside the potbellied stove in the middle of the crowded room. He let fly with a line of dark spit that missed an open can, spattering against the side of the stove, causing a sizzling sound. He had not risen to meet us and he did not move now.

Wynn jerked his head at the man. "Howdy, Charlie," he said. "Mind if we borrow your chair for a minute? My wife just gave her leg an awful whack on that tree stump you've got out front."

It was the room's only chair, and Charlie rose reluctantly with a grunt of disgust.

Wynn sat me down and lifted my skirt to get a good look at my injury.

"Bring your lamp, would you, Charlie?"

From the tone of Wynn's voice, I knew that, though it was Charlie's lodging, Wynn was in charge here. Everyone knew it.

Charlie brought the lamp. My leg was bleeding, seeping through my torn stocking, making a sticky dark patch.

"You've got to get out of those stockings," Wynn said to me.

I looked helplessly about the room. There was no place to go.

"But I can't," I insisted, casting a nervous glance at Charlie.

"Turn your back, Charlie," Wynn ordered, and the grumbling Charlie obeyed. The light of the lamp turned with him. I felt a bit more comfortable in the semi-darkness and hastened to raise my skirt and unfasten the garters that held up my ruined stocking. I slipped it down as quickly as I could and let my skirt drop back in place. Charlie shifted from one foot to the other and spit again. I don't know where that one landed. Weakly I sat back down.

"Okay," said Wynn, "let's have the lamp, Charlie."

Charlie turned around. For one awful moment, I feared he might spit in my direction. He didn't. He stood holding the lamp nervously, trying not to look at the leg that Wynn was studying.

"I don't think it's too deep," Wynn was saying. "Nothing broken that—"

"Except my stocking," I interrupted. Wynn's eyebrows went up.

"Legs heal," I said, to inform him. "Stockings don't—and I was able to bring only a limited number with me."

In spite of himself, Wynn smiled but made no reply.

"Charlie, do you have any first-aid supplies around here?" he asked.

Charlie grumbled and then muttered, "A few things."

"Set the lamp down and get them, please," said Wynn. "I don't want to have to unload the barge to get at my supply."

Wynn stood up to check the kettle sitting on the stove. It held water and that seemed to please him.

While Wynn cleansed and bandaged my swelling leg, the other men entered. Apparently they were satisfied that they had secured the barge against the storm, and now wanted to be in where it was warm and dry.

They greeted Charlie boisterously. In return, he greeted them with an oath, a spit, and a slap on the back.

I felt very much out of place. It was apparent that these men didn't spend much time in the presence of a lady. They joked and swore and jabbed at one another with harmless fists. One man soon produced a rum bottle, which they seemed to think was just the thing needed to take the chill out of their bones.

Wynn took charge because no one else seemed to have any mind to do so. He put on the coffeepot and asked Charlie for some tins of food for an evening meal. Charlie seemed reluctant to share until Wynn reminded him that he would be paid for anything that the Police Force used. Charlie then produced a couple of tins, and Wynn set about making some supper.

I offered to help him but he declined my offer. "I think you should rest that leg all you can. Here, let me help you."

Before I knew what had happened, Wynn lifted me from my spot on the chair by the stove to the pile of foul-smelling skins in the corner. I wanted to protest but the words caught in my throat.

"I'm sorry, Elizabeth," whispered Wynn, "but I guess this will be your bed for tonight."

I closed my mouth against the protest and the odor that came from the pile of furs as Wynn settled me gently on the bed.

"You mean this is all there is here?" I asked incredulously.

"This is it," answered Wynn.

"But what about you—and them?"

"We'll stay here, too. At least it's dry, and the fire will have our clothes dried out by morning."

I looked quickly at the tiny, crowded, overstocked room. Suddenly it seemed terribly stuffy and suffocating. I wished for the out-of-doors so I could breathe freely again. But when I heard the howl of the wind and the lashing of the rain, I closed my eyes and tried to be thankful for the warmth of the smelly little cabin. Wynn patted my shoulder in sympathy.

When supper was ready, a makeshift arrangement of a table was dragged up close to the stove. Wynn came to help me to it. I told him I really wasn't hungry and would gladly settle for just a hot cup of tea or coffee. He realized then that I was still in my wet clothes and shivering with the cold.

"I'm sorry, Elizabeth," he said. "I was so anxious to get some hot food in you that I forgot about your wet things. I didn't realize you got as wet as you did. I guess the slicker didn't keep out much of the rain, eh?"

"Oh, it did," I insisted bravely, comparing his soaked appearance to mine. "I only have a spot here and there, that's all."

Wynn reached out to feel my clothing. "You're wet," he argued, "through and through. We'll get you out of them as soon as you get some hot soup down you."

I wanted to protest further, but Wynn would have none of it. I allowed myself to be helped to the chair, and Wynn poured me a cup of the soup he had made. I sipped it slowly. It wasn't the best meal I had ever eaten, but it was hot, even tasty in a "canned" sort of way. My clothing on the side closest to the stove began to steam. I shifted around some to direct the heat on another section. I didn't really warm up, although a few spots of me were actually hot. It was a strange sensation to feel so hot in places and yet chilled at the same time. I finished my cup of soup and motioned to Wynn that I was ready to return to the heap called a bed.

"Got a couple of blankets, Charlie?"

Charlie lumbered up from the barrel on which he was sitting and spit at the stove as he reached up to a shelf.

"Hudson's Bay," he grumbled. "Hardly used."

"They'll still be hardly used come morning," Wynn answered, not to be intimidated by Charlie's growling. Wynn moved to where he could screen me from view with the blanket. "Now," he said, "get out of those wet things."

I looked at him, wondering if he really meant what he said. The room was full of men.

He meant it. I shrugged, unfastened my wet skirt and let it fall. I then removed my shirt and my petticoats, casting apprehensive glances at the blanket Wynn held for me.

I could tell by the noises on the other side of the make-shift wall that the four men were now enjoying Wynn's supper soup. There were slurps and smacking, and I was glad I wouldn't need to see as well as hear them eat. I wondered if Charlie could eat and chew tobacco at the same time, or if he actually disposed of his wad while he was dining.

"Now climb up there and lie down," Wynn spoke softly, "and I'll tuck you in."

He did as promised, using both of the blankets Charlie had provided. I lay there shivering. Wynn went back to the stove, took the cup I had used, and poured soup for himself. He then got a cup of coffee and came back to my bed. "Are you warming any?" I thought I was, though my teeth hadn't really stopped chattering.

Now that Wynn no longer claimed the stove for his meal preparation and I no longer occupied the one chair in the room, the men moved in closer to the heat. Their clothing began to steam and smell, not improving the odor in the room. I was glad I had already eaten. I couldn't have swallowed with that strong, offensive smell in the room.

I tried to move over to give Wynn room to sit down on the bed beside me, but this was truly a one-man bed. Wynn crouched beside me and sipped his coffee. I could see the clothes hugging tightly to him.

"You're still wet," I stated. "You'll get sick."

"I'll dry soon. I'll be okay. Why don't you try to get some sleep?"

I wanted to retort, "Here?" But I knew that "here" was the best he could offer, so I simply nodded.

Wynn moved back to the stove where the men were busy eating and joking.

"Hey, Sarge," quipped one of the boatmen. "Not bad soup for a lawman."

The other men joined in his guffaw at his tremendously funny joke. Wynn just nodded his head.

"Much obliged for your home and your bed tonight, Charlie," said Wynn sincerely.

Charlie looked over to the corner where I huddled. He had

finished eating, so he was free to chew and spit again, which he now did. It landed on one of the boatmen's boots. The fellow did not even glance down.

"No problem," Charlie assured Wynn. "Me, I ain't aimin' on usin' the bed tonight nohow."

The other men laughed and I wondered why. I didn't need to wonder for long. The makeshift table was quickly cleared of the few cups and a pack of cards was produced.

"Ain't got nothin' 'gainst cards, have ya, Sarge?" asked the chubby boatman.

"Not as long as they're fair and don't cause any fights," answered Wynn.

"Then I guess thet this here's gotta be a fair game, gents," the man said to his comrades; and they all laughed uproariously again, slapping their thighs and one another's backs.

Crates or barrels served as seats, and a couple of bottles soon joined the cards on the table.

"You wantin' to join us, Sarge?" invited the little dark man with the French accent and long mustache.

Wynn shook his head.

The four men hunched over the table, and the long night began. There wasn't much place for Wynn to go. Attempting to dry out his wet clothes, he pulled a block of wood close to the stove and sat down, leaning against a pile of crates.

The lamp flickered now and then, and an unwashed hand would reach out to turn the wick up a bit. The jesting got louder and more coarse. Wynn reminded them a lady was present, and then for a few minutes it was quieter in the cabin. As the night progressed and the bottles were emptied, the commotion grew. Wynn eventually watched it without comment, seeming to pay little attention to the whole thing; but I knew he was well aware of every movement in the room.

From my bed in the corner, I watched too. I was no longer shivering—the scratchy Hudson's Bay blankets were doing their job well. I nearly dozed once or twice, and then laughter or a stream of obscenity would jerk me awake again.

Wynn rose from his place by the fire to check on me. When I saw him coming, I closed my eyes lightly. I knew it might be considered deceitful, but I did not want Wynn to worry about me. He already had enough on his mind. I did not fool him, however.

"Are you all right?" he asked softly.

I didn't answer immediately. The truth was, I felt very strange, very out of place, in the room with the cursing, gambling men. I had never been in such a situation before. It was the kind of thing I had avoided all my life. If it hadn't been for the presence of my husband, I would have been stiff with fright. I glanced quickly at the four men in the room. The big one was taking another long drink from the bottle; and the dark, little one was impatiently waiting his turn, hand outstretched. I looked quickly back to Wynn. Concern showed in his face.

"I'm fine," I managed weakly; but then I repeated it more firmly, willing myself to realize I spoke the truth. "I'm fine."

"Your leg?"

"It doesn't hurt too badly at all."

"Are you warm?"

I merely nodded my head for this one.

He knelt beside me and shifted my blankets some, tucking them in tightly around me. "I'm sorry, Elizabeth. I planned the trip so you would have better accommodations than this. If this storm—"

"It's all right," I hurried to assure him. "You're here—that's what matters."

He leaned over and kissed me, the love showing in his eyes, but the worried look did not leave his face. "Try to get some sleep," he whispered.

I smiled at him and he kissed me again, and then went back to his place by the stove.

It was getting very late and the men were still playing cards, drinking, and cursing. Charlie rose from his crate and went to bring another bottle. When he placed it on the table, Wynn, hardly moving, stood slowly, leaned over and removed it. Four pairs of eyes turned to look at him.

"We've got a long trip ahead of us tomorrow. I want some sober barge-men. Charlie, you can drink if you want to. It's your liquor, but don't pass your bottle around."

There was authority in Wynn's voice; and, though there were some grumbles around the table, no one challenged him.

The card game went on, but it was clear that much of the "fun" had gone out of it.

At length, the men decided they'd had enough. They pushed back their makeshift seats, cleared a little space around the stove, and stretched out on the floor to sleep. For a few moments, it was blessedly silent. Then, one by one, they filled the room with a chorus of snores.

The snoring seemed even louder and more vulgar than the conversation had been. Resigned, I turned my face to the wall and tried to get some sleep in the little time that was left.

Once or twice I heard stirring as the fire in the stove was replenished. I knew without even looking that it was Wynn.

When morning came, I was still bone-weary. But at least the effort of trying to sleep was over. The rain was still falling, but the wind seemed to have died down. I was thankful for small mercies.

At my first stirring, Wynn was beside me.

"How do you feel, Elizabeth?" he whispered.

I ached all over, and my sore leg throbbed with each beat of my heart. I managed a faltering smile. "Okay," I answered. "Can you help me up?"

Wynn's strong arms helped me to my feet and shielded me with the blanket while I fumblingly got into my clothes. They were thoroughly dry now and felt much softer than the blankets had.

The men were still scattered around on the floor, sleeping off their binge of the night before.

"I need to go out, Wynn," I whispered. "Where do I go?"

Wynn nodded toward the one door.

"Anyplace in the woods," he answered me.

At my troubled look, he glanced back to the men. "Don't worry about any of them. They wouldn't wake up until next week if they were left alone. I'll watch them."

I was relieved but still apprehensive about the whole outdoors as a facility.

"Do you need help walking?" Wynn asked.

I tried my weight on my poor leg to be sure before I answered, "I'll be all right."

"Are you sure?"

I took an unsteady step. "I'll hang onto the cabin if I need support," I told him.

He helped me over to the door and opened it for me. Then he reached for his jacket. "Here," he said, "you'd better use this. It's still raining."

I wrapped the jacket tightly about me and stepped out into the misty morning. The nearby river was almost hidden by the fog that clung to it. Water from the trees dripped on the soggy ground beneath. Every step I took was in water. I was glad the wind was not blowing.

I took no longer out-of-doors than was necessary. Even then, by the time I hobbled back into the little, smelly, over-crowded cabin, my shoes were soaked through and the hem of my dress wet for several inches. I longed for the stove's warmth, but I hesitated to step over the sleeping men. Wynn helped me around them, and I took my place in the one chair and stretched my feet out toward the glow.

"Not very nice out there, is it?" Wynn commented.

"It's wet and cool, but the wind isn't blowing like yesterday."

Wynn seemed to approve of my healthy attitude. He gave me a smile and placed a hand on my shoulder as he handed me a cup of hot coffee.

"Now that you've seen the day, what do you think? Would you like to get back on the journey or wait out the storm here in the cabin?"

I looked at the four sodden men on the floor. The liquor from the night before mingled with the other smells. Snores still came forth from half-open mouths, sometimes catching in their throats in a rugged growl which snorted to a finish.

I glanced back at the makeshift bed in the corner. It was so narrow one could scarcely turn over and so lumpy I wondered how Charlie ever managed to get any sleep at all.

"Where will we be tonight?"

"There's a small post downriver."

"Are there—are there—?" I hesitated to say "houses," for I wasn't sure if there were any *houses* as such in the North. "Are there accommodations there?" I finally managed.

"Quite comfortable," Wynn replied.

"Then I vote to move on," I said without hesitation.

Wynn smiled and moved forward to stir the sleeping barge captain.

The man didn't even open an eye, just shifted his position and started to snore again in a different key.

"Blackjack," Wynn called loudly. "Time to hit the trail!"

The man just stirred again. Wynn knelt beside him and shook his shoulder. "Time to get up. Get this crew of yours off the floor," Wynn commanded the man.

Blackjack scowled up at him as if about to argue the point, but Wynn would take no argument.

"You're being paid to get us to River's Bend, remember? If you want the pay, then deliver the goods."

The man cursed and propped himself on an elbow.

"Coffee's hot," Wynn prodded him. "Get some in you and let's get going."

It was rather amusing to watch the revelers of the night before. They didn't look so lively now. Grumbling, holding their heads and muttering oaths, they tried to get their bodies to obey.

Wynn had little sympathy. "Let's get moving," he ordered again. "The fog's about to lift, and we have some time to make up."

They were finally on their feet and stirring. Wynn poured each a cup of coffee, except for Charlie. In spite of the commotion all about him, Charlie had slept on, only stirring now and then to reposition himself.

"Finished with the bed, Elizabeth?" Wynn inquired. When I gladly nodded that I was, Wynn unceremoniously lifted Charlie up and carried him to his bed. Wynn straightened out the unconscious body to what looked like a comfortable position and threw a blanket over him. Charlie slept on.

Two of the men went out to prepare the barge for departure while the other fellow mumbled and complained about the lousy day for traveling.

Wynn looked at his pocketwatch.

"Gotta be out of here in ten minutes, Wally," he stated flatly. "Ten minutes, no more."

Wally, still grumbling, went to join the others.

Wynn left money on the shelf by the coffeepot to cover our

expenses for the night's lodging and the food. Charlie was still snoring as we closed the door behind us.

Back in the boat with the slicker arranged around me, I discovered it was not raining hard. Without the wind, I was sure I would fare just fine.

In spite of the constant peppering with fine raindrops, I found myself enjoying the scenery on the riverbanks moving swiftly from view on either side. There was very little habitation, but occasionally I did spy the smoke of a woodstove and a cabin, half-hidden by the trees.

By midmorning the rain had stopped, the wind had died down to a light breeze, and early in the afternoon the sun actually came out. The slicker laid aside, I let the warm sun fall on my shoulders. We had not stopped except to eat a hurried noon meal consisting of a few tins of canned food heated over an open fire.

The country through which we passed was fresh and clean. No factory smells tainted the air with civilization. I appreciated the crispness of the air even more after having spent the night at Charlie's.

We passed through a marshy area, and Wynn moved close to me to point out two large moose. They put their heads completely under water for what seemed ever so long. When they finally lifted their heads, their mouths dripping with long marsh grass, they looked toward us almost with disdain, seeming to indicate that this was their territory and we were trespassers.

"Look at them," I said to Wynn in astonishment. "You'd think they didn't even have to breathe, they are under so long!"

"Oh, they breathe all right," Wynn assured me, "though they are unusual. They can even dive to get their food—some say as deep as thirty feet if need be. They scoop up the grasses on the bottom and then come back up again."

"Do they need to go back to land to eat it?"

"Oh, no. They just tread water. Moose are wonderful swimmers. Don't suppose there are many animals any better."

"Aren't they ugly, though? They look like—like leftover pieces of this and that."

Wynn laughed. "Well, there's a saying," he mused, "that a moose is a horse made by a committee."

We chuckled together at Wynn's joke.

Since the barge hands had started the day in bad spirits, I tried to stay as far away from them as I could. Now and then one of them would hold his head and weave back and forth. I wondered if they were in any condition to steer the barge, especially when we hit some white water; but they seemed to be alert enough when they had to be. Wynn did not seem worried, so I relaxed, too. Eventually their dispositions improved. In the later afternoon, I even heard Blackjack singing.

With the passing of the day, I guess my disposition improved as well. Wynn had often been by my side to point out interesting items in the water or on the riverbanks. The sun was swinging to the west, the men were no longer cursing with every breath, and the country all around me seemed mysterious and exciting. Yes, things were definitely improved over yesterday.

Lying in that little cabin, I had wondered if I'd ever make it as a Mountie's wife. How could anyone endure such conditions? Today I was confident I could. My leg wasn't even bothering me anymore. We would soon be at the post, and Wynn had said we would have good accommodations there. I wasn't sure how many nights it would take us to make the trip, but I was now certain I could endure. I had gotten through the first night, and it surely couldn't be any worse. From here on I would have no problem.

Chapter Eleven

Onward

The cabin was simple but seemed very adequate, and the best thing was that I didn't need to share it with four drinking men. Another nice thing was that I could share it in privacy with Wynn.

After we had gone to bed I heard a strange sound. It seemed to grow louder and louder until it was humming steadily in my ears. I was puzzled and wished I could ask Wynn about it, but I could tell by his breathing that he was already asleep.

In the darkness something stung me. I jumped and slapped at it. Another sting. I swatted again.

"Put your head under the covers if they are bothering you," said Wynn softly.

"What is it?"

"Mosquitoes."

Now I had seen mosquitoes before. I had even been bitten by a few; but this—this *din* was something new to me.

"Are you sure?" I asked Wynn.

"I'm sure," he answered. "This cabin doesn't have any screens on the windows."

"How do you ever sleep?"

"You get used to it."

Wynn turned over to pull me close and shelter my face with the blankets.

"Try to sleep, Elizabeth," he encouraged me. "You didn't get much last night."

I lay quietly in Wynn's arms, not stirring for fear I would keep him awake. The hum was a rising and falling crescendo. I wondered how many million mosquitoes it took to make such a sound.

In spite of the protection of Wynn's arms and the blanket, the mosquitoes still found me. I could hear their hum get closer and then I would feel the sharp sting as they sucked out my blood.

One thing is sure, I promised myself. *Our cabin in the North will have coverings over the windows even if I have to tear up my petticoats!*

In the morning I rose tired and grumpy. I would be so glad to get back on the barge and away from the mosquitoes.

My triumph was short lived; though we were soon back on the river, the dreaded mosquitoes swarmed around us, following us down the stream.

"Wynn," I said crossly, "they are coming with us."

"There are lots of mosquitoes in the North," Wynn informed me. "They are one of the area's worst pests."

"What are the others?" I muttered sarcastically, but Wynn didn't catch the tone of my question.

"Blackflies," he replied. "Blackflies are another real plague to man and beast alike."

Wynn was right. The mosquitoes were joined that day by the blackflies. I thought I would be bitten and chewed to pieces. Right before my eyes, new welts would rise on my arms. I hated to think what my face must look like. I was almost frantic with the intensity of the itching.

Wynn was sympathetic. "I might have something that will help," he offered and went to dig around in his medical supplies.

He came back with an ointment. It had a vile smell and looked awful, but I allowed him to rub it on anyway. It did help some, though it didn't seem to discourage the dreadful insects from taking further bites out of me.

"Why didn't they bother us yesterday?" I asked Wynn.

"The wind and the rain kept them away."

"Really?"

"They can't fly well in strong wind. They are too light, and they don't care for the rain either." I was ready to pray for more wind and rain. Anything to be rid of the miserable pests.

I guess I eventually got used to them. I was able to think about other things after a while and even to again enjoy, in a sense, my trip.

In the late afternoon, Wynn pointed out a mother bear and her two cubs. She was foraging at a bend in the river. Perhaps she was fishing, because she was staring intently at the water, seeming to ignore the barge completely as we went by.

The cute cubs took my mind off the mosquitoes and flies for a few minutes while I considered having a cub for a pet.

It was already getting dusk before we pulled into River's Bend, the place where we were to spend the night. Wynn lifted me ashore as there was no dock. This didn't make sense to me.

"Why is it," I asked, "that there's no dock and yet this is the place where all our things need to be unloaded? Isn't it going to be an awful job carrying all those heavy trunks and crates ashore?"

Wynn rewarded me with a broad smile. Apparently he liked a wife who was observant.

"The dock is around the bend in the river. Our things will be unloaded there. There are also a couple of temporary buildings and a Hudson's Bay Post, but I thought you might prefer to use this trapper's cabin. It is more private, though I'm afraid not luxurious. I've made arrangements with Pierre to use it for the night."

"Who's Pierre?"

"He runs the post."

"Is he married?"

"Nope. He batches. And his quarters are even worse than Charlie's."

I couldn't even imagine what that would be like.

"I don't want you to have to stay in those kinds of conditions again," Wynn stated firmly. "I know it must have been extremely offensive to you."

I thought back to Charlie's. The smelly, crowded cabin. The cursing, drinking, card-playing men. No, I wasn't particularly interested in that again either. I was pleased Wynn had made other arrangements.

Wynn opened the creaky, complaining cabin door; there was some quick scampering as some former resident took immediate cover. I stepped closer to Wynn. He put a reassuring arm around me. "Nothing that small could harm you," he smiled.

Wynn found and lit the lamp, and I placed my small case on the newspaper-covered table.

"Is this Pierre's cabin?" I asked, looking around me at the bare little room.

"No, it belongs to some trapper."

"Then why did Pierre—?"

"It's customary. Trappers always leave their cabins available for others to use. Pierre likely asked the trapper about using his lodgings for travelers like us; but even if he didn't, we still won't be considered trespassers."

Wynn moved about, swishing the heavy dust from the few pieces of furniture and checking what was available for making a fire. There was a good supply of dry wood in one corner, and Wynn soon had a fire going. "Remember your first experience with a wood stove at Pine River?" His eyes twinkled at me, and I had the grace to blush. It's a wonder I hadn't burned down the building! I wrinkled my nose at him and we laughed together at the memory.

Wynn went outside to the river, dipped the kettle full of water and placed it on to boil. Then he checked the bed. It was a very narrow one, and I secretly wondered how it would sleep two. Wynn flung back the Hudson's Bay blankets; they had seen a good deal of wear and very few washings. A heavy piece of denim material was spread across a mattress of spruce branches crisscrossing one another topped with moss. I winced and hoped Wynn hadn't noticed.

Our meal was a simple one of dried biscuits and canned police rations. Tasty it was not, but I was very hungry and ate heartily.

I insisted on washing the dishes. Wynn had been our wilderness cook all along our journey, and I was glad I could finally do something helpful.

It didn't take me long to wash the few things and place them back on the unknown trapper's shelf.

Wynn spread one of the worn blankets on the wooden floor in front of the fire and we settled down before it to talk. I looked about the simple, quaint little cabin and wondered if my own would look like this. I decided to ask.

"Do you know what our cabin will be like?"

"Not really. I haven't been to Beaver River before."

"But you have a pretty good idea?"

"Pretty good."

"Will it have just one room?"

"Not likely. A Mountie's home usually serves a double function—office as well as home. So it likely has at least two rooms."

I was pleased to hear that. I did want the privacy of a bedroom.

"It will be log?"

"I'm sure it will."

"With wooden floors?"

"With wooden floors."

We were silent for a few moments. Wynn broke the silence, his arm tightening about me as he spoke, "That must seem awfully crude to you, Elizabeth."

I turned so I could look into his eyes.

"In a way, yes—but really—I don't mind the thought of it at all. Look at this cabin now. True, it isn't much—but with a little fixing here and there—" I hesitated, wondering even as I spoke just what "fixing" one could do to make this very bare cabin look homey.

Wynn brushed a kiss against my cheek.

A strange, mournful, bloodcurdling sound interrupted us. I felt the hair on my scalp rise and my spine tingle. I had gotten used to the coyote's cry, but this—this was something entirely different. I pressed closer to Wynn.

"A timber wolf," he commented. I shivered as the cry came again and was answered from the other direction.

I had heard of timber wolves. Most of the tales had come from imaginative Julie. Wolves traveled in murderous packs, had menacing red eyes, and crept up stealthily on those whom they would devour.

"Are they all around us?" I whispered nervously, my eyes big with fright.

Wynn hugged me, sheltering me in the circle of his two strong arms.

"I doubt it," he said, without any trace of concern whatever. "But if they are, there is nothing whatever to be worried about. I suggest you just lie here in front of the fire and listen carefully,

Elizabeth. You can almost count how many there are in the pack by the difference in their cries. They are a part of our world here in the North—a part that needs to be respected but not feared. Accept them—maybe even enjoy them if you can."

I doubted I would ever live to enjoy the cry of a timber wolf, but I did try to be calm. Another cry tore through the night air.

"Hear that?" noted Wynn close to my ear. "I'm guessing that was the leader of the pack. Did you hear the authority in his voice?"

I tried to shake my head, but Wynn was holding me too close. Authority? Not particularly.

Another cry reached us. This one was shorter and farther away.

"That one now, he's answering the boss. Checking in. Could you hear the difference?"

This time I could. It was unbelievable.

There was another cry. It came from very near our cabin, yet it wasn't as spooky and bloodcurdling for some reason.

"A female," commented Wynn. "Probably the leader's mate."

"Are the females tamer than the males?" I asked, thinking that this one sounded so much gentler than others.

"Oh, no," laughed Wynn. "In fact, the female can be even more aggressive and more deadly than the males—especially if she has pups. The hunting pack always consists of some females. I'm not sure how the males would fare without them. The pack depends on their skill and aggressiveness for the kill. The female must have food not just for herself but to feed her young—and she will do anything to get what she's after."

The wolves were a part of Wynn's wilderness. I wasn't sure I would ever be able to listen to their howl without shivering, but Wynn's calm and easy acceptance of these wild creatures had certainly helped me to see them in another light.

Another howl. Another shiver. Another explanation from Wynn. He seemed to paint a picture of the pack around us, locating and identifying each member. He did not describe them with sparkling red eyes and drooling tongues. I was seeing them as needy, hungry creatures, depending on nature and their skills to feed themselves and their families.

"Contrary to what you may have heard," Wynn told me, "the

wolves only hunt to survive. In the wilderness, survival is not always easy."

I listened to the echoing calls of the wolves as they moved on, away from the cabin. My heart quit thumping. I found myself even wishing them good hunting.

Chapter Twelve

By Wagon

We took the trail the next morning to the small, hastily constructed buildings that formed the small outpost. Before we had left the little cabin, I had remade the bed and washed the dishes. Wynn had brought in a fresh wood supply, making sure he left more stacked against the wall than we had found the night before.

The trail through the woods crossed a stream on stepping-stones, and Wynn pointed east to where the beavers had dammed the water and made themselves a small lake. The morning sun was already promising a fair day, and the birds sang and winged overhead among the trees. The walk would have been perfect had it not been for the miserable insects. Even Wynn walked with a screen of cloth draped from his hat at the back.

When we reached the fort, I looked about at the sorry arrangement of small buildings. Even from the outside, I was sure I wouldn't have wanted to stay overnight in any of them. I was so glad Wynn had arranged for the cabin.

"I think you should wait out here," Wynn said to me. I wondered why, but did not question him. I found a nearby tree stump and sat down. No one seemed to be around, so I lifted my skirt to inspect my leg. It was no longer covered with a bandage; Wynn had decided the air would do it good.

Ugly scabs of various density and color covered the shin. I moved my foot back and forth. Almost all the pain was gone. Wynn had said that it was most important to have bodies capable of healing themselves when one was miles away from medical help. He seemed very pleased he had picked a woman with this quality.

Wynn was not in the cabin for long. He returned with a look of frustration on his face.

"What's wrong? Are they drunk?"

"Drunk isn't the word for it. They are *out*! Every last one of them. I couldn't even raise them."

"You're angry with them for drinking, aren't you? I don't blame—"

But Wynn didn't let me finish my intended consolation.

"Yes, I'm angry. With their drinking? I don't like it, but I can't stop it. That's their business, I guess—their way of life. That's the way they ease through the difficulties of life in the North. When men don't have God, they need substitutes. To my way of thinking, whiskey is a poor substitute—but many men depend upon it. But what I am angry about is that they didn't obey my orders."

I looked up in surprise.

"They were supposed to unload the barge last night before they started their drinking. I knew very well they wouldn't be any good for anything this morning. There sits the wagon, nothing on it; and in there, sprawled out on the floor, are the men who were to load it and the man who was supposed to drive it."

"What do we do now?" I finally asked in a small voice.

Wynn roused and reached over to cup my chin. He smiled then for the first time since emerging from the house.

"We do it ourselves, my love," he answered, strength and confidence back in his voice.

It was a long, hard job. The morning sun was high in the sky before we finished. I really wasn't much help. The crates and trunks were all too heavy for a woman's shoulders, and Wynn would not even let me try. Wynn had driven the wagon down as close to the dock as possible in order to save unnecessary steps. I volunteered to hold the team, as there was no hitching post. Wynn seemed pleased that I was willing to help, but the job I had did not go well.

The horses were skitterish. The mosquitoes and flies were plaguing them, and they kept tossing their heads and stamping around. Wynn watched my efforts warily for a while and them decided to unhitch the horses, take them up the bank and tie them securely to a tree. Now I had nothing to do.

I tried to give a hand now and then but soon found I was more in the way than anything else. At length I gave up and found a tree stump in the shade.

As I sat there, I angrily thought about the men in the nearby cabin. There they slept in a drunken stupor while my husband labored to do the work they had been hired to do!

Finally the loading was completed and the horses rehitched to the wagon.

Wynn made one more visit to the cabin to check on our hired driver.

"Any luck?" I asked when he returned, his lips set in a thin line.

"None." It was a crisp, blunt reply.

"What do we do now?" I asked. "Do we have to wait here until he wakes up?"

"No, we don't wait. We are late enough getting away now. We'll never make it as far as we should today. We *drive*. When he wakes up he *walks*."

The horses were not made for speed and the wagon was clumsy and heavy. It had been much faster traveling on the river. The sun grew hot on my back and the insects buzzed persistently.

We didn't talk much. Wynn concentrated on his driving, and I tried to keep my mind busy with things other than my discomfort. The river barge seemed like a pleasure boat compared to this lumbering wagon.

We stopped at noon for a quick meal. Wynn ate with one eye on the sky, for clouds were gathering. I knew he feared a storm before we reached our destination. Neither of us voiced the concern, but I noticed that Wynn pushed the horses a little faster.

The track could, at best, be referred to as a trail. It wound up and down, around and through, following the path of least resistance, much like a river would do. At times there was no way but to challenge the terrain head-on. The horses strained up steep hills, then slid their way to the bottom again, the wagon jolting behind. Fortunately, Wynn was an expert teamster, and I breathed a prayer of thanks whenever we reached fairly level ground again.

At one point, even Wynn feared for the safety of the horses and wagon. He asked me to climb out and walk down the incline. It seemed to be almost straight down. On further thought, Wynn crawled down from the wagon, rustled through some of his belongings, and came up with the horrid men's pants. They had been washed since I had seen them last, which I assumed Wynn had done himself.

"You'd best put these on," he said. "You might spend part of the descent in a sitting position."

Without question I quickly obeyed and stuffed my simple skirt and petticoat into the overnight bag lying on top of the load.

Wynn went first. I didn't really want to watch, but I couldn't tear my eyes away. A good brake system on the wagon kept the wheels skidding downhill, always on the heels of the sliding horses.

I stood there with bated breath, now and then gasping and covering my eyes, then quickly uncovering them again to make sure Wynn was still all right.

I forgot to follow. When Wynn finally rolled the wagon to a halt on comparatively even ground, I still stood, with my mouth open, at the top of the hill.

I blushed and hurried down to join him. His call, "Slow down," came too late. Already I had picked up more speed than I could control on the steep slope. I tried to brace myself against the momentum, but soon my body was moving far too fast for my clumsy feet, and I felt myself falling and rolling end over end. The next thing I was aware of was Wynn's white face bending over me.

"Elizabeth," he pleaded, panting for air, "Elizabeth, are you all right?"

I moaned and tried to roll over into a more dignified position. I wasn't sure if I was all right or half dead. I did have enough presence of mind to be glad for the horrible pants.

Wynn began to feel my bones. I roused somewhat, my dizzy head beginning to clear.

"I think I'm okay," I told him, struggling to sit up.

"Lie still." he ordered. "Don't move until we are sure."

He continued to check. By now my head was clear.

"I'm okay," I insisted, feeling only a few places on my body smarting. "Just embarrassed to death, that's all."

Wynn satisfied himself that nothing was broken and sighed with relief. He then turned his attention to the scratches and bruises.

"Let me up," I implored him and he carefully assisted me to my feet.

He brushed the dirt from my clothing and the leaves from my hair, showing both relief and concern on his face.

"I wanted you to walk down to keep you from injury," he said softly, shaking his head in dismay.

I began to laugh. Wynn looked at me with more concern in his eyes and then he smiled slowly.

"That's some record for coming down that hill," I said between gasps of laughter.

"I think," he remarked, "I might have set a record for coming back up—Hey!" His shout made me turn to follow his gaze. The deserted team had decided to plod on without us. They were not far ahead, but they were still traveling; and if we didn't hurry or if something spooked them, we might be walking for a long way. Wynn ran down the remainder of the hill, chasing after them. I followed, but at a much slower pace. I didn't want a repeat performance. I was already smarting and aching quite enough.

Wynn caught the team about a quarter of a mile down the road. They had not exactly followed the trail though, and Wynn was hard put to back them out of the dead end they had led themselves into among the trees.

Finally back on the trail again, we noticed the clouds had gathered more darkly overhead. It had cooled off noticeably and the wind was picking up.

"Is there anyone living nearby?" I asked him, sensing his uneasiness.

"Not that I'm aware of," he answered.

Even the horses seemed to sense the coming storm and tossed their heads and complained at the load.

They balked when we came to a stretch of marshy land where they were required to cross on corduroy (wooden logs placed side by side). Wynn coaxed and then forced them to take the first steps. The logs rolled and sucked, squeezing up oozy marsh soil as we passed over. I felt as reluctant as the horses. I wished I could walk but then rethought the matter. In places the logs lay beneath the surface of the water.

The horses clomped and slipped, snorting and plunging their way ahead. One horse would balk and refuse to take another step while its teammate was still traveling on. Then the horse would give a nervous jump and scramble on, slipping on the logs as he did so. By then, his teammate would have decided to balk. We jerked our way across the precarious floating bridge, and I breathed a sigh of relief when the wagon wheels finally touched solid ground again.

The horses, sweating more from nerves than from exerted energy, were even more skittery now, so when the first loud crack of thunder greeted us, they jumped and would have bolted had Wynn not been prepared and held tightly to the reins.

I moved uneasily on the seat, my eyes on the clouds overhead. It would pour any minute and there was no place to go for shelter.

Wynn urged the team on. It was impossible to expect them to run. The wagon was much too heavy and the track too poor, but he did ask of them a brisker walk. They obliged, seeming as reluctant as we were to be caught in the storm.

Just as the rain began to spatter about us, we rounded a corner and there before us was a shed! It was not in good repair and we weren't sure what its use had been in the past; but it was shelter, and Wynn turned off the rutted track, heading the team quickly for it.

"Run in before you get soaked, Elizabeth," he urged, helping me down from the wagon seat. I did not stop to argue.

Wynn hastened to unhitch the team and then he was there, bringing the horses right in with him. He moved them to the far end of the shed and tied them to a peg in the wall. A loud crack of thunder made me jump and the horses whinney in fright. Now the rain came in sheets. I had never seen it rain so hard.

The shelter we had found was in no way waterproof. We had to watch where we stood in order to prevent the rain from running down our necks.

There was one spot along the south wall where it seemed to be quite dry. Wynn pointed to it and suggested we sit there to wait out the storm. The building had a dirt floor and again I was glad that I still wore the pants. We sat on the floor and leaned against the wall of the building. Outside the angry storm continued to sweep about us, flashing and booming as it passed over our heads.

It did not last long. In less than a half hour or so it was over. The dark clouds moved on, the thunder continuing to rumble in the distance.

The storm had not improved our road any. Where we had, a few minutes before, been traveling in dust, we now were in muck. Wynn said we were lucky—such a hard rain had a tendency to run off rather than to soak like gentler rain would have done. But I wondered how the trail could possibly have gotten any muddier.

I felt sorry for the horses as they labored through the mud which made the already heavy load even heavier. We both walked whenever we could find halfway decent footing to save them the extra weight. Wynn stopped frequently to let them catch their breath. Their sides heaved and their backs began to steam; but they seemed impatient to get on with it and were soon chomping at the bit at every stop.

The storm brought one blessing. For a few merciful minutes, the mosquitoes stayed away. I was just about to share my joy with Wynn when the pests began to buzz around us again.

"I've been told that there are some trappers who live along this route," Wynn informed me as we trudged on. "I had hoped to make it to their cabin tonight."

I was glad to hear there were people living along the trail. Then I remembered Charlie.

"Just men?" I asked.

"No, they have womenfolk—and children, I believe."

That was even better news.

"How far?"

"I'm not sure. I've never been up this way before."

"Do you think we'll make it by dark?"

"I'm hoping so—but, if not, we'll be fine camping out if we need to. Remember, you had wanted the experience of sleeping under the stars on our Banff honeymoon."

I nodded. I remembered well. And then our honeymoon had been cut so short there wasn't time.

"It might be fun," I answered Wynn. "Do you think it will rain some more?"

Wynn checked the sky. "I don't think so. Not tonight. Maybe a little tomorrow."

"Oh, dear," I fairly groaned at the news. "Will we get held up again tomorrow?"

"I hope it won't be stormy enough to stop us—but it might be rather miserable traveling for a spell."

The long summer day of sunlight allowed us to continue traveling till after ten o'clock. We had not even stopped to eat, munching instead on hard, dry sandwiches and sipping water from the flask Wynn had filled that morning.

"Well," Wynn said, just as I was beginning to realize how very weary I was, "I'm afraid we are going to have to give up on that cabin. We need to stop. You must be exhausted, Elizabeth, and the horses need a chance to rest and feed."

I looked around at the scraggly evergreens. We had passed through much prettier spots earlier in the day.

"It looks like there might be a clearing just up ahead. The grass should be better there. Let's have a look."

Wynn was right. Much to our surprise, at the opposite side of the clearing stood a small log cabin.

"Well, look at that," said Wynn, relieved. "The trappers. And right when we need them."

The cabin appeared to be very small. I looked around for another one. Wynn had mentioned more than one family. I couldn't see another cabin. It must be hidden in the trees.

"Do you think one of the families might have room for us?" I asked Wynn.

Wynn smiled. "Oh, they'll have room all right. Even if we all have to stand still to manage it, there'll be room."

I looked perplexed and Wynn explained. "Hospitality in the North is as much a part of life as eating and sleeping. They might not have much, but whatever they have is yours."

As we approached the cabin, I looked down at myself in embarrassment. Wynn had said there were women here, and I would be turning up at their door in my male attire looking like a pincushion—bites and scratches and bruises indicating a much-used pincushion at that. I didn't have the time or the opportunity to make any repairs on my appearance. We had already been spotted.

We were met in the yard by four small children—three boys and a girl. I had never seen such chewed-up hands and faces in my life. I was a mess, but they were even more so. They seemed to take it all for granted, chatting with us and swatting insects as though it was the most natural thing in the world.

The children ushered us into the house and, to my surprise, we found that it was home to two families. The men saw no reason to furnish and supply wood for more than one cabin. It was one long, open room shared by four adults and four children. Another baby was on the way, probably due any day.

The woman who met us at the door and welcomed us in was just as mosquito-bitten as the children, as was the one who turned from the stove and smiled a shy welcome. I relaxed about how I looked, but at the same time I winced. Would I look like this the entire time I lived in the north country? *Surely not, God,* I whispered in dismay.

With great ceremony we were immediately seated at a crude table, while the woman at the stove brought huge bowls of steaming stew and set them before us. They had been about to have their evening meal; and upon our arrival, the women had given us their places at the table. I wanted to protest, but Wynn nudged me forward and I understood that to decline their invitation as welcomed guests might offend them. With mixed feelings I sat down and smiled at them appreciatively. I was hungry and the food smelled delicious.

I recognized none of the vegetables I saw in my dish. Wynn informed me that the women were experts at combing the forest for edible plants. I smiled at them again, thanking them for sharing their supper.

"We be so glad to see ya, yer doin' *us* the favor," declared the older one with simple courtesy.

No grace was said before we began, so I offered, unobtrusively, my own short prayer of thanks. I blessed Wynn's food as well, as the men did not give him any time for such an observance. Immediately they began plying him with questions about the outside world.

The children ate noisily. It was plain that manners were not considered necessary around this table. A common cup passed from person to person with the hot drink that went with the meal. I smiled and passed it on. To my chagrin, Wynn lifted it without hesitation and drank deeply. I fervently prayed again— that God would keep him from getting some dreadful disease.

"That was very good," I said to the cook when we had finished. "I wish we had time to let you show me how to make it."

She dipped her head shyly.

"Wasn't nothin'," she stated. "It's the bear that gives it the flavor."

"Bear?" I echoed, feeling my stomach contract.

"Bear meat's 'bout the best there is," observed her cabin-sister.

For a moment, I thought I would bolt from the table; but then I saw Wynn's amused eyes on my face and I swallowed hard and smiled.

"Well, it certainly is," I answered her evenly. "That was very tasty."

I saw the look of unbelief cross Wynn's face, and I smiled again—directly into his eyes. "Maybe when we get settled, you can shoot a bear," I challenged him, "and *I* can make *you* some stew like this."

He laughed outright. I'm sure no one else at the table understood our little joke.

We did spend the night with the trappers and their families. There were two beds in the room. We were given one of them. The two women took the other; and the two men, without comment or protest, took robes and blankets from a stack in the corner and spread out on the floor with the children, everyone sleeping fully clothed.

Chapter Thirteen

The Last Day on the Trail

After Wynn had dressed my injured leg the next morning and expressed again his pleasure at how nicely it was healing, we were on our way. With luck, this would be our last day on the trail.

I followed Wynn's advice and draped a scarf over my head and down around my neck, but the pesky little mosquitoes and flies still got at me. The hairline at the back of my neck seemed to be their special delight.

"How do the people stand it?" I asked Wynn as I scratched at the swelling lumps.

"It's one of the things they learn to live with," he shrugged.

I didn't like the answer. Mostly because I knew that it implied I must learn to live with it as well.

It was a beautiful July day; and, though clouds passed by overhead, it did not rain. The warm sun soon had dried the rain of the day before from the track. Only in spots did we still plow through messy, gooey, wet places, the horses throwing themselves against their collars and straining to pull the heavy wagon. Wynn would always stop them for a breather and soon they were chomping and straining to be on the way again.

Occasionally, we traveled along the banks of a stream or beside a still lake. The fish would jump to feed on the swarming insects that got too near the water's surface. I wished them good hunting—each fish's dinner was one less to bother me!

We stopped around noon in an area covered with tall fir trees. I recognized several different varieties, but I didn't know enough to be able to separate them by name. Wynn was much too busy unhitching the horses and getting the fire going to answer questions, so I walked off alone, observing as I walked and storing questions for later. I kept Wynn in sight so I wouldn't get lost.

By the time the fire was burning briskly, I was back to help with our meal.

We did not stop for long.

In a swampy area I spotted a mother moose and her young one, even without Wynn pointing them out to me. I was pleased with myself.

"Look!" I cried. "A moose—two mooses."

Wynn smiled and nodded his head as he followed my pointing finger. He turned to me and said simply, "I must correct you, Elizabeth, so you won't be laughed at.—Moose is both singular and plural."

I guess I had known that; but, in my excitement, I had forgotten. I nodded in appreciation of Wynn's concern for me. I also appreciated the fact that he had not laughed.

I watched the moose until they were lost from sight and then I turned to Wynn. "What else?" I asked.

"What else, what?" he puzzled.

"What other animal names are both singular and plural?"

"Deer. Elk. Caribou." Wynn stopped.

"Bear?" I asked him.

"Bear? No, it's quite all right to refer to 'The Three Bears.' "

"Any other?"

"Likely."

"Likely? You mean you don't know?"

"They don't come to mind right now."

"How will I know what to say if—?"

He smiled at me and reached to push back a lock of unruly hair that insisted upon curling around my cheek. "You'll learn. You're very quick."

I flushed slightly under his smile and the compliment. It was good to know Wynn was not afraid that he might be embarrassed by his city-bred wife.

"Are we almost there?" I asked Wynn like a child for the tenth time. We had stopped for our evening meal.

He smiled at me and spread out his map. He carefully studied our surroundings, looking for some identifying signs. I couldn't make head nor tail of Wynn's map. After a moment of study, he pointed to a spot on the map. "We are about here," he said. "That should leave us about nine or ten miles to go. No, not quite," he corrected himself. "More like seven to eight."

"Will we make it tonight?"

"I certainly hope so—but it won't be early. It's a good thing we have lots of daylight for traveling. I'm afraid we're going to need it."

I loaded our supper things back in the wagon while Wynn hitched the horses, and we were on our way again. Perhaps we had made our last stop—I certainly hoped so. Excitement took hold of me as I thought of how close I was getting to my *new home*.

The horses seemed to sense they were getting close to home, too; and Wynn had to hold them back in spite of their tiredness and the heavy wagon they pulled.

I felt too excited and tense to even talk, so the last leg of our journey was a quiet one. But my mind was full of questions— some that even Wynn would not have been able to answer, not having lived at Beaver River himself. *What will our little cabin be like? What will our neighbors be like? Will there be any white women at the Post? Will the Indians like me and accept me? Will I ever be able to converse with them?* The thoughts whirled about in my head, making me almost dizzy.

The sun dropped into the west, closer and closer to the horizon. Still we had not reached Beaver River, and I was beginning to wonder if Wynn had made an error in his estimation— easily forgiven considering the little information he had been given. I was about to wonder aloud when Wynn spoke.

"Would you spread out that map on your lap, please? I want to take another look at it while it's still light enough to see well."

I spread out the map and, without comment, Wynn began to refigure.

"If I've got it worked out right, the settlement should be right over this next hill."

I wanted to shout for joy. In my excitement I reached over and gave Wynn a quick and unexpected hug which sent his stetson tumbling into the dust of the roadway. By the time

Wynn got my arms untangled and the team stopped, his Royal North West Mounted Police hat had been run over by the steel rim of the heavy wagon wheel. Horrified, I watched Wynn walk back to retrieve the poor thing from the dirt. It was now quite flat where it should have been nicely arched. I covered my remorseful face with my hands but Wynn returned to the wagon smiling; and, after a bit of pummeling and a punch here and there, he settled the hat back on his head—a few unsightly lumps, but it was in better shape than I had dared to hope.

Wynn was right. As we rounded the brow of the hill before us, there lay the little settlement at our feet. I refrained myself from hugging Wynn again. Instead, it was Wynn who hugged me.

"There it is, Elizabeth," he whispered against my cheek. "There's home."

"Home," I repeated. It was a magic word and brought tears to my eyes. I tucked my arm within Wynn's, even though he did need both hands on the reins. To think of it! We were almost home.

In the gathering dusk, it looked like a friendly little village to me. We could see the flag flying high over the Hudson's Bay Company Store. Scattered all around that central building were others of various sizes. At our approach, dogs began to set up a howl. People appeared in doorways and looked our way. A few of them even waved an arm to the approaching team. I suppose everyone in the settlement knew well who was in the coming wagon. They would be waiting to size up the new lawman and his wife. I held Wynn's arm more tightly.

"Tell me again," I asked, "what did you say the name of the Hudson's Bay man was?"

"McLain," said Wynn. "Ian McLain."

"And he's not married?"

"I couldn't find anyone who knew. I asked, but no one had heard of a Mrs. McLain."

"I suppose that means there isn't one," I said in resignation.

"Not necessarily. There really isn't much reason for the records to show if there is a wife or not. The agent is listed, not his family."

I took this as a spark of hope, but I wasn't going to count

too strongly on another white woman in the village.

Darkness was closing in quickly now that we had passed down the hill. Windows were beginning to light up with lamps. The noise of the dogs increased as more people gathered around. I looked over the crowd of white men and several Indians. My eyes searched on. Who was Mr. McLain? Was he alone?

Wynn pulled the team to a halt before the large Hudson's Bay building and called out a friendly greeting to the men gathered there. A tall, square man with a heavy beard stepped forward. "Welcome to Beaver River, Sarge," he said. "Name here is Ian McLain."

He was alone.

Chapter Fourteen

Home

Wynn shook hands with many of the men who had gathered around and nodded his head to others as he moved about. For a moment I felt forgotten. I didn't know whether to climb down from the wagon or to stay where I was until someone noticed me. Eventually I could feel eyes turning my way. Wynn invited the Hudson's Bay Post employee closer to the wagon and smiled up at me. "My wife, Elizabeth. Elizabeth, Mr. McLain."

McLain reached up and gave my hand a hearty shake.

"Come in. Come in," boomed Mr. McLain, but Wynn cut in rather quickly.

"We've had a long six days, and Elizabeth is anxious to get settled. If you could just point out the cabin for our use, we'd be grateful."

Mr. McLain nodded in understanding. He pointed west toward a stand of trees. The outline of a cabin showed faintly against the last glimmer of daylight.

"Right on over there," he informed us.

"Is there a place there to keep the horses?"

Mr. McLain took a look at the team and suddenly remembered something.

"Where's Canoue?" he asked.

"Sleeping when I last saw him. He got to sharing whiskey with the boys and I wasn't able to rouse him. I couldn't wait, so we left him behind."

The Hudson's Bay man shook his head. "He has his problems with the bottle. I warned him. 'Canoue,' I said, 'don't you go messin' this one up. I can't keep findin' you work if ya ain't able to stay with it.' Needed that money." McLain shrugged his shoulders. "There ain't no place for horses over to 'the law'; you can bring 'em back on over here. I got a corral out back," the man continued.

All the time this conversation was taking place, I could feel eyes studying me. Mostly we were surrounded by men, but now I saw a few Indian women and some young people and children. I smiled at them, though I must admit I felt as out of place and uncomfortable as I ever had in my life. I was anxious for Wynn to end his conversation and get us out of there and home.

At last he climbed back up into the wagon, turned the team around and headed for the little cabin which was to be our first home.

I felt tingles go all through me. What would it be like? Would it be in good repair? Would it have that private bedroom I wanted so badly? I fought the temptation to close my eyes until I actually got there. I was anxious and afraid—all at one time.

When Wynn said "whoa" to the team, I knew the moment was at hand. He turned to me and drew me close. "Well," he murmured softly, "are you ready?"

I couldn't get my lips to move, so I just nodded my head against him.

"What will you need tonight?"

I really didn't know. I had no idea what I might find in the cabin.

Then we heard voices behind us and turned to see a group approaching. It was McLain's voice that called out to us.

"Thought we might as well unload that there wagon tonight and save ya the trouble in the mornin'. Then ya won't need to fuss with the team ag'in."

It was a thoughtful offer, and I was sure Wynn appreciated it. I should have appreciated it, too, but I had wanted to enter our new home in privacy—just the two of us. Now we were to be ushered in by the Hudson's Bay trader and a host of local trappers. I felt disappointment wash over me. If only Wynn would quickly send them all away and tell them the load could wait until morning. He didn't. He withdrew his arm, climbed down from the wagon, and turned to help me down. "Appreciate that," he responded. "Shouldn't take long at all with the good help you've brought along." I blinked away tears in the semi-darkness and knew instinctively that Wynn would not understand how I, as a woman, felt about the intrusion. He would consider the practical fact that the wagon loaded with heavy trunks and crates needed unloading. I sentimentally thought that a man and his wife deserved to walk into their first home alone and together. Perhaps foolishly, I realized now, I had had visions of being carried over the threshold.

By the time my feet were firmly planted on the ground, the men were already bustling about the wagon.

"Perhaps you'd like to go in and show them where you would like things put," Wynn suggested.

I wanted to sputter that *I* would prefer things left right where they were, but I knew that was foolish and would be misunderstood; so I walked numbly to the door as Mr. McLain, who had taken the first crate forward, stood aside to let me get the door for him. How romantic!

The door was stuck, and I had to put both hands on the knob and pull hard. It finally gave and, in the process, skinned my knuckles. The injured hand stung smartly, and the tears in my eyes multiplied and spilled down my cheeks before I could stop them.

The house was dark. I had no idea where to find light. It was quite dark outside by now and the few small windows let in very little light. I hesitated. McLain shuffled his feet. He was waiting for me to make up my mind so he could rid himself of the heavy load he carried.

"Just set it down against that wall," I told him.

I guess he realized I was a little at a loss, for he volunteered, "I'll see if I can find the lamp." He soon had it lit and placed where it could bring the most benefit to the men who were unloading our belongings.

In and out they went. Men I had never seen before were clumping in and out of my new home, never stopping to wipe their feet. One of them even spit on *my* floor. Wynn did not enter himself. He was far too busy overseeing the unloading. I stood dumbly in the middle of the room, wondering what I should do; and then I remembered I did indeed have a responsibility: I was to tell the men where to put things. How did I know where to put things? I still didn't even know what rooms we had to furnish. So I just pointed a finger, which they probably couldn't see anyway from behind their big loads, and said, "Over there," until one wall was stacked high with our belongings.

Finally the stream of groaning, heaving men stopped. There was only the sound of their voices from the yard. Wynn was talking to the men before they returned to their own homes. I tapped my foot impatiently. Why did he take so long? Why didn't he just thank them and send them away?

I noticed a soft hum, which was soon a whine. Then another and another, and I realized we had given the mosquitoes a wonderful welcome. The open door, with the lamp burning in the room to light their way in, had not been ignored. Already our cabin must be filled with hundreds of them. With an angry little cry, I rushed over and slammed the door shut.

Wynn was still talking to the men. I turned dejectedly to the stack of our belongings and wondered just where I might find some blankets to make a bed. Picking up the lamp, I went over and began to check the pile. Labels of contents didn't help me much. All the crates on the top seemed to be things for Wynn's use as northern-law-enforcer and area-medical-supplier.

How would I ever make a bed? The past few nights on the trail I had promised myself that I would need to endure sleeping in such makeshift ways only for a few nights, and then I would be in my own home and sleeping in my own clean and fresh-smelling bed. And now I couldn't find my bedding. As a matter of fact, I didn't even know if there was a bed. Just as I was leaving the room, lamp held high, to find out if there was a bed in the cabin, Wynn poked his head in the door. I sighed with relief until I heard his words, "I'm going to take the team over, Elizabeth. I shouldn't be long. You make yourself at home."

I don't suppose he could have chosen any words that would have upset me more. *Make yourself at home.* This was home? Piled boxes. No husband. No blankets for my bed. And me, bone-weary. All I wanted was a warm bath to remove the messy trail dirt and a clean bed to crawl into. *Then* I might have been able to make myself at home. And Wynn. I wanted Wynn—my husband. After all, it was because of him that I had come to this strange, faraway land.

I let the tears flow freely then. Wiping my eyes and sniffing dejectedly, I stumbled into another room with the lamp held before me. There was a table, a stove, some rough shelves, and a cot—but no bed, at least not one that would hold two people.

I did not stop to look further but went on through another door. This room had pegs along one wall, a dilapidated stand with drawers and, yes, a double bed. It even had a mattress rather than spruce boughs—at least it was a mattress of sorts. It wasn't very clean, and it was rather lumpy; but it was a mattress. There was no bedding. I looked around for a shelf and found one, but there was no bedding on it either.

Going back to the other room again, I looked all around but still found nothing that would provide bedding for the night. There were three chairs I had missed before. Two of them were wooden and the third an overstuffed chair sitting in front of a fireplace. I was pleased with the fireplace, and then I realized it was probably more functional than anything else. It was likely the only source of heat in the cabin. I flashed the lamp around the room once more. It was quite bare—and not too clean. And then I spotted something I had missed in my first perusal. Over the fireplace hung a large fur that had been tanned and used as decoration or heat-retainer—I wasn't sure which. I put my lamp down and walked over to it. I gave it a pull. The fur was firmly attached. I pulled again. It still stayed in place. I grasped it in both my hands and put all my strength into the pull. With a tearing sound and a billow of dust, it came tumbling down from the wall and I went tumbling down to the floor.

I pushed the heavy fur off and got to my feet. It felt rather unyielding and bristly, not soft like the furs I was used to seeing. I pulled it to the bedroom and worked it through the door. I then went back for the lamp. I did finally manage to get the fur up on the bed and spread out in some way.

I looked around me. This was my new home! It was bare and dirty and had a lumpy bed, with no sheets, no blankets, and a smelly fur hide. There were no curtains, no soft rugs, no shiny windows—nothing. Even the chimney of the sputtering lamp was dirty with soot. But, worst of all, I was alone! That thought brought the tears streaming down my face again. I carried the lamp back out to the other room and set it on the table—I'm afraid it was more to coax the mosquitoes out of the bedroom than to provide a safe and welcome light for Wynn. Then I walked back to the bedroom, kicked off my shoes, crawled under the awkward animal skin, and began to cry in earnest. I didn't even have my evening talk with God. I was so miserable I thought He'd rather not hear from me. And in my present state, I really didn't want to hear from Him. I was very weary, so I did not cry for long. Sleep mercifully claimed me.

Chapter Fifteen

Making a Home

When I awoke the next morning, it took me several minutes to sort out where I was. With the knowledge came some of the hurt of the night before, but it wasn't as painful as it had been then. I looked down at myself. I was now covered with blankets. The fur I had struggled with was spread out on the floor by the bed, looking soft and even inviting. I was still in my clothes, my skirt and blouse now wrinkled as well as travel-stained. I knew my hair must be a sight—I had not even removed the pins the night before. They had worked loose in the night, so now part of my hair hung wildly about my face while part of it was still caught up with one pin or another. I removed the last pins and let my hair all tumble about my shoulders, combing my fingers through it to make some order out of the mess.

At my faintest stirring, Wynn was there, concern and pain in his face.

"Are you—?" But he didn't finish. Instead, he pulled me into his arms and held me so tightly I had to fight for air. "I'm so sorry, Elizabeth," he whispered, and there was a tremble in his voice.

I looked up at him then and saw his eyes were misted with unshed tears. It brought my tears again. I clung to Wynn and cried away all the feelings I had bottled up the night before. He let me cry.

When the tears finally stopped, Wynn tipped my head and looked deeply into my eyes. Perhaps he was looking for answers to some unspoken questions. I wasn't quite ready to smile yet, but I was ready to carry on. I avoided his eyes by shutting mine. He kissed me softly and then let me go.

"Are you hungry?" he asked. It wasn't until then that I

smelled coffee. Surprisingly, I realized I *was* hungry. I looked again at my clothes and my hands.

"I'm not sure what I need the most," I said, "food or a bath."

"How about the food first? Then we'll look after that bath."

I slipped into my shoes and futiley smoothed my skirt. Then I looked at Wynn. "Where do I go here?" I asked him.

He understood my question. "Out," he answered.

"Just—out?"

He nodded.

"You mean they don't even have any—any—outbuilding here in the village?"

"We're a quarter of a mile from the village."

"Still—"

"I'll make arrangements as soon as possible," Wynn stated and turned away to return to whatever he had been doing before I awakened. The pain was in his eyes again. I thought he might be thinking that he had been right—a girl like me didn't belong in the north country. I blinked back some new tears that stung my eyes and went *out*.

The day was filled with sunshine. A large flock of birds chattered in the nearby trees where they were already gathering, making their plans to return to lands where winter snow would not blow. In the village, a quarter of a mile away, I heard distant voices and barking dogs. I breathed deeply of the morning air. The hillsides were covered with evergreens and scattered with poplar and birch trees.

It was beautiful country. I would make it. I would! I would fix the house and—and—clean myself up, and I'd prove to Wynn that I could be happy here—as long as he was with me. A nagging fear gripped me then. What about all the times Wynn's duties would take him elsewhere? Like last night? He had to care for the borrowed team. He couldn't just turn them over to the Hudson's Bay trader. That man had his own responsibilities. Wynn had done only what needed to be done, and yet . . . It was going to take a lot of resolve on my part to create a home, a happy home, in Wynn's wilderness. I couldn't crumble like I had last night every time I faced difficulties, every time modern conveniences were not at my disposal. I wanted to be happy here. Most of all, I wanted to make Wynn happy. I was going to need help. I knew of only one true source readily available to me. I stopped for a few moments of prayer.

By the time I returned to the cabin, I had myself in hand again. Wynn was busy with the crates. He had carried my trunk to the bedroom and placed it beside the wall under the one lone window. I opened the lid, hoping to find a more suitable skirt and blouse in which to be seen at breakfast; but the ones I lifted from the trunk were just as wrinkled as those I wore. I gave up and went to see if I could find a basin to wash my hands. Wynn had already set one out, and a towel was hanging on a peg beside it.

I washed and moved on to the stove. The coffeepot was sending out a delightful aroma and Wynn had made a batch of pancakes that needed only to be poured on the griddle. It was hot and ready, so I began to spoon out the batter. The sizzle and the good smell made my stomach beg for a taste.

Wynn was soon in the kitchen beside me. "Smells good," he said, his hands on my shoulder behind me. "I had a tough time waiting."

"Why didn't you go ahead—or waken me?"

"I thought you needed the rest. And I didn't want to start my first day without you."

I swallowed hard and willed away the tears. That was all over now. I needed to put it firmly behind me.

"So what do you think?" I said, in order to initiate conversation.

"Think?" asked Wynn.

"About the cabin," I went on.

"It's bigger than I had dared to hope." Wynn sounded pleased, and I realized for the first time that he was right. I had seen three rooms in the darkness. I had been hoping for at least two. I had not even thought till now to be thankful.

I smiled at Wynn now. "That's right. I had hoped for a private bedroom, and it has a private living area as well." I looked around me. It wasn't much, this living area, but it had possibilities. There was the fireplace, with one small chunk of the fur I had yanked down the night before still dangling over it. There was a window looking out to the east and the village. There was the cot with the hard-looking covering, the, well—

the *easy* chair. Nearer at hand were the stove, some makeshift cupboards, the table and two chairs, and a stand where the basin and two large pails of water rested.

"Where'd they come from?" I asked Wynn. I had not noticed the pails the night before, and they weren't the ones from the teacherage that I had given Wynn to pack for our use.

"I borrowed them," he answered simply. "I thought you'd be aching for a bath last night so I asked McLain for them. It took us awhile to heat that much water—I guess I would have been wiser to have hurried back instead of waiting on it."

I looked at the heavy pails. They were filled almost to the brim. Wynn had carried them full of hot water the night before—for a quarter of a mile—hurrying and stumbling through the dark so I might have a bath. And what had he found? A childish woman who had cried herself to sleep under a musty old hide.

I crossed to Wynn, the pancake turner still in my hand. I reached my arms up and tightened them around his neck. "I'm sorry," I whispered.

He held me and kissed me. We didn't speak. I guess we were both busy sorting out thoughts. The smell of burning pancakes pulled me back to reality. Fortunately, they weren't so burned we couldn't eat them. In fact, after the dried and canned trail fare, they tasted good.

Wynn helped unpack our crates and trunks. It took us all morning to sort through our things and get them into the rooms where they would be used. After a light lunch, Wynn had some things to attend to at the store. I assured him I would be just fine. I was going to be very busy with a scrub brush and hot, soapy water.

I was scrubbing out the shelves which would be our kitchen cupboards when I heard men's voices. I expected a knock on our door, but after several minutes when none came I went to the window and cautiously looked out. Two men, with a team of horses and a dilapidated old wagon piled with rough lumber, were busily studying a large sheet of paper and arguing over the right way to go about their assigned task. They must have figured something out, for soon shovels, hammers and saws were industriously put to work. I was puzzled at first; and then as the small building began to take shape in the late afternoon, I realized Wynn had lost no time in keeping his promise. There was to be a private outbuilding—and soon. I felt a pang at having caused Wynn this additional problem, but at the same time I was greatly relieved. I couldn't imagine living for very long without some kind of accommodation.

I kept scrubbing and cleaning, and the men outside continued pounding. My back began to ache and my arms cramp. Still I kept on. I was determined to have a clean house by nightfall.

I did the cupboards, the windows, the floors. I wiped off the mattress of the bed and managed to drag it outside for a bit of air and sunshine. I pulled the hard seat covering of the cot out into the sun, too. Then I washed all our dishes and pots and pans and put them on the newly scrubbed shelves. I arranged tins and cans of food on the remainder of the shelves, stacking some things on the floor. There just wasn't room for everything to be put away. Certain items, like the dishpan, the frying pan, and some of the utensils, I hung on the pegs on the wall.

It didn't make a particularly tidy-looking kitchen, but it was clean, and I was pleased. I put away the thought of asking Wynn for doors on my cupboards to conceal all the clutter. It was enough that I was getting the little outbuilding and, as I considered it the far more important of the two, I would just do without the cupboard doors—or I would think of some way to conceal the shelves myself.

It was getting late in the afternoon when I went out to retrieve the mattress from the stumps where I had propped it in the sun. It was even harder to drag back in than it had been to get it out; but after much tugging and yanking, I finally managed to get it back in on the bed. I made up the bed then with clean sheets and blankets. How good it would be to have our own clean bed to sleep in again. I took my clothes from the trunk and hung them on the pegs in the wall. They were still wrinkled, but I would have to wait to get to that. I couldn't do everything in one day.

By the time Wynn arrived home, the house was in quite good order—that is, the two rooms which we considered our house. The large room that was to be Wynn's office still needed to be arranged, but Wynn had told me to leave that to him. We had been delighted and surprised at the discovery of a storage room off the bedroom. Our crates, boxes, and supplies could all be kept there, out of our living accommodations. Wynn had placed the crates in the little room as we had emptied them that morning.

Our supper that night came from tins of North West Mounted Police rations. I had no other meat and no vegetables of any kind. It was a simple meal, but we ate with a deep feeling of satisfaction. We were where we belonged, doing what we felt called to do. We had a home, and we had one another. True, there was much more that needed to be done before we were *settled,* but we had made a good start. I forgot my tired arms and back and chatted with Wynn about all the possibilities the little cabin held. I looked out of my window to the rough little shanty with its crooked door and crude shingles and felt more thankful for it than for the fanciest bathroom. "Thanks, Wynn," I said, "for having that little building built so soon. I appreciate your thoughtfulness."

"I want to make you happy and as comfortable as possible," he said with a smile.

This was our start in our new life. After a good, hot soak in the tub I had found hanging on the outside wall, I was sure that I would feel content with my world.

Chapter Sixteen

Neighbors

Wynn was very busy taking on his Mountie responsibilities in the next few days, and I managed to keep just as busy. I was trying so hard to turn our little cabin into a real home. The material I had purchased in Calgary came out of the trunk, and I set to work in earnest with needle and thread. It was not an easy task. The material was heavy and, as I had no access to a sewing machine, I had to do all the sewing by hand. There were no frills. I made things as simple as I could. Soon the windows had curtains and the cot resembled a couch with its new spread over the hard foundation. I hand-stitched some cushions to toss on the cot, and it took on a homey look. Wynn surprised me with some fur rugs he purchased from an old trapper who tanned his own. They were much nicer than the old one I had pulled from the wall. Wynn moved that one onto his office floor. I placed the two new ones on the floor in front of the fireplace and beside our bed. They added a nice touch to the rooms, though I still couldn't get used to the odd smell lingering around them.

I had found the irons Wynn had packed for us and constructed a makeshift ironing board on which I was able to remove some of the wrinkles from our clothing. I wasn't satisfied with the job, however, but I shrugged it off as the best that could be done under the circumstances. We came to our first Sunday in the North. It was strange not having a church to attend. I asked Wynn what we would do in the place of a Sunday service. I suggested we might have our own and invite the people from the village to join us, but he felt it would be wise to take our time with any such plans. Then he proposed that, if I liked, we could take our lunch and go for a hike along the river. I was pleased with his idea and at once went to see what would be suitable for a picnic.

The countryside was beautiful. A few of the trees were already beginning to show their fall colors. It seemed awfully early to me, but I was reminded that we were now much farther north than I had been used to.

We didn't walk far. Everything was so new to me that I kept stopping for a good look and questions. Wynn answered them patiently. We saw a couple of cabins back in the bush, not far from the stream, and I asked Wynn if he knew who lived there.

"Not yet," he answered. "This next week I expect to find out more about our neighbors. I'll be gone a good deal of the weekdays, Elizabeth. Some nights I won't get home until quite late."

I nodded my head but said nothing.

"Does that bother you?"

I was slow to answer. I wouldn't look forward to long days without Wynn. But I had spent some time in prayer my first morning in the settlement, and some of my praying had been about that very issue.

I was able to say honestly now, "I'll miss you, certainly. But I'll be all right. I had a—a long talk with God about it and—I understand. I know that you can't stay in your office all the time. Or even around the settlement. I'll be fine. I still have so many things to do that I'll keep busy."

I managed a smile.

Wynn reached for my hand. "I know you've been very busy. Our little house looks much different since you've fixed it up, and I'm proud of you." His smile of appreciation filled me with a warm glow. "I've been wondering, though, if you might find some time now to get acquainted with some of our neighbors," he went on. "We will be living among them; it would be nice if you could soon find some friends."

"I've been meaning to," I told him. "Every day I've been telling myself, 'Today I will walk over to the store and meet some of the people.' But each time I find something more that needs to be done, so I put it off again."

Wynn nodded in understanding.

"I'll take some time this week. Tomorrow I need to do the washing, but maybe Tuesday I can go to the store."

"I'd like that. I'd like you to get to know some of the women so you might have company on the days I'm away."

I was quiet for a few moments. Wynn noticed.

"Something's bothering you," he commented, more as a statement than a question.

"Not 'bothering' really. It's just—well, I worry some about how I'll ever—" I didn't know just how to express that strange little fear twisting inside of me. Finally I just blurted out, "How do you get to know people when you can't talk to them?"

"You'll be able to talk to them. Oh, I know it will be hard and there will be times when you'll have problems expressing yourself. But you will pick up a few of their words quickly—many of the Indians already know a number of English words. Then there are always signs. The Indians are very good at making one understand them by using their limited English and their hands. They point out all kinds of messages. You'll catch on quickly—but you can't learn about them if you are not with them."

I knew Wynn was right, and I determined I would no longer hide behind my work but would venture forth and meet my new neighbors. It would be so much easier for me if Wynn could be along, but I knew his duties did not allow time for him to escort me around.

The sky was beginning to cloud over, so I picked up our picnic remains and we hurried to our cabin. The day suddenly went from sunshine to overcast to a thunderstorm. Wynn made a fire in the fireplace and we stretched out before it on the bear rug and talked about the people we had left behind and the folks who were our new neighbors here.

Thus far, my contact with the villagers was only on the night we had arrived. I had seen and been seen by a circle of friendly looking faces. Thinking back on it, though, I would have called them more curious than friendly. I could not remember even one smile except from the big man, Ian McLain. From my window I had watched as the two workmen had constructed our little shanty out back, and I had seen a few Indian women and children at a distance as they walked one or another of the paths that passed by our place. They always looked toward our cabin with a great deal of interest. But none of them had stopped and, as I hadn't known what to say to them, I had not called a greeting or invited them in.

Well, all of that must change. Even if it did mean learning a difficult new language, I must somehow break down the barriers and get to know my northern neighbors. *If only*, I mourned to myself, *one of them were a white woman*. There would be a common ground, a common bond, with her.

"You haven't even been in the Hudson's Bay Store, have you?" Wynn was asking.

"Not yet."

"I think you'll be surprised at the number of things available there. Of course, they are quite expensive. The shipping charges added to the cost make it far wiser to bring all you can with you rather than pay the extra price."

I remembered the heavy wagon loaded with all the crates, barrels, and boxes that brought our belongings to the settlement.

"Did that driver ever turn up?" I asked suddenly, my thoughts going back to our experience on the trail.

"Driver?"

"The one who should have driven us here but who was sleeping—?"

"Oh, him. Yes, he came walking in a couple of days ago—with all kinds of excuses and stories. Ian gave him a good scolding—like one would scold a child. Then Mrs. McLain filled the fellow up with roast duck and baking powder biscuits."

"Mrs. McLain?"

"Didn't I tell you? There is a Mrs. McLain after all."

My face must have beamed. I could hardly wait now for the opportunity to go into the settlement for my first visit. It would be so nice to have a chat with another woman. Perhaps I would even be able to invite her for tea on one of the afternoons when Wynn was away. It would help to fill in a long day.

"What is she like?"

"I haven't met her. I just overheard McLain telling about the wayward team driver and the lecture and then her feeding him."

Attempting to picture Mrs. McLain, I began by imagining a woman my age, then quickly amended that. If she were married to McLain, she must be a good deal older than I.

"Do they have a family?" I queried.

"I haven't heard."

"Well, I'll find out all about them when I go to the store," I said, quite satisfied with the thought of my new venture.

Over our breakfast the next morning, I shared with Wynn my revised plans of going to the store that afternoon. He seemed pleased that I was making the venture to get acquainted.

"What can I say?" I asked him.

He looked puzzled. "What do you mean, what can you say?"

"Well, I can't just march in there and announce that I came to meet his wife."

Wynn smiled. "I'm not sure that would be so bad. People would be pleased to think that you are anxious to meet them. But—if you are hesitant to do that, do your purchasing first; and then, if you have a chance for a little chat with McLain, you shouldn't feel enbarrassed to mention the fact that you are most anxious to meet his wife."

"Purchases? I hadn't thought of purchasing anything."

"There must be something there you could use. Look around a bit."

I hesitated. Wynn looked at me questioningly.

I went on, slowly, picking out the words to voice my concern.

"You said it's a trading post, right? Well, I've never been— I've never bought anything at a trading post. I don't know how to . . . I've never *traded* for things before. What do I trade? I don't have any furs or—"

Wynn began to laugh. He reached out and lifted my chin and kissed me on the nose, but the laughter was still in his eyes. I knew I had just showed my city breeding. I either could get angry with Wynn for laughing at me or choose to laugh with him. For a moment I was very tempted to be angry. Then I remembered my father's prayer—the part about humor for the difficult times—and I began to laugh with Wynn. Well, not laugh really, but at least I smiled. "I take it I'm off-track?"

He smiled and kissed my nose again. "A little. It's true that it's a trading post and that the trappers bring their furs there. But Mr. McLain is very happy to accept good hard cash as well. However, for you that won't even be necessary. We have a charge account there with Mr. McLain. You pick what you need and he will enter it in his little book under my name. I also would like you to keep an account of what you spend, so I can enter it in my little book. That way, when Mr. McLain and I settle up each month, hopefully our accounts will agree."

I nodded. It all seemed simple enough.

After Wynn was gone, I hurried with the laundry. Wynn had already filled every available pail and the boiler that sat heating on our woodburning stove.

The clothes were all hand-scrubbed on a galvanized board we had brought with us from Calgary. On any other laundry day I would have taken my time, but today I was so excited about the prospects of meeting Mrs. McLain that I rushed through everything. I was hoping to finish the wash around noon. Then I would have time to walk down to the store while the clothes dried on the outside lines.

Wynn did not come home for the noon meal, so I had a simple lunch and then hurried to tidy myself for my trip to the store. I was still a bit concerned as to exactly how to approach the subject of meeting Mr. McLain's wife. Maybe if I was really lucky, she would be in the store as well.

The afternoon was a bit breezy and my carefully groomed hair threatened to be undone from its pinning. I had chosen one of the best dresses I had brought along. It swished in the loose dirt of the trail into the settlement. I held my hat with one hand and my skirt up with the other.

Many small, sometimes shabby, shacks lined the sides of the clearing as I neared the store. They were not placed in any regular pattern but rather built wherever a man had a mind to build. Some had smoke streaming forth through small chimney pipes. Some of them had no chimney pipe, and the smoke billowed instead out of unglassed windows. Children of various sizes and states of dress played in the dusty areas surrounding them, stopping to stare at me out of dark eyes in round brown faces. Dogs seemed to be everywhere. Some of them looked ferocious, and I was glad a few of the meaner looking ones were tied up. I dared not imagine what might happen if they were given their freedom. Once or twice I took a brief detour in order to stay a little farther away from a dog that didn't seem to be friendly.

The little children weren't too friendly either. I smiled at many of them, but the expression on the small faces did not change. I could not blame them. To them I must have looked strange indeed with my piled-up, reddish-gold hair and my long, full skirt swishing at the ground as I walked. I decided that the next time I ventured forth I would wear something less conspicuous, but this time I had so wanted to make a favorable impression on the settlement's only other white woman.

When I reached the Hudson's Bay Store, Mr. McLain was busy with another customer. The man did not look totally white nor did he look totally Indian. I assumed this was one of the mixed race people who Wynn had said were common in the North. He spoke English, even though rather brokenly, and there were some words mixed in with it that I did not understand. Mr. McLain seemed to have no difficulty. The two got along just fine. In fact, Mr. McLain himself also interchanged his English with words I had never heard before.

Mr. McLain spoke to the man and then moved my way. "Goodday to ya, ma'am," he said with a big smile, "an' may I be helpin' ya with something?"

"I'll need a while to look," I assured him. "You go right ahead with your customer. I'm in no hurry."

He nodded to me and went back to the other man.

I looked around the store. Wynn had been right. I was surprised at the amount and variety of merchandise carried. I was also shocked at the prices. Three times I selected something from the shelf, and three times my frugal nature made me put it back. I was about ready to give up and leave the place in embarrassment when I spotted some tacks. Now I did need some tacks. They, too, were expensive; but as I truly did need them and as I couldn't possibly get them from anywhere else, I decided to buy them.

I had just made my selection when the other customer left the store and Mr. McLain came my way.

"Have ya found what you're needin'?" he boomed.

"Yes. Yes, I think these will be just fine," I fairly stammered.

Mr. McLain led the way to the counter. I laid the box of

tacks on the wooden square by the cash box. They looked very small and insignificant.

"And will this be all?" asked Mr. McLain.

I guessed he was used to his customers coming in and buying supplies to last them for many weeks. Here I was buying only a box of tacks. It must seem to him very much like a wasted trip. I flushed.

"I'm still not settled enough to know my needs," I tried to explain, "and we brought most of our supplies with us." Then I wondered if that was good news to a man who ran the only local store. I flushed more deeply. "I—I mean—we'll certainly be needing many things as the winter sets in and all—"

Mr. McLain seemed not to notice my discomfiture.

"Everything in good shape at the cabin?" he asked.

"Fine," I answered, not too sure just what he meant. "Just fine."

"The man before you wasn't much of a housekeeper," he commented. "I had to send one of the trappers' wives over to sorta sweep out the place after he left. The fella before him— now, he was some fussy. Made the men take their boots off when they went to his office—finally got so many complaints, the department said he had to stop it." Mr. McLain shook his head. "He was some fussy all right, that one."

I appreciated his consideration in sending over a woman to clean our cabin. I had thought it dirty when I arrived—I couldn't imagine what it might have been before.

As Mr. McLain talked, he got out a big black book and flipped to a page marked "Delaney, R.N.W.P." and began to make an entry. There were already several items listed on the page. In my brief glance I noticed some of them were to do with lumber— probably the building the two men constructed for us.

I took one more glance around the room and then let my mind go back to Mrs. McLain. How did I broach the subject of meeting the trader's wife? Mr. McLain solved the problem for me.

"My wife's out back in the garden. She's right anxious to meet ya. Got a minute to step around with me and say howdy?"

A smile flashed across my face. "I'd love to," I stated as I tucked the small box of tacks in my handbag and prepared to follow Mr. McLain.

The garden was weed-free and very productive. I wished with all my heart that I had one just like it. Next year I must try. It would be so nice to have some fresh vegetables. Some of them here were unfamiliar to me, though there wasn't much variety. I knew the frosts came much earlier this far north. I had also been told that, because of the long summer days, some vegetables did very well, with the added hours of sunshine to make them grow rapidly.

I took my eyes from the plants and looked about for a woman. She was at the far end of the garden patch, her dark head bent over a row of beets to which she was giving her total attention.

"Nimmie!" Mr. McLain hollered. "Got Mrs. Delaney here."

The dark head lifted; then, in one graceful movement, the woman was standing and facing me. A quiet smile spread over her face. She moved to meet me, extending a hand as she came.

"I am so pleased to meet you," she said softly.

She was Indian.

Chapter Seventeen

Adjustments

I walked home slowly, paying little attention to the staring children or the barking dogs. I had not stayed long to chat with Mrs. McLain. After my initial shock, there really didn't seem to be much to say. I hoped with all my heart that my shock hadn't shown on my face. Why hadn't Wynn warned me? Or had he known? And why hadn't I expected it? Wynn had told me that often the men in the North married Indian women. They were used to the lifestyle, the hardships, the work and weather, and weren't always fussing for their husbands to take them back to civilization. So why hadn't I prepared myself for that possibility?

I guess it was simply because I had so much wanted to have one white woman in the area, and it seemed that the Hudson's Bay man was the only candidate. In spite of telling myself that I was being foolish, I felt an intense disappointment. There wouldn't be a woman in the area after all with whom I could share intimacies. No one for little tête-à-têtes over an afternoon cup of tea. No one to understand women's fashions and women's fears. It was going to be a lonely time, the years ahead. They would be sure to get me down if I didn't take some serious steps to avoid allowing myself to be caught in the trap of self-pity.

I wasn't quite prepared at the moment to take those steps or to make future plans. For now it was enough just to sort out my thoughts and to spend some time in prayer concerning my feelings.

I did pray as soon as I got home, and I was feeling much better by the time I went to bring in the clothes and apply the irons to the garments.

As I ironed, I thought, *What might I have to offer these In-*

dian people? What things do we as wives have in common? What could I do to improve their living conditions? I knew Wynn didn't want me rushing in trying to change their way of life, but weren't there little things we might enjoy doing together?

Perhaps a sewing class? I was a good seamstress, though I did admit difficulty in adjusting from machine to hand work. It seemed so clumsy and slow to me, and my poor fingers always seemed to be pricked full of holes in spite of a thimble.

Sewing might be a good idea. Then we could have tea. Maybe Indian ladies enjoyed tea every bit as much as white ladies did. I began to feel excited about the prospects. By the time the ironing was completed, my plans had begun to take shape.

The first thing to do was to make friends with them. At the first opportunity, no matter how difficult it seemed, I was going to speak to the Indian women. Even if I made blunders, it would be a start. I would never learn unless I tried.

But first I had another little project. The open cupboard shelves bothered me. I had lots of material I had brought along; and now, with the help of the tacks obtained from Mr. McLain, I would do something about covering them.

As soon as my ironing was done, I put away the laundry and the makeshift board and went to Wynn's office in search of a hammer. I found one hanging on a nail with the rest of his few tools and went to work. With material, scissors, hammer and tacks, I soon had the open-cupboard area nicely draped with curtains. They hung in attractive folds and I was quite pleased. They certainly were an improvement on the exposed dishes, pots and pans, and food stuffs. I cut matching place mats for the table, hemming them up as I hummed to myself.

I was finished just in time to get busy with the supper preparations. I could hardly wait for Wynn to get home and see how much nicer the kitchen looked. Again I wished for a white woman to share with. She would have understood my satisfaction and pleasure with the accomplishments of the day. Wynn, being a man and troubled with the duties of a law officer, might not be able to fully appreciate just how important this little addition was to me. A woman would, I was sure.

Wynn did notice my kitchen, complimenting me on how nice

it looked. I beamed with pleasure.

As we had our evening meal together, he asked me if I had met Mrs. McLain as planned. I did not want Wynn to know about my great disappointment in not finding a white woman, so I tried to make no comments that would give away my true feelings.

"She seems to be somewhat younger than Mr. McLain," I began.

"I understand that he was married before," commented Wynn.

"She has a garden," I said with some enthusiasm. "I would love to have one like it next year. It would be so nice to have fresh things."

Wynn agreed. "You shall have your garden next year," he smiled. "I'll even see that the ground is broken for you. I think fresh vegetables would be a treat, too. That's one thing, I must confess, I miss about Calgary."

"I didn't recognize all her vegetables," I confided, "but she had lots of carrots, beets, potatoes, and onions."

"What's she look like?" Wynn asked, remembering that looks might be considered important to a woman.

I hesitated. I hadn't really looked at Mrs. McLain too closely. I drew from my memory in the brief glances I had afforded her.

"She's dark, not too tall, rather slim."

It wasn't much of a picture; but I couldn't really remember much more.

"Was she pleasant?"

"Oh, yes. Most pleasant," I hurried with my reply.

"That's nice," said Wynn. "I'm glad you have a white woman to—"

So he hadn't known. "Oh," I interrupted him, hoping my remark sounded very offhand and matter of fact, "she isn't white. She's Indian."

I turned from Wynn to get the teapot, so I didn't see if his surprise equaled mine or not. When I turned back to him, his face told me nothing.

"I'm sure she'll be good company," he encouraged. "I hope you'll be good friends."

The next morning I heard some women's voices approaching

our cabin on the trail to the west; and, true to my resolve, I went outside so I could greet them. Three Indian women approached me, talking rapidly as they came.

They were dressed in a combination of Indian buckskin and calico purchased at the trading post. Lovely beadwork made a splash of color against the natural tan of the soft deerskins.

At my appearance, things were suddenly very quiet.

I knew no Indian words. I had to take the chance that they might know a few English ones.

"Good morning," I said with a smile.

There was no response.

I tried again. "Hello."

They understood this. "Hello," they all responded in unison.

"I'm Elizabeth," I said, pointing a finger at myself. That seemed like such a long name to expect anyone to learn. I changed it. "Beth," I said, jerking my finger at my chest.

The youngest woman smiled and nodded to the others.

"Beth," I said again.

She giggled, hiding her face behind her hand.

I didn't know what to try next. I wanted to invite them in but didn't know what words to use. Well, since I only had English, I would use English.

"Would you like to come in?" I asked, waving my hand toward the cabin.

They looked puzzled.

"Come in?" I repeated.

The middle one seemed to get my meaning. She held up a basket she was carrying and said distinctly, "Berries."

I understood then that they were on their way to pick berries and didn't feel they had time to stop. At least, my logic came up with this information.

I nodded, to assure them I understood. The other two women lifted their containers to show me that they were berry-pickers as well.

I nodded again. How did one tell them that she wished them great success in their picking. I scrambled around in my mind for some words; but before I could come up with something, the young woman surprised me by pointing a finger at me, lifting her basket in the air, waving a hand at the trail ahead, and saying, "Come?"

It caught me off-guard, but I was quick to respond.

"Yes," I smiled. "Yes, I'd love to come. Just wait until I get a pail."

I ran into the house, hoping they wouldn't misunderstand and go off without me. I quickly scribbled a note for Wynn in case he should come in while I was out, grabbed a small pail, my big floppy hat and a scarf to ward off mosquitoes, and dashed back out the door.

They were still waiting for me.

They took one look at my hat, pointed at it, and began to laugh loudly. There was no embarrassment, no discourtesy. They thought it looked funny and enjoyed the joke.

I laughed with them, even making the hat bounce up and down more than was necessary to give them a good show. They laughed harder, and then we moved on together down the path to the berry patch.

I had no idea where we were going. I decided to watch closely for landmarks in case I had to find my own way home. I wasn't much of a woodsman, and I would have hated to require Wynn's leaving his other duties to come looking for me.

We followed the path to the stream and the stream to the river and then followed the trail that paralleled the twists and turns of the river. I was sure I could find my way home so far.

We had gone maybe a mile and a half when the women cut away from the river and headed through the bush. There was no path now and I began to get worried. I could never find my way home without the aid of a path. I sincerely hoped the other women could. We might all be lost!

We walked for about another mile before we came to the berry patch. The bushes were thick with them, and they were delicious-looking. The women talked excitedly as they pointed here and there. Then they set right to work.

I couldn't begin to keep up with them. Their hands seemed to flash as they whipped berries into their containers. I tried to follow their examples but ended up spilling more berries than I got to my pail, so I decided it was wiser for me to take my own time and get the berries safely where they belonged.

While the women chatted, I listened intently. I tried so hard to formulate some pattern in their speaking, to pick out a word that was repeated and sort out its meaning; but it was hopeless. As they chatted, they often stopped to double over in joyful, childlike laughter. It was clear they were a people who knew how to enjoy themselves. I wished I could share in their jokes. Then I wondered if I might indeed be the butt of their jokes; but, no, they didn't seem to be laughing at me.

It was almost noon when the youngest one came over to where I was picking. She looked in my pail and seemed to be showing approval on my good job. Then she showed me her basket. She had picked twice as many. She knelt beside me and quickly picked a few handfuls which she threw in my pail. The others came with their full containers. They gathered around me and they, too, began to pick berries and deposit them in my pail. I was the only one who still had room in my container. With four of us picking, the pail was full in no time. I thanked them with a smile, and we all got up and stretched to ease the ache in our backs.

"Ouch," said the oldest lady, and everyone laughed.

We started home then, full containers of berries carefully guarded. It was well after noon when we arrived at my house, and none of us had had anything to eat. I was starving. I wondered if they were, too.

"Would you like to come in?" I asked them, motioning toward the door.

They shook their heads and nodded toward their baskets, informing me that they had to go home to care for the berries. I lifted my pail then. "Some of these are yours," I reminded them, pointing to the berries and then at their baskets.

I began to scoop out berries to add to their already full containers, but they shook their heads and pulled the baskets away.

"Keep," one of them said, the others echoing, "Keep."

I thanked them then and they went on their way, while I went to find something to eat and then to care for my own bountiful supply of berries. Such a delightful surprise! The berries were sweet and juicy and would be such a welcome addition to our simple meals. And the contact with the Indian women had been just as pleasant a surprise.

I wondered where they lived and if I would see them again.

I told Wynn I had a surprise for supper that night.

"Where did you get these?" he asked in astonishment when I brought out the pie.

"I picked them myself—well, at least most of them."

"How did you find them?"

"You'll never believe this," I began enthusiastically. "Some Indian women came by today; and when I greeted them, they said they were going berry picking and they invited me to go along . . . so I did. I didn't quite fill my pail on my own. They helped me."

"So you found some women who could speak English?"

"No. Not really."

"Then how—?"

"Oh, they said 'hello' and 'berries' and 'come.' "

Wynn smiled.

"We sort of filled in the rest with gestures. Oh, Wynn, I wish I could understand them! They had so much fun."

"Give yourself a little time. You'll soon be joining in. Who were they?"

"That's part of the problem. I don't even know their names. I couldn't ask them where they live or anything."

Wynn reached out and gently stroked my hair. "It's hard, isn't it?" he said.

"I might have found some friends—and lost them—in the very same day," I mourned.

I was working about my kitchen the next morning, wondering how I was going to fill my long day, when a loud call—almost in my ear—spun me around. There stood the youngest member of the trio who had shared the berry patch the day before. After my initial fright, I was able to smile at her and indicate a chair for her. She shook her head and held up her basket. She was going to pick berries again.

"Yes, I'll go," I nodded to her. "Thank you for stopping for me. It will take me just a minute to get my things."

I thought as I bustled about finding my hat and my pail that she probably hadn't understood one word of what I had just said.

We went out into the sunshiny day and there, waiting at

the end of our path, were four more women. Two of them had been with us the day before and the other two were new to me. I smiled at all of them, pointed to myself and said, "Beth," which they repeated with many giggles and varying degrees of success, and we started off. This time we went in a different direction when we came to the river. All along the way, the women chattered and laughed. I could only smile.

We picked berries until noon again. As before, they filled their containers before me and helped me to finish.

We walked home single file, the women laughing and talking as they went. How I wished I could join in. I wanted to at least ask them their names and where they lived. I might as well be mute for all the good my tongue did me.

When we got to our cabin, I again motioned for them to come in. They showed me their brimming pails and pointed to the settlement. I wouldn't let them go without *some* information. I would try it again. So I pointed at myself and said, "Beth." Then I pointed at the youngest woman who had been the one to walk right into our home. The women looked at one another and smiled.

"Evening Star," the young woman said carefully, and then she went around the little circle pointing her finger at each of the ladies and saying their names. It was a strange mixture. The middle-aged woman was Kinawaki, the older woman Mrs. Sam, and the two new ones who had gone with us were Little Deer and Anna. I reviewed each of the names one more time to make sure that I had them right. The ladies nodded. I turned back to Evening Star, aching to communicate.

"Where do you live?" I tried.

She shook her head, not understanding. I looked at the other women grouped around her. They all looked blank.

"Your house? Where is your house?" I pointed at my house.

Evening Star's face lit up. "Law," she said. She must have thought that I was asking something about my own home.

I pointed toward the settlement. "Do you live over there?" I asked again.

"McLain," said the woman. At least she knew the name of the Hudson's Bay trader.

I knew I couldn't hold them any longer. I smiled and stepped back, nodding them a good-day. They smiled in return and started one by one down the path. Anna, the small, thin woman with the missing tooth, was the last to turn and go. Just as she passed by me, she stopped and leaned forward ever so slightly. "She doesn't understand English talk," she whispered, and then followed the others down the path. I stared after her with my mouth open.

Chapter Eighteen

Teas and Such

We went for berries the following day, too. Anna was there, and I directed my inquiries to her. I would not be cheated again out of conversation. I found out that the five women all lived in the settlement. Two of them, Mrs. Sam and Anna, were married to white trappers. Mrs. Sam had wished to be called as white women are called, by their husband's names. She did not understand quite how the system worked. Sam was her husband's first name; his last name was Lavoie.

Anna spoke English well because she had attended a mission school in another area. Beaver River had had no school. Anna did not consider herself superior, just different from the others. I found out later that she had had more schooling than her trapper husband, even though it was only the equivalent of about grade four. She was the one who did the figuring when she and her husband went to the trading post.

I also asked Anna about the families of the women. Anna didn't offer much on her own, but she did answer my direct questions. Evening Star was married to Tall One and had four children. She had had two others who had been lost at a young age to *dark blood*. I wondered what *dark blood* meant to the Indian. I tucked it away to ask Wynn. Kinawaki had been married—twice. Both her husbands had died. I decided that it would be improper and insensitive to probe for details. Kinawaki had borne nine children, five of them still living. Mrs. Sam had never had children. She had much time to do nothing, according to Anna. Little Deer, the short, round woman, had two boy-children who were always in the way; and she, Anna, had five—two in Indian graves and three at home.

The mortality rate appalled me. The resigned way in which

they seemed to accept it bothered me even more. Was it expected that one would raise only half of one's family?

I was learning how to fill my pail more quickly than I had previously, but the women still gave me a hand before we left for home. On our way home, I walked along beside Anna. The path was not made for walking two abreast—now and then we would come to thick growth where I would have to step back, allowing her to go on without me, and then hurry to catch up to her again. I wanted to be sure to let her know that I would welcome any of the women into my home at any time.

"Not today," said Anna. "Today we have much work. We must dry berries for cold. Takes much work."

I agreed.

"Berries almost gone now," she went on. "Bears and birds get rest. Not pick anymore."

"When the women are finished with their berries, then will they have time to come?"

"I'll ask." She spoke rapidly to the other ladies, who were trudging on single file down the trail. No one stopped and no one turned to enter the conversation; they just called back and forth. After a few minutes of exchanges, Anna turned to me.

"Why you want us come?" she asked forthrightly.

I was a bit taken aback. "Well, just to—to—to get to know you better. To make friends—to maybe have some tea—"

She interrupted me then. "Tea," she said. "That's good."

She talked again to her companions. I heard the word "tea," which seemed to be a drawing card. There was a general nodding of heads.

"We come—sometime," said Anna.

"Good!" I exclaimed. "How about tomorrow?"

Anna looked puzzled. "Why?" she said. "Why tomorrow?"

"Well, I—I'd like you to come as soon as possible."

"Come when ready," responded Anna, and I nodded my head.

"Come when ready," I agreed.

Two days later I looked up from my sewing to see Little Deer standing in my doorway. I had not heard her knock. She came in smiling and took the seat I offered her. I got out the teapot and made the tea. We couldn't talk, so we just sat smiling and nodding at one another. She had watched with great interest as I lifted china cups from my cupboard. I didn't have any cake or cookies, so I cut slices of fresh bread and spread it with the jam I had made with some of my berries.

We had just taken our first sip from the cups when Evening Star walked in. She had not knocked either. I got another cup and we continued our tea party. When we finished I decided to show the two ladies around our house. They carefully looked at everything, their faces showing little emotion. I couldn't tell if they were pleased, puzzled, or provoked at what they saw. Nothing seemed to move them in the least.

I came to my kitchen and proudly demonstrated how I could sweep aside my curtains and reveal the dishes and food stacked on the shelves. Evening Star reached out a hand and tried it herself. She lifted the curtain, peered in behind it and let it fall back in place. Then she did it again. She turned to Little Deer and spoke a word in her native dialect. Not only did she say it once, but she repeated it, and Little Deer said it after her. At last, I had found something that impressed them! I said the word over and over to myself so I would remember it. I wanted to ask Wynn about it when he got home.

It wasn't long after our tea party until Wynn was home for supper. I still had the Indian word on the tip of my tongue. I wanted to be sure to ask him before I lost it.

Almost as soon as he entered the door, I asked him. It was a difficult word for my tongue to twist around, and I wasn't sure I could say it correctly.

"What is *winniewishy*?" I asked him.

Wynn puzzled for a moment and then corrected my pronunciation.

"That's it. What does it mean?"

"Where'd you hear that?" asked Wynn.

"Two of the ladies were here today for tea," I informed him excitedly. "What does it mean?"

"Well, in English, I guess we'd say *nuisance*. Why?"

Nuisance! They had viewed and touched my curtains and pronounced them *nuisance*? For a moment I was puzzled and hurt, and then it struck me as funny and I began to laugh.

"What's so funny?" asked Wynn.

"Oh, nothing, really. That was just the opinion of the ladies about the pretty, unpractical curtains over my cupboards."

It was Sunday again, though I had a hard time really convincing myself of that fact. It seemed so strange not to be preparing for church. I missed the worship. I missed the contact with friends. I missed being with my own family. But, most of all, I missed the feeling of refreshing that came from spending time with other believers in praise and prayer.

We set aside some time, just the two of us, in a manner that would become our practice for the years ahead in the North; and, with Bible in hand, we had our own brief Sunday worship service.

The next day, my washday, I was busy with ironing when a call from within my doorway announced another visitor. It was Evening Star. Right behind her came Mrs. Sam and Little Deer. I put aside my ironing and fixed the tea. The women seemed to enjoy it, smacking their lips appreciatively as they drank. We had just finished when Anna appeared. I made another pot and we started all over again.

With the coming of Anna, I was able to talk to the women. "I thought you might like to do some sewing," I said to them. "I have things all ready."

I went to my bedroom trunk and brought out material that I had already prepared to make pillows. I also brought needles and thread and proceeded to show the ladies how to go about stitching up the pillows. They started somewhat clumsily with the lightweight material, but seemed to catch on quickly enough. When they had finished, they handed the pillows back to me.

"Oh, no," I told them. "You may keep then. Take then home with you." I pointed to the many pillows I had on the cot. "You can use them in your own homes," I said, and Anna passed on the information. The women still looked a bit hesitant, but they all left with their pillows.

The next day the women came again, all walking right in as they arrived. I decided I would talk to Anna about it—explain that one did not just walk into another's house without knocking first. She would be able to inform the other ladies. It was uncomfortable for me, not knowing when someone might suddenly appear at my elbow.

Again we had our tea. I began to wonder just what I had started. Did the ladies think they needed to come to my house every day of the week for a tea party? I was glad they liked to come, but I wasn't sure how to put a stop to this as a daily event.

After tea I was all prepared to go and get some more sewing. They seemed to easily have mastered the simple cushion; now perhaps they would like to try something a little more difficult. I excused myself and went to my bedroom. While I was gone, there was a shuffling in the kitchen. Little Deer left the room and went to the outside step. I had returned to the kitchen-living room when she came back with some baskets on her arm. The ladies had each brought her own sewing. I stood dumbstruck as I watched the deft fingers move rapidly in and out of the material. Intricate designs in thread and bead-work were quickly forming under skilled hands. I could feel embarrassment flooding my face with deep color. To think that I, Elizabeth Delaney, had had the foolish notion that I could teach these women how to sew! Why, their work would put mine to shame any day. I didn't even know the right words to apologize.

Well, Elizabeth, I said to myself, *you certainly have a lot to learn.*

I did speak to Anna about my desire for the women to knock before entering. She looked puzzled. It seemed that even at the mission school knocking was not a custom. However, she nodded her head and passed the word on to the other women. They, too, seemed at a loss for the reason behind this, but they also nodded. I was relieved that the matter had been well taken care of.

The next day I was in the yard shaking a rug when Anna arrived. She was alone, but I expected that a number of the others would soon follow. I led her into the house, opening the door for her and letting her pass on ahead.

She hesitated. Neither of us moved for a moment, and finally Anna said, "You not knock."

"Oh, no," I tried to explain. "That's fine. Go ahead. It's only at your house that I would knock. Not at my house."

She looked at me like I had really lost my senses, but she went in.

That day we were joined for tea by Mrs. Sam and Kinawaki, both of whom knocked before entering even though they arrived together. Evening Star and Little Deer did not come.

When Wynn got home that night, he took off his heavy boots and stretched out his long legs to rest his tired muscles. I knew he had been working very hard during these first few weeks on the post. He wanted to know his area thoroughly before the bad weather set in, so he might be well-prepared for trouble spots. I was bustling around with last-minute supper preparations.

"You know," he said to me, "I saw the strangest thing when I came through the village tonight. There was Anna, knocking on her own door. They never have a lock on their doors, so she couldn't have been locked out. I couldn't imagine what in the world she was doing. I asked McLain. He said that somewhere she had picked up the notion to knock, to chase out any evil spirits that were in the house before she entered."

I gasped. How could she have misunderstood me so? I certainly had no wish to be fostering false ideas about the spirit world. I explained it all to Wynn and he smiled at my dilemma. I was horrified.

The next time Anna came to see me, I informed her that I had been wrong, that it wasn't necessary to knock after all. She could enter at any time and call as she had always done.

Anna nodded impassively, but I was sure she was wondering about those crazy white people who couldn't make up their minds! From then on I never knew for sure if I had company until I had checked over both shoulders, and I made a habit of doing that frequently.

Chapter Nineteen

Friends

"Did you know that Ian McLain's sister lives here?" Wynn asked one morning at the breakfast table.

I looked up in astonishment. I certainly didn't know that. I wondered where she had been hiding. Then I checked myself—that wasn't fair. I hadn't been to the settlement more than two or three times myself.

"No," I said now. "Have you seen her?"

"Just at a distance."

"What's she like?"

"She's rather tall, like Ian. Not broad though. She walks very erect and briskly—that's all I know. All I saw was her retreating back."

"Where does she live?" I asked next, thinking eagerly about visiting her.

"I think she has one of the rooms at the back of the store, but I'm not sure even about that."

Well, I would find out. When I tracked her down, I would invite her for tea. Perhaps some morning. The Indian ladies still came often in the afternoon.

I switched my thoughts back to Wynn. "Have you heard her name?"

"She's a Miss McLain. I don't know her given name."

"She's never married? Is she quite a bit younger than her brother?"

"I don't know that, but I wouldn't expect so."

Wynn rose from the table and reached for his stetson. The poor thing still had the telltale wagon-wheel marks.

"I won't be home until late tonight," he said. "I have a lot of ground to cover today."

I dreaded having him gone from morning to dusk. It made the day so long. I said nothing but stepped over to him and put my arms around his neck for my goodbye kiss. "Be careful," I whispered. "Come home safely."

He held me for some minutes before he gently put me from him; and then he was gone, walking out our door and down the footpath in long, even strides.

I watched him until he had disappeared. With a sigh I turned and began clearing the table. Then I remembered Miss McLain.

So there *was* another white woman in the settlement! I couldn't wait to meet her. I wondered what she would be like. She would be older than I, certainly. Perhaps even twice my age. Had she been raised in the North? Or had she come up from the city, like I had?

I needed a few items from the store anyway, so I would just take a walk after I had done the morning household chores and see what I could find out.

I wasn't too eager to walk into the village. I didn't quite trust some of the dogs with their snapping teeth and snarling jaws. I was fine if they were kept tied; but the trappers and their families were sometimes a little careless about that, being so used to the dogs themselves. I had seen some of the Indian women carrying a heavy, thick stick as they walked through the village. When I asked Wynn about it, he nonchalantly remarked that it was needed against the dogs.

This morning, I was so enthused about meeting the white woman that I decided to even dare the dogs. As soon as I had finished up the dishes, tidied up the two rooms that composed our home, and swept the step, I freshened myself and started for the store. This time I had a respectably long list of needed items.

Fortunately, the dogs did not give me too much cause for concern. The more ferocious ones were all securely tied. Children played in the dirt of the roadway. Since we were now into September, I was very conscious—as a schoolteacher—that they really should have been in school. Again I longed to start some classes, but I realized I had none of the words of their dialect—well, just "nuisance"—and they had only a few of mine.

Mr. McLain was busy waiting on some Indian women. One

of them was Mrs. Sam. I greeted her as an old friend, but we were still unable to say more than hello to one another.

I purchased my items, even adding a couple of things I hadn't thought about but spotted on the stacked shelves. Mr. McLain listed the items under our account, and I carefully itemized each one in my little book to give Wynn an accurate account for his records.

"Care for some coffee?" offered Mr. McLain in a neighborly fashion, jerking his thumb at the pot which ever stood ready on the back of his big airtight heater. A stack of cups was scattered around on a nearby stand. Some of them were clean, but most of them were dirty, having been used by former customers that morning. At first reluctant, I changed my mind.

"A cup of coffee would be nice," I said and walked over to the stove to help myself. I still wanted a chance to talk some with Mr. McLain, and a cup of coffee might prolong my stay enough to be able to do so.

"My husband was telling me that you have a sister living here," I ventured, after taking a deep breath. To make the statement seem less important, I then took a swallow of coffee. It was awful. It was so weak it hardly tasted like coffee at all—and so stale that what little flavor was there was almost completely eclipsed. It was hot though—I had to give Mr. McLain credit for that. I burned my tongue.

Mr. McLain kept figuring. Finally he lifted his head. "Katherine. Yeah, she lives here. Has lived here now for almost twenty years."

I wasn't sure what to say next. Katherine was such a pretty name. I tried to visualize the lady to whom it belonged.

"Where was she from, before that?" I asked rather timidly. Maybe the answer would tell me something about her.

"From St. John."

"St. John? My, she has come a long way from home, hasn't she?"

"Guess you could say that," agreed McLain. "She was a schoolmar'm back there."

"Really?"

Already I was warming up to this unknown lady. She had been a schoolteacher, educated, cultivated. I was confident we would have much in common.

"I was a schoolteacher, too," I went on. "I'd love to meet your sister. I'm sure we'd have much to talk about."

McLain looked at me in a strange, quizzical way. He didn't answer for many moments and then he said simply, "Yeah," very abruptly and curtly.

I waited, hoping to discover how I could go about making the acquaintance of this woman. Mr. McLain said nothing.

Finally I ventured, "Is she—does she live around here?"

It was a stupid question. "Around here" was the only place there was to live—that is, if she was considered a part of this settlement.

"Out back," said McLain shortly. "She has the room with the left door."

I stammered on, "Do you—do you suppose she would mind if I called?"

McLain looked at me for what seemed like a long time and then jerked his big head at the door. "I don't know why she'd mind. Go ahead. Leave your things right here 'til you're ready to go off home."

I thanked him and went out the door and around to the back of the building to look for the door on the left.

Mrs. McLain was in the backyard hanging out some laundry. I felt embarrassed. What if she saw me? But, then, what did it matter? She had her back to me, anyway, as she sang softly to herself.

I rapped gently. There was no response. I knocked louder. Still no response. I hesitated. Clearly Miss McLain was not in. I decided to try one more time. To this knock there was a loud call of "Come," and I opened the door timidly and went in.

The room was dark, so it took me a few minutes to get accustomed to the lack of light and locate the room's occupant.

She was seated in a corner, her hands idly folded in her lap, staring at the blank wall in front of her. I wondered if she might be ill and was about to excuse myself and depart for a more convenient time, but she spoke. "You're the lawman's wife."

Her voice was hard and raspy.

"Yes," I almost whispered, wondering if her statement was recognition or condemnation.

"What do you want?"

"Well, I—I just—heard that—that a white woman lived here, and I wanted to meet you."

"White woman?" The words were full of contempt. "This is no place for a white woman. One might as well realize that anyone who lives here is neither white nor a woman."

I couldn't believe the words, and I certainly could not understand the meaning behind them. I turned and would have gone, but she stopped me.

"Where are you from?" she demanded.

"Calgary. I was a schoolteacher near Lacombe before coming here. I was born and raised in Toronto."

"Toronto? Nothing wrong with Toronto. Why'd you come here?"

"Well, I—I—married a member of the Royal North West Police. I—"

She turned from me and spit with contempt into the corner. When she turned back, her eyes sparked fire. "That's the poorest reason that I ever heard for coming to this god-forsaken country," she said. "Some people come because they have to. My brother came for the money. Nothing else, just the money. Buried his first wife here, and still he stayed. But you—"

She did not finish her sentence but left me to know that I had done something incredibly wrong or stupid, perhaps both.

I felt condemned. I also felt challenged. Suddenly I drew myself up to my full five feet, three inches. "Why did *you* come here?" I asked her.

Again her eyes flashed. I was afraid for a moment that she might throw something at me, her anger was so evident. But she would have needed to leave her chair in order to do that—she had nothing near at hand.

"I came," she said deliberately, hissing out each word, "I came because there was nothing else that I could do—nowhere else where I could go. That's why I came."

I was shaken. "I'm—I'm sorry," I murmured through stiff lips. I stood rooted to the spot for a moment and then I said softly, "I think I'd better go."

She did not comment, only nodded her head angrily at the door, indicating that I was quite free to do so, and the sooner the better in her estimation.

I was glad to step out into the warm sunshine and close the door behind me on the angry woman inside. I stood trembling. I had never seen anyone behave in such a way. *My, what deep bitterness is driving this woman?* I wondered. It could completely destroy her if something wasn't done. But what could one do? Personally, I hoped I would never need to encounter her again.

A soft song caught my ears and I remembered Mrs. McLain. She was still there hanging up her laundry. I didn't want to make contact with the woman, especially not in my present shaky condition. I hastily headed down the path in hopes of dodging around the building, but she saw me.

"Good morning, Mrs. Delaney," she called pleasantly.

I had to stop and respond. I managed a wobbly smile. "Good morning, Mrs. McLain," I returned. "It's a lovely morning, isn't it?"

"It is. And I am just finishing my washing and stopping for a cup of tea. Could you join me?"

I thought to wonder then about her excellent grammar. She had only the trace of an accent.

I still wanted to head for the security of my little home, but that would be very rude; so I smiled instead and said, "That is most kind. Thank you."

She pegged the last dish towel to the line, picked up her basket and led the way through the right-hand door.

The room was very pleasant and homey, a combination of white and Indian worlds. I noticed what a pleasant atmosphere the blending gave the room.

She seated me and went out to her small kitchen. Soon she was back with a teapot of china and some china cups. She also brought some slices of a loaf cake made with the local blueberries. It was delicious.

"So, are you feeling settled in Beaver River?" she asked me.

"Oh, yes. Quite settled."

We went on with small talk for many moments, and then she became more personal. Eventually it dawned on me that this was the kind of conversation I had been aching to have with a woman. The kind for which I had been seeking white companionship.

"Does it bother you, being left alone so much?" she asked sympathetically.

"I guess it does some. I miss Wynn, and the days are so long when he is gone for such a long time. I don't know how to make them pass more quickly. I have sewed up almost all the material I brought along, and there is really nothing else I can cover, or drape, or pad, anyway," I said in truth and desperation.

"When you have a family, you won't have so much free time," she observed. "In fact, when winter comes, you will be busier. It takes so much more of one's time even to do the simple tasks in the winter," she went on to explain. I hadn't thought about that, but I was sure she was right.

I switched back to her earlier comment. "Do you have a family?" I asked.

"No," was her simple answer, but I thought I saw pain in her eyes.

"Have you always lived here?" I said, partly to get on to another subject.

I expected her to say she had come to Beaver River from another area, so I was surprised when she said, "Yes. I have never lived more than a few miles away. My father used to have a cabin about five miles up river. I was born there."

I know that my surprise must have shown on my face.

She smiled.

"You are wondering why I speak English?"

I nodded.

"I'm married to an Englishman." She laughed then. "Not an Englishman, really. He is a Scotsman. He was raised from childhood by a Swedish family. At one time he went to a French school, he was apprenticed under a German, and he speaks three Indian dialects—but his mother tongue is English."

"My," I said, thinking about McLain with new respect. I had wondered why he didn't speak with a Scottish accent. His sister did not have one either, come to think of it. "My," I said again. "Does he speak all of those languages?"

"Some French, some Swedish, some German, and much Indian." She said it with pride.

"But that still doesn't explain your English."

She looked at me as though she thought I should have understood, and perhaps I should have. "If my husband can speak seven languages," she said, "it seemed that at least I should be able to learn his."

I nodded. What spirit the young woman had.

"And how did you learn?" I persisted, feeling very at ease with her.

"Books. When he saw that I was really interested, he got me books; and he helped me. In the long winter evenings, we would read to one another and he would correct my pronunciation and help me with the new words. I love English. I love reading books. I wish my people had all these wonderful stories to read to their children."

Excitement filled me. "Have you ever thought of writing the stories for them? You know, putting the Indian stories down on paper for the children to read."

"None of them can read," she said very sadly.

"But we could teach them," I was quick to cut in.

She smiled, and her smile looked resigned and pitiful.

"They do not wish to learn. It takes work. They would rather play."

"Are you sure?" I asked incredulously.

"I'm sure. I have tried." She looked older then. Older and a bit tired.

"I'll help you. We can try again."

A new spark came to her eyes. "Would you? Would you care enough to really try?"

"Oh, yes. I've just been aching to get going, but Wynn said that I should wait. That I shouldn't go rushing in. I even brought some books along so that I might—"

I stopped. I was getting carried quite away with it all.

She reached out and took my hand. "I thank you," she said sincerely. "I thank you for feeling that way. For caring. Maybe we *can* do something."

"I'll show you my books and the things I have and—"

She stopped me. "Your husband is quite right, Mrs. Delaney. We mustn't rush into this unprepared. The Indian people have waited for many generations for the chance to read and write. A few more weeks or months will make little difference."

I supposed she was right. I swallowed my disappointment

and glanced at the clock on the wall. It was almost noon, I discovered with surprise.

"Oh, my," I said, "look at the time. I had no idea. I must go."

I stood quickly, placing my empty cup on the nearby small table.

"Thank you so much for the tea—and the visit. I enjoyed it so much."

"I've enjoyed it, too. I do hope that you will come back again soon, Mrs. Delaney."

"My name is Elizabeth," I told her. "Elizabeth, or Beth—you can take your pick. I'd be pleased if you'd call me by my given name rather than Mrs. Delaney."

She smiled. "And my name, Elizabeth," she said, "is Nemelaneka. When I married Ian, I thought he would like a wife with an English name, so I spent days poring over books and finally found the name Martha. 'Martha,' I told him, 'will be my name now.' 'Why Martha?' he asked me. And I said, 'Because I think that Martha sounds nice. Is there another name that you like better?' 'Yes,' he said, 'I like Nemelaneka, your Indian name.' So I stayed Nemelaneka, though Ian calls me Nimmie."

"Ne-me-la-ne-ka," I repeated, one syllable at a time. "Nemelaneka, that's a pretty name."

"And a very long and difficult one," laughed the woman. "Martha would have been much easier to say and spell."

Just as I was taking my leave, Nemelaneka spoke softly. "Don't judge poor Katherine too quickly," she said. "There is much sorrow and hurt in her past. Maybe with love and understanding—" She stopped and sighed. "And time," she added. "It takes so much time, but maybe with time she will overcome it."

I looked at her with wonder in my eyes but asked no questions. I nodded, thanked her again, and hurried home after retrieving my shopping from the store.

Chapter Twenty

Change of Direction

No ladies came for tea that day. I had thought I would welcome a day to myself, wondering at times how I was ever going to put a stop to the daily visits; but now, with none of them coming, I found that I really missed them. I fidgeted the entire afternoon away, not knowing what to do with myself. Eventually, I laid aside the book I was trying to read and decided to take a walk along the river.

I did not go far and I did not leave the riverbank since I was still unsure of my directions.

It was a very pleasant day. The leaves had turned color and, mingled among the dark green of the evergreens, they made a lovely picture of the neighboring hillsides.

The river rippled and sang as it hurried along. Occasionally I saw a fish jump, and as I rounded one bend in the trail I saw a startled deer leap for cover. I was enjoying this wilderness land. But Nimmie had been right. I was lonesome at times as well.

I thought now about all the family I had left in Calgary and Toronto. I thought, too, about my friends and school children at Pine Springs. *I wonder if the school has a new teacher?* I certainly hoped so. The children who had finally been able to start their education needed the opportunity to continue.

I wished there was some way to learn what was going on back home. I seemed so far removed from them all, so isolated. *Why, something terrible could happen to one of them and I would never know!* The thought frightened me, and I had to put it aside with great effort or it would surely have overwhelmed me with depression.

I firmly chose to think of other things instead. It was easy to go back to my visit with Nimmie. I was so glad to have found a kindred spirit. One who was just as concerned—no, *more* concerned—about the need of schooling for the village children. I could hardly wait to get something started, but I knew Nimmie and Wynn were right. One must go slowly and do things properly.

Reluctantly, I turned my steps homeward again. I earnestly hoped Wynn wouldn't be too late. I had so many feelings whirling around inside, and I needed so much to be able to share them with someone—someone who would listen and understand.

The day passed slowly. Dusk was falling and still Wynn had not returned. I walked around the two rooms we called home, looking for something to do but finding nothing that interested me.

I paced the outside path, back and forth, and tried to formulate in my mind just where I would plant my next year's garden.

I stirred the supper stew and rearranged the plates on the table and stirred the stew again.

I sat with a book near the flickering lamp and pretended to myself that I was interested in the story.

Still I was restless and edgy. My agitation began to turn to anger. Why did he have to be so late? Was the job really that important? Did his work matter more than his wife? Was this dedication to his job really necessary, or was he just putting in time, choosing to be late every day?

My angry thoughts began to pile up, one on top of the other. *Wynn could have been home long ago had he chosen to be!* I finally concluded.

It was now quite dark. Even Wynn had not expected to be *that* late. My thoughts took a sudden turn. What if something had happened? What if he were lost? Or had had an accident? What if some deranged trapper had shot him? Mounties were warned of this possibility. Suddenly I was worried—not just a little worried, but sick-worried. I was sure something terrible had happened to my husband and here I sat not knowing how or where to get help. What if he were lying out there somewhere, wounded and dying, and I sat idly in my chair fumbling with the pages of a book and fuming because he was late?

What could I do? I couldn't go looking for him. I'd never find my way in the darkness. Why, I could barely find my way in the broad daylight! Besides, I had no idea where Wynn had gone. What should I do?

Indians! They were good at tracking. Didn't they have some sort of sixth sense about such things? I didn't know any of the Indian men, but I knew their wives. I would go to them for help.

I ran for my light shawl. I would go to the village and knock on doors until I found someone.

Then I remembered the dogs. They were often untied at night because the owners were not expecting anyone after dark. Out in the darkness of the woods by our pathway, I searched the ground for a heavy stick.

Footsteps on the path startled me. I swung around, my breath caught in my throat, not sure what I would be facing.

"Elizabeth!" Wynn said in surprise. "Did you lose something?"

I wanted to run and throw myself into his arms but my embarrassment and my remembered anger stopped me. I wanted to cry that I had been worried sick, but I feared that Wynn would think me silly. I wanted to run to my bedroom and throw myself down on the bed and cry away all my fear and frustration, but I did not want to be accused of being a hysterical woman. I did *not* want to explain what I was doing out in the tangled bush by the path in the darkness, and I would not; so I simply said, rather sharply, "What took you so long? Supper is a mess," and brushed past him into the kitchen.

Wynn said nothing more at the time. He ate the nearly ruined supper and I pushed mine back and forth across my plate with my fork.

Supper was a long and silent meal.

I had had so much to tell him, so much to talk about; and here we sat in silence, neither of us saying anything. It was foolish, and well I knew it.

I stole a glance at Wynn. He looked tired, more than I had ever seen him before. It occurred to me that he might have things to talk about, too. What had happened in his day? Were there things that *he* wished to talk about?

Taking a deep breath, I decided I should lay aside my hurt pride and ask him.

"You were very late," I began. "In fact, I was worried. Did something unexpected happen?"

Wynn looked up, relief in his eyes.

"A number of things," he answered. "Our boat got a leak, we were charged by an angry bull moose, the trapper we went to see chose not to be home and we had to search for him and we ended up bringing him in handcuffs; and the Indian that I had taken along to act as my guide took a nasty fall and had to practically be carried the last two miles on my back."

I stared at Wynn in unbelief. Surely he was joking. But the look on his face told me he was not.

"Oh, my," was all that I could say. "Oh, my."

Wynn smiled then. "Well, it's over," he said. "That's the only good thing I can say about this day."

But it wasn't over.

We hadn't even finished our poor meal when there was a call from outside our window. A man in the village had accidentally shot himself in the leg while cleaning his gun and Wynn was needed to care for the wound.

Wordlessly, he put on his hat and followed the excited boy.

It was very late when Wynn returned home. I was still waiting up for him. He crossed to me and kissed me. "I'm sorry, Elizabeth," he said; "you should have gone to bed."

"I couldn't sleep anyway," I said honestly.

The truth was that while Wynn had been gone, I had been doing a lot of thinking. I really had no idea how Wynn filled his days. When he came home at night, after a long day being— well, somewhere—we talked about what I had done with *my* day. I had never really asked Wynn about his before. What were Wynn's days like? Surely they weren't all as difficult as this one had been.

I had been anxious to tell him about my tea with Nimmie and about meeting Miss Katherine McLain. He had faced grave problems and possible death and likely would have made no comment about either if I hadn't made an opportunity just to make idle conversation. I felt ashamed. *From now on,* I determined, *I'm going to pay more attention to my husband and be less concerned with my silly little doings.*

By the time Wynn had returned from dressing the wound, I was feeling quite meek. Hadn't I come north with him to be his companion and support? I had been living as though I had come merely for his decoration.

I tipped my face now to receive Wynn's kiss, then asked, "How is the man?"

"He'll be okay, though he does have a nasty flesh wound. Barring infection, he should have no problem."

I shivered thinking about it.

"You're cold," said Wynn. "You should be in bed."

"No, I'm not cold, just squeamish," I answered. "Would you like a cup of something hot to drink? Coffee? Tea?"

"Tea sounds good. Is the water still hot?"

"I kept the fire banked. It will just take a minute."

"It's very late, Elizabeth. I know you're tired. I don't need—"

"It's no trouble," I assured him as I moved to the kitchen area.

Wynn sat down in the one easy chair and I could hear him removing his high-topped boots. *He must be nearly dead of exhaustion,* I thought.

I brought Wynn's tea and he gulped more than sipped it.

"You wanted to talk?" he said, lifting tired eyes to me.

"It can wait for morning."

"It doesn't need to wait," maintained Wynn.

"It's not that important. I just met Miss McLain today and had tea with Mrs. McLain. I'll tell you all about them at the breakfast table."

I took Wynn's empty cup from him and carried it to the table. Then I turned to him. "Come," I said. "This day has been long enough already."

Chapter Twenty-one

The Storyteller

The next few weeks were rather uneventful. Wynn still was busy; but now that he had carefully patrolled all the area to which he was assigned, he was able to do more of his work from his one-room office. I liked having him around more, and it also helped me to become more familiar with what he did.

He was police, doctor, lawyer, advisor, handyman, and often spiritual counselor—and so much more. The people came to him for any number of reasons. He was always patient and just, though sometimes I wondered if he wasn't a little too frank. They seemed to expect it. If he said, "No, Cunning Fox, that is not your territory for trapping; and, if you insist upon using it, I will need to lock you up," the Indian did not blink. At least he knew exactly what to expect.

The Indian women came often for tea, though not nearly as regularly as they had at first. Mrs. McLain, my friend Nimmie, called, too: and I always enjoyed her visits. Miss McLain did not come, though I had bolstered up my courage to invite her on more than one occasion.

We still did not have a school. Nimmie and I had spent hours poring over books, both hers and mine. I was so anxious to get started; but she felt it was far more likely to succeed if we could convince the chief, or at least some of the elders, that it would be good for the children. This would take time, she assured me. As the chief of the band did not live in our village, but in a village farther west, we had no way to hurry our negotiations.

One Wednesday morning, a swollen-faced Indian came to see Wynn. After a brief examination, Wynn came into the kitchen.

"Got any hot water?" he asked me.

I indicated the kettle on the stove, and Wynn pulled out a pan and put some simple instruments in it, then poured the water over them and set the whole thing over the heat.

"What are you doing?" I asked, curious.

"Reneau has a bad tooth. It's going to need to come out."

"You're going to pull it?" I asked in astonishment.

"There isn't anyone else," Wynn answered. Then he turned teasingly to me. "Unless, of course, you want the job?"

"Count me out," I was quick to reply.

Wynn became more serious.

"In fact, Elizabeth, I was about to do just that," he said, turning the instruments over in the pan. "How would you like a little walk, for half-hour or so?"

I must have looked puzzled.

"I have no anesthesia. This man is going to hurt."

I realized then that Wynn was giving me opportunity to get away from the house before he began his procedure.

"I'll go to the store," I said quickly.

It didn't take me long to be ready to leave the house. Wynn was still with the shaking Reneau. I wondered who was dreading the ordeal ahead more—Reneau or Wynn.

There really wasn't anything I needed from the store, so I decided to drop in on Nimmie. She didn't answer my knock on her door. I turned to look around me, and then I spotted her in a little grove of poplar trees just beyond her garden. She had gathered about her a group of the village children. I hoped I wasn't interrupting things and approached quietly. Nimmie was telling a story, and all eyes were raptly focused on her face. *She must be a good storyteller—not a child is moving!* I marveled.

I stopped and listened.

". . . the man was big, bigger than a black bear, bigger even than a grizzly. He carried a long hunting spear and a huge bow and arrow with tips dipped in the poison potion. Everyone feared him. They feared his anger, for he roared like the mighty thunder; they feared his spear, for it flashed as swiftly as the lightning. They feared his poison arrows, for they were as deadly as the jaws of a cornered wolverine. They all shook with fear. No one would go out to meet the enemy. They would all be his slaves. Each time they came from the trapline they would have to give to him their choicest furs. Each time they pulled in the nets, he would demand their fish. Each time they shot a bull elk, they would have to give him the meat. They hated him and the slavery, but they were all afraid to go out to fight him.

"And then a young boy stepped forward. 'I will go,' he said. 'You cannot go,' the chiefs told him. 'You do not have the magic headdress. You do not have the secret medicine. You are not prepared for battle.' 'I can go,' said this young boy named David, because I take my God with me. He will fight for me.' "

I stood in awe as the story went on. I had never heard the story of David and Goliath told in this fashion before. I was surprised to hear Nimmie telling it now. Where had she heard it? She had not attended a mission school. And why was she telling it to the children in English? Few of them could understand all of the English words.

I was puzzled but I was also intrigued. How often did Nimmie tell the local children stories, and how often were they taken from the Bible? Did she always interpret the stories with Indian concepts and customs?

" 'See,' said David, 'I have here my own small bow and five tried arrows. God will direct the arrow. I am not afraid of the bearlike Goliath. He has spoken against my God and now He must be avenged.'

"And so David picked up his small bow and his five true arrows and he marched out across the valley to the wicked enemy. Goliath laughed in scorn at David. 'What are you doing,' he cried, 'sending out a child instead of a brave? You have shamed me. I turn my head from you. I shall feed this little bit of meat to the ravens and foxes.'

"But David called out to the man as tall as the pine tree, 'I come not as a child, nor yet as a brave; but I come in the name of my God, whom you have insulted,' and he thrust one of the tried arrows in his bow, whispered a prayer that God would guide its flight on the wings of the wind, and pulled the bow with all of his strength.

"The arrow found its mark. With a cry, the big warrior fell to the ground."

If I for one moment had doubted that the children were able to follow the story, the shout that went up at the moment of

Goliath's defeat would have convinced me otherwise. They cheered wildly for the victorious David.

When the noise subsided, Nimmie went on, "And so David rushed forward and struck the warrior's head from his body and lifted his huge headdress onto his own head. He picked up the long spear and his big bow and arrows and carried them back to his own tribe. They would never be the slaves of the wicked man again. David had won the battle because he had gone to fight in the name of his God."

Again there was a cheer.

"And now you must go," said Nimmie, shooing them all away with her slim hands.

"Just one more. Another one. Only one," pleaded a dozen voices.

"You said that last time," laughed Nimmie, "and I gave you one more and you say it again. Off you go now."

Reluctantly the children began to leave, and Nimmie turned. She had not been aware that I was standing there. A look of surprise crossed her face, but she did not appear to be disturbed or embarrassed.

"What a bunch," she stated. "They would have one sitting all day telling stories.—Come in, Elizabeth. We will have some tea. Have you been waiting long?"

"Not long, no. And I enjoyed it. Do you tell the children stories often?"

"Often? Yes, I suppose so—though not often enough. I don't know who enjoys it more, the children or I. Though I try to make it sound like they are a nuisance."

She laughed again and led the way to the house.

"But you told it in English," I remarked. "Do they understand?"

"They understand far more than you would think. Oh, they don't catch all the words, to be sure; but as they hear the stories again and again, they pick up more and more."

"And you told a Bible story," I continued, still dumbfounded.

"Yes, they like the Bible stories."

I wanted to ask where she had learned the Bible stories but I didn't.

"I love the Bible stories, too," she explained without being asked. "When I was learning to read English, the Bible was one of the books I read. At first it was one of the few books my new husband had on hand, so he taught me from it. I enjoyed the stories so much that, even now that I have many books, I still read from the Bible. They are such good stories."

She opened the door and let me pass into her home.

"I like the stories about Jesus best," she continued. "The children like them, too. I tell them often. The story about the little boy and his fish and bread; the story about the canoe that nearly was lost in the raging storm; the story about the blind-man who could see when Jesus put the good medicine on his eyes. Ah, they are good stories," she concluded.

"You know, Nimmie," I pointed out, "those aren't merely stories. Those are true reports of historical events. All those things really happened."

She looked so surprised and bewildered that I said, "Didn't—didn't Ian tell you that—that the Bible is a true book, that those events, those happenings—?"

"Are they *all* true?" asked Nimmie incredulously.

"Yes, all of them."

"The ones about Jesus?"

"Every one."

"And those wicked people really did put Him to death—for no reason?"

I nodded. "They did."

There was silence. Nimmie looked from me to the Bible that lay on the little table, her eyes filled with wonder and then anger. "That's hateful!" she protested, her voice full of emotion. "How could they? Only a white man could do such a thing—destroy and slay one of his own! An Indian would never do such a shameful thing. I would spit on their graves. I would feed their carcasses to the dogs." Her dark eyes flashed and her nose flared.

"It was terrible," I admitted, shocked at her intensity. "But it wasn't as simple as you think. The reason for Jesus' dying is far more complicated than that. We could read it together if you'd like. I'd be glad to study the story with you, right from the beginning, and show you why Jesus had to die."

She began to calm herself.

"He didn't stay dead, you know," I went on.

"Is that true, too?" she asked in disbelief.

"Yes, that's true, too."

She was silent for a moment. "I might like to study that."

I smiled. "Fine. Why don't we start tomorrow morning? At my house?"

She nodded and rose to prepare the tea. She turned slightly. "Elizabeth, I'm sorry—sorry about what I said concerning the white man. It's only—only that sometimes—sometimes I cannot understand the things men do. The way they gnash and tear at one another—it's worse than wolves or foxes." This time she did not say *white* man, though I wondered if she still thought it.

"I know," I agreed shamefacedly. "Sometimes I cannot understand it either. It isn't the way it was meant to be. It isn't the way *Jesus* wants it to be. It isn't the right way. The Bible tells us that God abhors it, too. He wants us to love and care for one another."

"Does the white man know that?"

"Some of them do."

"Hasn't the white man had the Bible for many years?"

"Yes, for many years."

"Then why doesn't he read it and do what it says?"

I shook my head. It was a troubling question. "I don't know," I finally admitted. "I really don't know."

Chapter Twenty-two

Studies

Our Bible studies together started the next day as planned. We did not meet together every day, but we did meet regularly. Ian did not seem to object, and Wynn was most encouraging.

Nimmie was a good student; and as we began to piece together the whole plan of God for His creation, she became excited about it.

"Katherine should be here! She needs to hear this," she insisted.

I wondered about Katherine. I doubted that she would come out of her bitterness long enough to even listen, but Nimmie kept insisting.

"Do you mind if I bring her?" she continued.

"Well, no. I don't mind. I'm not sure—I'm not sure she'd come that's all. I've asked her to my house many times, and I've never been able to get her to come."

"For Bible study?"

"Well, no, not for Bible study necessarily. Just for tea. But if she won't come even for tea, I surely don't think she'll want to come for study."

"She might," persisted Nimmie. "I'll ask her."

When Nimmie arrived for the next study, she had Katherine with her. I never will know how she effected the miracle. I tried to keep the shock out of my face as I welcomed them both in.

Katherine scowled as we opened our Bibles and began to read. She had brought a Bible of her own, but it didn't look as though it had received much use. She said nothing all morning long, even though Nimmie often stopped in the reading to comment or ask for an explanation. She was eager to know not just the words but the *meaning* of the words, now that she knew each of the stories was true.

When the two ladies left that morning, I told them I would be looking forward to our next time together. Katherine frowned and informed me in unmistakable tones, "Don't expect me back. I came just to get this here woman off my back. There's nothing in this book that I don't already know. I'm not a heathen, you know—I was raised in church."

"Then you must miss it," I said softly.

She wheeled to look at me.

"I was raised in church, too," I continued, "and if there is one thing about the North that I miss more than any other, it is not being able to go to church on Sunday."

She snorted her disgust, pressed her lips together and marched out the door.

Nimmie looked at me sadly and followed the other woman.

I don't know how it came about; but the next time Nimmie came for her study, Katherine was reluctantly trudging along behind her, her Bible tucked under one arm.

I made no comment except to welcome them both, and we proceeded with our reading and discussion.

The weather was getting colder. Daily, large flocks of ducks and geese passed overhead as the birds sought warmer climates. Almost all the leaves were dancing on the ground rather than clinging to the now-bare branches. The animals' coats began to thicken; and men talked about a long, hard winter.

Wynn hired some men to haul a good supply of wood for the fire, and we prepared ourselves as well as possible for the winter weather ahead.

The inevitable day came. The north winds howled in, carrying sub-zero temperatures and swirling snow. We were in the midst of our first winter blizzard. I was so thankful that Wynn was home, safe and sound, instead of out someplace checking on a far-off trapper.

In spite of the fire in the stove, the temperature in the cabin dropped steadily. Wynn lit the fireplace and hung some blankets over the windows to shut out the cold. Still the chill did not leave the air. We piled on the clothing to keep our body heat in.

That night we banked our fires and retired early, hoping that the next day might bring a break in the storm. During the night, Wynn was up more than once to be sure the fire was still stoked with wood.

"I do hope there are no casualties," Wynn said. "This is unusually severe for this time of year. Some folks might not have been prepared for it."

I hoped, too, that there were no casualties. It would be terrible to be caught out in such a storm.

When we awoke the next morning, we were disappointed to find the fury of the storm had not slackened. Still it raged about us.

"Look," I said to Wynn when I found the water in the washstand basin frozen, "it *really is* cold in here!"

I was about to empty the chunk of ice into the slop bucket when Wynn stopped me. "Don't throw it out," he instructed. "Heat it and reuse it."

"Use *this*?"

"Who knows when we might be able to get more water. We only have three quarters of a pail, and we will need that for drinking and cooking. We'll make the wash water last as long as possible."

When I had finished the breakfast dishes, I did not throw out that water either. Instead, I left it in the dishpan at the back of the stove. It would have to serve for washing the dinner dishes and perhaps even the supper dishes as well.

I was all set to enjoy a lovely day with Wynn in spite of what the weather was doing outside; but he came from the bedroom drawing on a heavy fur jacket.

"Where are you going?" I questioned in alarm.

"I need to go down to the Hudson's Bay Store and make sure there are no reports of trouble. I shouldn't be gone too long; but if something comes up and I don't get back right away, you're not to worry. There is plenty of wood. You shouldn't have any problem keeping warm and dry."

He stopped to kiss me. "Don't go out, Elizabeth," he cautioned, "not for any reason. If something happens so I can't get back to you by nightfall, I'll send someone else."

By nightfall? What a dreadful thought!

Wynn slipped out into the swirling snow, and I was left standing at the window watching his form disappear all too quickly.

I don't remember any day that was longer. There was nothing to do but to tend to the fires. Even with both burning, the cabin was cold. I borrowed a pair of Wynn's heavy socks and put on my boots. Still my feet were cold.

I walked around and around the small room, swinging my arms in an effort to keep warm and to prevent total boredom. The storm did not slacken. It was getting dark again. Not that it had ever been really light on this day, but at least one had realized it was day and not night.

I fixed some tea. I had quite forgotten to eat anything all day. I was sorry I had not thought of it. It could have helped to fill in a few of my minutes.

It was well after I had lit the lamp and set it in the window that I heard approaching footsteps. I rushed to the door. It was Wynn. He was back safe and sound. I could have cried for joy.

"Is everything all right?" I asked, hugging him snowy jacket and all.

"As far as we know," he replied, stamping the snow from his boots. "We had to go and get Mary. She had no fuel for a fire and wouldn't have made it through the storm, I'm sure."

"Who's Mary?"

"She's a woman who lives alone since she lost her husband and family three or four years ago. They call her Crazy Mary— maybe she is; maybe she isn't, I don't know. But she refuses to move into the settlement, and she has a tendency to rant and rave about things. She was mad at me tonight for bodily removing her from her cabin and bringing her to town."

"Bodily?"

He nodded. "She absolutely refused to go on her own."

"What did she do? Did she fight?"

"Oh, no. She didn't fight; she just wouldn't move, that's all. I carried her out and put her on the sled, and she rode into town like a good girl. But I had to pick her up and carry her into Lavoies' cabin as well."

I smiled, thinking of this determined Indian lady. She certainly had gotten her point across.

"Well, she should be all right now," said Wynn. "Mrs. Sam is sure she will stay put as long as the storm continues."

I was glad Crazy Mary was safe. *What is the real story behind her name?* I wondered.

Chapter Twenty-three

Winter

With the coming of the winter, many of the men had to leave their warm cabins to go out to their traplines. The furs they trapped in winter were the most profitable because of their thickness, and each trapper had a designated area that was considered his. When I asked Wynn how they made the arrangements, he said it seemed to be by some kind of gentleman's agreement rather than by any legal contract. I did learn that trapping another's territory was considered a major offense.

There was the problem of stealing, as well. There wasn't much common thievery in the North. No one felt over-concerned about locking up what he owned. Houses were left open and belongings left about the yard. The cabins that were constructed by the trappers for protection while working the traplines were free to be used by others who were passing through. Most trappers even made sure there was an adequate wood supply and blankets, matches and rations for any guests who might drop in during their absence. Of course, they knew the other trappers would extend the same courtesy.

So in an area where usual theft was not much of a problem, a very serious temptation and offense was stealing from another's trapline. Such a criminal was considered to be the lowest of the low, not only a thief of valuable animal pelts, but of a family's livelihood as well. Vengeance was often immediate and deadly, and few felt that the wronged man could be blamed for taking the law into his own hands. The Royal North West Policeman must be on guard all the time for this. Any suspected thieves must be spotted and the guilty party apprehended immediately before a brutal beating or even a murder might occur.

Wynn watched the lines and kept his eyes and ears open for any complaints of offenses.

Mostly it was the men who worked the traplines, but Crazy Mary also claimed a small territory as her own. So, once the storm had blown itself out, she refused to stay at the Lavoies' and headed back, poorly clothed, to protect her interests. She hinted rather loudly that there might have been someone messing with some of her traps.

Most people shrugged off the story as one of Crazy Mary's fancies, but Wynn could not dismiss it so easily. It must be checked and proven false to put everyone's mind at ease. When the storm ended, Wynn took snowshoes and dog team out to investigate.

Wynn did not keep his team at our cabin but in an enclosure by the Hudson's Bay Store. One reason was that the food supply for the dogs was over there, and also their clamor would not keep us awake at night.

Each dog had been carefully picked by the men of the Force who had preceded Wynn. The dogs were chosen for their endurance, dependability, and strength, not particularly for their good disposition. Many of them were scrappers and, for that reason, they had to be tied well out of range of one another. Some of them had ragged ears or ugly scars from past fights. I didn't care much for Wynn's sled dogs. Harnessing them to the sleigh was a tough job. Things could be going well; and suddenly one of the dogs would get mad at something another dog did, and a fight would break out. Before long the whole team would be in a scrap, tangling the harness and making a general mess of things. Yet the dog team was very necessary. Wynn used his dogs almost every day during the winter.

He had been talking about choosing his own team and training them himself for harness. With different training, he thought the dogs might be better-tempered and make less problems on the trail. It sounded like a good idea to me. It was going to take time and work, but Wynn was watching for promising pups.

When he went out after the storm to check on Crazy Mary's story, he informed me he also planned to swing around and see a litter of pups which a trapper by the name of Smith had for sale near the west branch of the river. I found myself wishing I could go with him, but I didn't even mention the thought to Wynn. It was still very cold and the snow was deep. The sled dogs were enough trouble on the trail. He certainly didn't need me along to complicate matters.

Wynn didn't return until late that night. He had talked with Mary and gone over her trapline with her. She had shown him "signs" and ranted on about her suspicions. This was the trapline her late husband had managed, and Mary was steadfast in her belief that it now was her exclusive property. But someone was moving in, she maintained, infringing on her area. She hadn't found any evidence yet of stolen pelts, but the new traps were getting in too close. They found no traps that belonged to another trapper, but Mary was sure one or two had been there. She could see the marks on the ground; she dug around in the snow to prove her point. But Wynn could not accept her "evidence" as valid. He left her, promising to keep a sharp lookout and asking her to get in touch with him if she still suspected anything.

Then, as planned, Wynn pulled his team around and went to see Smith. Smith was away from his cabin when Wynn arrived, so Wynn went in, started up a fire and made himself a cup of tea. The pups were in a corner of the cabin, so he had a good chance to look them over well for potential sled dogs. There were some possibilities. Wynn watched them play and tussle, liking what he saw.

It was getting late in the day and Smith had still not arrived at the cabin; so Wynn banked the fire to try to keep the cabin warm for the trapper's return, carried in a further wood supply, and turned his team back on the trail for home.

Wynn had learned to appreciate one thing about his sled dogs. While on the trail they usually laid aside all grudges and pulled together. They were considered to be one of the fastest teams in the area. Speed could, at times, be important to a policeman. A few minutes might mean the difference between life or death.

The team was in a hurry to get back to the settlement, so Wynn was hard pushed to keep up with his dogs. On the smoother terrain, he rode the runners; when the way was rough, he snowshoed behind it, guiding it over the crusted snow.

When Wynn told me about his day as we sat in front of our fireplace that night, I found myself almost envying him. It sounded exciting and almost fun to be swinging along the snow-crisp trail behind the sled dogs. Wynn must have seen the wistful look in my eyes, for he surprised me a few days later.

"Want to take a little ride?"

I looked out the window. The day was filled with sunshine, the wind was no longer blowing, and the snow lying across the countryside made a Currier and Ives Christmas card of the scene.

"I'm going back out to check on Crazy Mary."

"Do we have to call her Crazy Mary?" I objected.

Wynn smiled. "There are four Marys in the area—Little Mary, Old Mary, Joe's Mary, and Crazy Mary. All the people refer to them in this way."

"Well, I don't like it. It's—it's degrading."

"You're right. But, from what I've been hearing, her neighbors are probably right. I think she does have mental problems. It sounds like it started when she lost her children in a smallpox epidemic. Her husband was away at the time and Mary was all alone. She watched all five of them die, one at a time. She hasn't been quite the same since. If she were in one of our civilized areas, she would have been institutionalized and cared for. Here, she is still on her own. She doesn't care about people and won't take help when it is offered. Now and then, if the weather really gets bad, one or another of the men leaves a quarter of meat on her doorstep. They have never been thanked for it, but it does disappear; so they assume she does make use of it."

I felt sorry for Mary. *What an awful way to live! What an awful way to be known,* I mourned. I had never seen her, but I was sure that if people really tried, *something* could be done.

"You haven't answered my question," Wynn's voice broke into my thoughts.

"The ride? I'd love to, though I have no idea what you have in mind."

"I want to keep a close eye on Mary and her problem. I also plan to stop and see if Smith is home. I'd like to get two or three of those pups."

My face lit up then. "I'd love to go," I said again.

"I'll go get the team. Wear the warmest clothes you have. Those old pants are a must."

I hurried to get ready. I didn't want to keep Wynn waiting. I borrowed a pair of Wynn's long drawers and pulled the old pants over them. The combination of the two meant I could hardly move. I also borrowed Wynn's wool socks and pulled on my own heavy sweater. The footwear had me concerned. All I had were the old hiking boots, and common sense told me they would not keep my feet warm.

Wynn soon returned, leaving the team lying fan-style on the ground when he came in for me. I was still trying to struggle into the heavy boots.

"Here," he said, "I think these will be much warmer."

He handed me a pair of beautiful, fur-lined Indian moccasins. They had elaborate designs in bead and quill work, and I exclaimed as I reached for them.

"They are wonderful! Where did you get them?"

"I had Mrs. Sam make them. I knew you would be needing something warmer for your feet. Fortunately, they were ready this morning."

"They are so pretty," I continued.

"They are pretty," agreed Wynn. "They are also warm."

I caught his hint that they were for wearing rather than for admiring, and I hastened to put them on. Then, donning my heavy mittens, I followed Wynn out to the sleigh.

Since I could not maneuver showshoes, I was privileged to ride. Wynn ran along beside or behind me, calling out orders to the dogs. They obeyed immediately. Maybe Wynn's "secondhand" team wasn't so bad after all. They certainly behaved themselves better in harness than out. I was gaining respect for them as we glided over the crisp winter snow.

"This is fun!" I shouted to Wynn as the sled flew over a slight rise in the trail. He laughed at my little-girl exuberance.

We came to an area where the wind had swept across the path, leaving the snow only a few inches deep.

"Would you like to walk for a while?" Wynn asked me. I did, so I scrambled from the sleigh and set out to follow him and the team.

The team would have left me far behind if I had just walked along behind. I had to run. I could tell Wynn was holding the team back with his commands. Still they seemed to gain ground. I hurried faster, but it was hard to keep at it with all the clothing I was wearing. Wynn soon stopped the team, and I laughingly tumbled back onto the sled. I was out of breath and panting, but it had been good for me.

Wynn found Crazy Mary out working her traps. She was a little woman. *Too small to be handling this man-sized job,* I reasoned, and my concern for her deepened.

She had straight, black hair which had been chopped off at the jawline. In the morning sunshine, she wore her parka hood back, and her hair kept flopping forward, covering her face. She peeped out from between strands of it, her eyes black and flashing. There were some scars on her face, and I realized that somehow she alone had survived the smallpox epidemic. Over her back she wore a skin sack of some kind, and I could see fur pieces sticking out of it. Apparently, Crazy Mary skinned the animals just where she found them, then threw aside the carcasses and stuffed the fur into her sack. Wynn had told me that as soon as the trapper got back to his cabin, he cleaned and stretched the pelts onto a wooden frame for drying. Crazy Mary would still have work to do when she got home at the end of the day.

I stayed near the sleigh while Wynn talked to her. I could not hear their conversation. But I could tell she was still agitated. She waved her arms and pounded her fists together and then gave little shrieks like a wounded animal. I didn't know if she was giving Wynn a demonstration of something that had happened or just expressing her feelings.

After some minutes Wynn came back to the sled.

"Well?" I asked.

"She still says someone is pushing back her boundary lines."

"Do you think they are?"

"I don't know. It's hard to tell when there really aren't any actual, visible lines in the first place."

I waved to Crazy Mary as we moved away. There she stood, one little woman alone fighting against the elements and an unseen, unknown enemy. I felt very sorry for her. I refused to refer to her as "crazy." If she had to be identified, they could call her *Brave Mary* or *Trapline Mary*. There was no need to call her Crazy Mary at all.

At Smith's cabin, his dog team was tethered in the yard and began howling and barking as our team swung around to the front. Smith himself came to the door. Seeing Wynn's uniform under his parka, he waved an arm to us, beckoning us to come in. I didn't suppose that he got many visitors.

He wasn't much for conversation, but he grinned and went about making up a tin pot of very strong, hot tea.

We sipped slowly. I was given the honor of the only chair in the room, the men half crouched, supported by the wall of the cabin.

They talked about lines, furs, and the economy. I didn't join in. I was too busy watching the litter of puppies that ignored us and went about their play. What fluffy round balls they were, with sparkling eyes and curly tails. It was hard to believe they could grow up into snarling, fighting, mean-spirited dogs. They were good-sized already, and I knew that they were well past the weaning stage.

After a few minutes, Smith seemed to feel there had been enough small talk.

"So what brings you out this way, Sarge?" he asked Wynn.

Part of Wynn's job was to gather information where he could, and another part of his job was to scatter a little information, too.

"Mary has reported that someone is getting a little too close with their traps," Wynn said, carefully studying the man's reaction.

"That crazy woman! She's the one broadening *her* boundary. She's been mismanaging her traps for years; and now that she can't find the animals, she's moving her lines. Did you see where she's got her traps?"

Wynn agreed that he had.

The trapper pulled a hand-drawn map from the shelf in the corner and spread it out on the table.

"Looky here," he said, agitated. "This here is my trapline. I've had it for years. Goes right along the river here, swings to the north by that stand of jackpine, follows up the draw, dips down to that little beaver dam, turns around west here, and comes back along this chain of hills. Every trapper in the territory knows those are my boundaries. So what does she do? She's sneaking traps in here and a few over in here." His finger stabbed at the map, punctuating each statement. "And the last time I was out, she even had a couple in here."

It was clear that Smith was upset.

"If she wasn't a woman," the man exploded, "an' a crazy one at that, I'd—" But he didn't finish the statement.

Wynn continued to study the map. "I'll do some checking," he said quietly. "It's clear that we've got to find out who's crowding who."

Then Wynn turned his attention to the pups snapping and fighting playfully on the dirt floor.

"I'm looking for some new sled dogs," he said. "Hear that you raise good animals. They look pretty good to me. Planning to sell these, are you?"

It was the first time Smith smiled. He reached down and scooped up a fluffy pup. It rewarded him by chewing on his thumb. He roughed its woolly back and clipped its ears playfully.

"Hate to, but I gotta. Got all of the team dogs now that I need. Another litter due in a couple of weeks. Which one you got your eye on?"

I knew which one I had *my* eye on. It was a little fellow with a full fluffy tail that curled over his back. He was a silver grey in color with shining black eyes and a sticky red tongue. He had been licking the snow off my boots.

I waited breathlessly for Wynn to name his dog.

"What do you think, Elizabeth?" he surprised me. "Which ones would you pick?"

"How many do you need?"

"I thought I'd start with two."

"For sled dogs?"

"What else would we need them for?"

I reached down and picked up the cute pup. He turned from licking at my boots and began to lick at my hands. *I think he likes me,* I exulted.

"Well, I was just thinking that it wouldn't be a bad idea to have a dog at the house. I mean, it would be company and—"

"You want a *dog*?"

I did not hesitate but answered him with the same intensity with which he had asked his incredulous question.

"Yes."

He laughed then, softly. "I thought you were afraid of dogs."

"The ones in the village, yes. They snarl and growl and snap when you go by. But I like dogs, generally. Really. A dog of my own, there at the cabin, might make me feel—well, less lonely— and more secure when you are away."

Wynn could see that I really wanted the pup.

"Okay," he smiled. "You go first."

"Go first?"

"You take your pick first."

That was no problem for me. I held up the pup already in my arms.

"This one," I said without a moment's hesitation.

Smith and Wynn were both grinning at me when I looked up.

"What do you think, Smith?" asked Wynn in a teasing way.

"I think the little lady got you," grinned Smith.

I must have looked puzzled.

"I think she did, too. Picked the best one in the bunch. I had my eye on that one for lead dog." Wynn reached over and tussled the pup's fur. It growled playfully and pawed at his hand.

I felt very happy with myself. I had picked a winner. Still, if Wynn had wanted this one for the lead dog, perhaps I should—

"You can have him if you like," I said, offering the pup. "You need him. I just want him."

Wynn lifted his hand from the pup and touched my cheek. "You keep him. I think he'll be just right for you. There are plenty of others for me to choose from. They look like the makings of good sled dogs, too."

Wynn made his two selections. They were pretty little dogs as well, but I was glad I'd had first choice. Wynn paid Smith and we bundled up our armload of pups and headed for home.

The pups were not easy to transport. Wynn fared better with his. He put them in a knapsack with only their furry heads protruding and secured them on his back. They watched, wide-eyed, as we hurried over the trail.

My little fellow was more difficult. I insisted on carrying him on my lap. He didn't like being confined, and wiggled and squirmed and whined and yapped. I was about to give up on him when he decided that he had had enough, curled up and went to sleep.

I kept my hand on him, gently stroking the soft fur. I was so happy to finally have a dog of my very own. Being raised in the city, my folks thought our house and yard were too confining for pets. I guess I had secretly always wanted one. Maybe that was why I had enjoyed the small mouse, Napoleon, for the short while he had been with me in the teacherage. And now I had a dog! And a beautiful dog it would be. I would name it myself. I began to go over names in my mind. *A dog like this should have a name that is rather majestic, like King or Prince or Duke.* But I rejected each of those as too common.

Suddenly I thought of something. I turned slightly in the sleigh.

"Wynn," I hollered against the swishing of the sled runners and the yipping of the dogs. "Do I need a boy-name or a girl-name?"

There was laughter in Wynn's voice as he called back, "A boy-name, Elizabeth."

Chapter Twenty-four

Settling In

I named my dog Kip. If someone had asked, I really wouldn't have been able to explain why. It just seemed to suit him somehow. He was a smart little thing, and Wynn said that it was never too early to begin his training. So I started in. I didn't know much about training dogs. Wynn told me obedience was of primary importance. A dog, to be useful and enjoyable, must be obedient. Wynn gave me pointers, and in the evenings, if duties did not call him out, he even worked with me and the young dog.

It was amazing how quickly Kip grew. One day he was a fluffy pup, and the next day it seemed he was a gangly, growing dog. He turned from cute into beautiful. His tail curled above his silver-tipped, glistening dark fur. He was curious and sensitive and a quick learner. I loved him immediately and he did so help to fill my days. Aware of his needs, physical and emotional, my own life was enriched.

Kip needed exercise, so I took him out for walks, bundling myself up against the cold. It was a good way to get my exercise as well. When the snow got deeper and more difficult to navigate, I asked for snowshoes so that I might still keep up the daily exercise program. Wynn brought some home and took me out to introduce me to the use of them. They were much more difficult to manage than it seemed when watching Wynn maneuver in them. I took many tumbles in the snow in the process of learning. Kip thought it was a game; every time I went down, he was there to lick my face and scatter snow down my neck.

Eventually I did get the feel of snowshoes. The cold or the snow no longer kept me confined. I walked along the river trails, along the treeline to the west, and to the settlement. Whenever

I went to the store with Kip, I picked him up and carried him. He was getting heavy and he was also getting impatient with me. He hated to be carried; he wanted to run. But I was fearful about all the dog fights I had seen on my trips to the village. I did not want Kip to be attacked. And so, as the weeks went by, each time our outings included the store, or Nimmie's for Bible study, I picked up my growing, complaining dog. I wondered just how much longer I could manage it. I hated to be stuck in the house, and I hated to leave Kip at home alone. I guessed that eventually all our walks would have to take us away from the dogs and the village and into the woods instead.

As the weeks went by, more snow piled up around us. The people began to be concerned about food and wood supplies. It took all their time and attention to provide a meal or two for the day and to keep their homes reasonably warm.

Christmas seemed unreal to me. There was no village celebration, no setting aside of this important day. Wynn and I celebrated quietly in our home. We read the Christmas story, and I shed a few tears of loneliness. I tried not to let Wynn see them, but I think he was suspicious. We did not have a turkey dinner with all of the trimmings. We had, instead, a venison roast and blueberry pie made from the berries I had gathered and canned. The Indian women had dried theirs, but I knew nothing about the drying process. Besides, I thought I preferred the canned fruit; to my way of thinking, they did taste awfully good in that Christmas dinner pie.

In the afternoon, Wynn suggested we take Kip for a run. It was fun to be out together, but the weather was bitterly cold, so we did not stay out for long. I think even Kip was glad to be back inside by our warm fire.

We were soon beginning a new year. Repeatedly, Wynn had to dig us out from a new snowfall in the mornings. If it had not been for Kip, I'm sure I would never have left my kitchen. He would whine and scamper about at the door, coaxing for a run.

The trappers now and then brought home meat for their families. The women supplemented this with some ice fishing in the nearby river. It was cold, miserable work; and I ached in my bones for them. Children and women alike were often out gathering wood from the nearby forest. I wondered why more of them did not prepare for the winter by stacking up a good fuel supply. Most of the Indians gathered as they needed it, and that was a big task when the fires had to be kept burning day and night.

I still met for studies with Nimmie and Miss McLain, though she still had not thawed out much. She seemed so deeply bitter and troubled. Little by little I learned her story. She had been orphaned at the age of three; Ian was five at the time. A fine Swedish family in the East had taken pity on the two children and raised them along with their own six. They had been treated kindly enough, but the family was poor and frugal, and all the children were required to work at an early age.

Schooling was one thing the family had felt was important, so each one of the children had been allowed to attend the local school as high as the grades went. When they reached their teen years, they were soon on their own. When Ian left the family, he apprenticed to a merchant in a nearby town as a bookkeeper and stock-checker. The man was German, and Ian lived in his home and learned German. Katherine had her heart set on being a schoolteacher, and so she found employment in the home of a doctor as housemaid and took classes whenever she could crowd them in.

The woman of the house was impossible to please, and young Katherine often found herself the victim of fits of fury. She would have left if she had had any place to go. At length her schooling was completed and she was able to obtain a position at a local school. The doctor's wife suddenly realized that she was losing good help, and she tried to bar Miss McLain from getting the job. It didn't work. Miss McLain was hired and moved out of the home and into a boarding house. There was a young man staying at the boarding house as well; and, after some months, they became attracted to one another and eventually engaged. Miss McLain was now a happy girl. For the first time that she remembered, she had a job she loved, a salary on which she could live, and—most importantly—someone who loved her.

The young man seemed happy, too, and he was anxious for the wedding to take place. Miss McLain told him she had to wait until she could afford her dress and all the other things she needed. The man declared that he hated to wait longer and then came up with a lovely plan. He had a sister in town. He was sure she would be ever so glad to help them.

They boarded a streetcar and went to see the sister. Miss McLain was excited. If her John was correct in assuming his sister would help, she would soon be a married woman with a husband and home of her own.

When the streetcar stopped and they walked the short distance to the sister's home, Miss McLain could only stand in frozen bewilderment. There must be some mistake. They were at the home of her former employer.

She did go in, but things did not go well. Not only did the angry woman refuse to help her, but she raged and ranted about her dishonesty, her ill temper, her laziness, and even her bad name. John only stood there like a statue, not even defending his Katherine.

In the end, the rift between them was so great that it could not be repaired, and John called off the engagement. Miss McLain left behind her school and her dreams and headed for her brother, who was by now living in the North.

She had never buried her bitterness. In her twenty years in the North, she had nursed it and fostered it and held it to her until now it was a terrible, deep festering wound in her soul. She was miserable; she deserved to be miserable; I think she even enjoyed being miserable; and she did a wonderful job of making those around her miserable, too.

In spite of her bitterness and her anger with life, I began to like Miss McLain. I felt both sorry for her and angry with her. Other people had suffered; others had been treated unfairly. They had lived through it. There was no reason why Miss McLain could not pull herself out of her misery if she had a mind to.

Nimmie was always patient and loving with her. Miss McLain, in turn, was spiteful and cutting with Nimmie. She didn't bother much with me. Perhaps she didn't think I was worth the trouble, or perhaps she thought I would not be intimidated by her; I do not know.

In spite of the difficulty, we were able to proceed with our Bible study. As we went through the lessons together, I was sensing a real change in Nimmie.

There was an eagerness, a softness, an openness that really thrilled me. She was so disappointed if a storm kept us from meeting. After a morning of study, she would share with Ian at night the things that she had learned. I was surprised and delighted that Ian seemed interested in what Nimmie told him. He, too, seemed eager to hear truth from God's Word.

In the middle of January, a bad storm hit. In all of my life I had never seen so much snow fall in so short a time. I was worried about Wynn; he was somewhere out in that whiteness with the dog team. I knew that dogs had an unusual sense of direction even in a storm, but I paced and prayed all day that the animals wouldn't let us down now.

The temperature dipped and the water in the basin again glazed over with ice. I worked hard to keep the cabin warm, adding fuel to the fire regularly. Kip whined at the door to go for a run, but I put him off. He was so insistent that eventually I sent him out for a few minutes on his own. I had never let him out alone before and I was afraid he might not come back. But he was soon crying at the door to be admitted to the warmth.

I fed Kip and made myself tea. Still Wynn did not come.

It was dark outside when there was a thumping at the door. I ran to it with my heart in my throat. Who could it be? Wynn did not knock at his own door. Who else would be coming and why? *Has something happened to Wynn?*

But it *was* Wynn, and in his arms he had a bundle. I opened the door wide for him.

"It's Crazy Mary," he said. "She was alone in her cabin with no heat and no food."

I hurried ahead of Wynn and tossed the cushions from the cot to make a place for her.

He opened the blankets, and she lay shivering. For a moment, I wondered if she was conscious, and then her eyelids fluttered and she looked at us. I smiled, but it was not returned.

"Do you have any food ready?" asked Wynn.

"There's soup in the pot, and I just made tea."

"A little soup. Not too much. I'll have to feed her."

While I went for the soup, Wynn finished unbundling the

blankets from Mary, and now he removed the moccasins and wrappings of hide from her feet. He was working over her feet when I came with the soup. He went to take the bowl from me, but I indicated her feet. "I'll feed her," I said. "You do whatever is necessary there."

At first she refused the soup on the spoon; but when I was able to trickle a little of it into her mouth, she opened it ever so slightly and I was able to give her more. She swallowed several spoonfuls before I decided it was enough for the time.

"Should I give her some tea?" I asked Wynn.

"A little," he replied, and I got a cup of tea and spooned some of it into the woman's mouth.

She still shivered. I had never seen anyone who looked so cold. I went for more blankets.

We fixed a bed for Mary on the cot and looked after her throughout the night. Several times I awoke to find Wynn absent from bed and bent over the old woman, spooning hot soup or massaging her frostbitten feet.

The next few days were taken up with nursing Mary. Her toes swelled to a disturbing size. There didn't seem to be much more we could do for them. About once an hour I would spoonfeed her. She ate more heartily now, though she still was unable to feed herself.

I knew she could talk, but she did not speak to me. I had heard her talking to Wynn the day we had visited her on her trapline. She had been quite vocal then. I knew her silence now was not because she couldn't speak but because she chose not to. For whatever reason, I decided to respect it. Oh, I talked to her. I talked to her as I fed her and as I cared for her feet. I talked to her about the weather as I moved about the house doing the dishes or feeding the fire. I talked to her much like I talked to Kip—including her in my activities but not expecting an answer.

She lay on the cot, her black eyes watching every move I made; but she said nothing.

When the worst of the storm was over, Mrs. Sam and Evening Star came for tea. It had been some weeks since I had had their company and I was so glad to see them. I suspected they had come to see Mary. They may have, but if so they certainly kept it well hidden. After one glance in the woman's direction, they completely ignored her. They crossed to my kitchen table where they knew they would be served, and seated themselves.

They talked about the storm, the need for wood for the fire, the difficulty in catching fish—mostly communicating with waving, expressive hands, though they did add a word here and there. Evening Star played with Kip, seeming to like my dog. The Indians were not accustomed to having a dog in the home, and it must have seemed strange to her.

When they rose to leave, I followed them to the door.

"Mary is getting much better," I said quietly, to introduce the subject of her stay with us into the conversation. "In a few days, we hope she will be able to sit up some."

There was no response.

"As soon as she is able to sit, we think she will be able to feed herself, and then before too long she will be able to get around again. It's going to take awhile, but she is getting better."

I wasn't sure how many of my English words the two women understood, so I used hand gestures to accompany them.

Mrs. Sam was shaking her head. She turned at the door and looked at me.

"Not stay," she said clearly.

"Oh, she must stay," I persisted. "She needs lots of care yet. She couldn't possibly care for herself for many days."

But Mrs. Sam still shook her head. "Not stay," she insisted. "She go—soon."

Mrs. Sam was right. When we got up the next morning, Mary was not there. How she ever managed to drag herself from our home and back to her cabin I'll never know. She had been so weak and her feet so swollen, and yet she was gone. Wynn immediately went after her. She was already home—sitting in her cold cabin, her scanty blankets wrapped around her. She refused to move.

He gathered wood and built her a fire and made her a cup of tea from the supplies he always carried with him. Then he spent the morning gathering a wood supply for her.

He went out with his rifle and was rewarded in his hunt

with a buck deer which he cleaned and hung in a tree close to Mary's cabin. Preserved by the cold, it would supply meat for many weeks for the lone woman.

He gave her instructions about caring for her feet, unloaded all of the food supplies he had with him, and left her.

I cried when Wynn told me. I felt so sorry for the little woman all alone there.

"There is nothing more we can do," Wynn comforted me. "If we brought her back here, she would only run away again; and next time she might not make it."

I knew he was right. He had done the best he knew how for Mary. We hoped it was enough to keep her alive.

Chapter Twenty-five

The Storm

Storm after storm hit the little settlement. We lived from one day to the next, accepting the weather as it came. On the good days, when the wind calmed down, I went out with Kip. On the days of snow and wind, I shivered and stayed in. I came to hate wind. Not only was it cold and miserable, but it was confining and, I was soon to learn, deadly.

One brisk, windy morning, Wynn returned from the Hudson's Bay Store where he had gone for a few needed supplies and reported that he had to take a trip south.

"Today?" I asked incredulously. It was bitterly cold. The windchill must have lowered the temperature to −50°F or worse.

"Now," he answered, "I'm on my way as soon as I get the team."

Wynn came into the cabin long enough to add some extra clothing to what he was already wearing and to pack his supply sack with more food and medical equipment. I felt panic seizing me as I noticed his precautions. It looked as though he expected delays.

"I may not make it back home tonight, Elizabeth," he said, straightening up and drawing me into his arms. "Don't worry about me. There are several trappers' shacks along the trail, and if the storm gets any worse I can take cover. Do you have everything you need?"

Me? I was all right. He was the one going out into the storm. Wynn checked the wood supply.

"There is plenty more wood stacked right outside the door if you should run out," he informed me. "Don't leave the cabin until you are sure the storm is over. And then if you do go out, be sure to take Kip."

I nodded. It sounded as if he was planning to be gone *forever*! Tears welled up in my eyes.

"I'll be fine," he said, brushing the tears away tenderly. "I love you."

I tried to tell him that I loved him too; but it was difficult to get the words out. My throat felt tight and dry.

"Where—where are you going?" I finally managed to ask.

"Word just came in that a trapper out near Beaver Falls hasn't been seen for a couple of weeks. His friend says he always shows up at his place for a Friday night card game, but he hasn't been there for two Fridays now. He's worried about him."

"Doesn't he have a cabin?"

"They checked it out. He's not there."

"If he's been gone for two weeks," I said, annoyed, "why didn't someone report it before—when the weather was decent?"

"I can't answer that; but it's been reported now, and I have to go."

I was angry with the careless trapper. I was disgusted with his friend who had let it go for so long without reporting it. I was even a little put out with Wynn for taking his duty so seriously. Surely it would be wiser to wait until the weather improved.

I kissed him goodbye and let him go, because there was nothing else I could do.

Even Kip wasn't much help in filling in the long day. I talked to him and fed him and petted him, but my heart was with Wynn. *I hope he makes it home before dark,* I anguished inwardly.

Night came and Wynn did not come. I sat up, curled in a blanket and tucked between pillows, on our cot. Kip snuggled at my feet, now and then lifting his head to listen intently to the sounds of the night. I heard the howl of a wolf above the wind, and Kip heard it too. He stirred restlessly but did not answer the cry.

I watched the fire closely. If Wynn returned—no, *when* Wynn returned—he would be chilled and would need the warmth.

I dozed off now and then; each time I awakened, I strained to hear footsteps approaching the cabin. They did not come.

Toward morning I finally gave in and fell asleep.

I awoke to find the cabin fairly shaking with the wind. The fire was nearly out, and I quickly went for more fuel to build it up. The wind seemed to scream through every crack and crevice of our little home. The temperature dropped further and the snow swirled all around the cabin. Even Kip seemed to be uneasy.

All day I kept the fires burning. I knew I would soon be drawing on the supply from outside. I wondered about the Indian families. They weren't as well stocked for wood as I had been. Surely by now they would have exhausted their supplies. I wished there was some way of bringing them to the warmth and protection of our cabin. With my fingers, I scratched a spot in the frost on the window and looked out. I could not see the buildings of the settlement. I could not even see the birch tree that grew about fifteen feet from the door. All I could see was angry, swirling snow.

I tried to drink a cup of tea, but my hands shook when I lifted the cup to my mouth. I was on the verge of tears, but I knew that tears would do no good.

I fed the fire, I prayed, I walked the floor, I prayed, I read my Bible, I prayed; and somehow this even longer second day of storm passed by, hour by hour.

Another night, and still Wynn had not come. Again I did not go to bed. Kip whined uneasily and pressed his nose against my hand. I stroked his rich, fluffy fur and spoke to him in caressing tones, but I could not keep my tears from falling as I did so.

Somehow we made it through another night. We awoke to another day of snow and wind. I thought I couldn't stand it any longer. The wind was driving me mad with its incessant howling. I clung to my Bible and prayed until I felt utterly exhausted. Mid-morning, after reading, weeping, and praying for what seemed like hours, I fell asleep. The long days and sleepless nights had taken their toll, and my body demanded some rest even if my mind fought against it.

When I awoke, I could scarcely believe my eyes. Sunshine! The wind had stopped. The snow was no longer falling. The storm had passed. I wanted to shout; I wanted to run. I wanted to break out of my confining cabin and find human companion-ship. How had they all fared through the storm? And I won-dered about Wynn. Now that the storm was over, he would soon be home. I must have a hot meal ready for him.

It was then that I realized the fires were no longer burning. I must get them started again quickly. I had only a few more pieces of wood that I had brought in from outside, but there was plenty more by the door. I rushed to get some. But I could not budge the door. I pushed again, not understanding; but it would not give. *The snow!* It had drifted us in. I tried again. Surely we wouldn't be shut in here for long. Surely, with enough strength, I could get it open. I tried again and again, but the door would not move.

I let the fire in the kitchen stove go out and just kept the fireplace burning in order to conserve the little fuel I had. Wynn would soon be here. Surely the fuel would last until then. When he came, he would dig us out and all would be well again.

But the day wore on and Wynn did not come.

I walked to my window and scratched a spot to look down at the settlement. I could see smoke rising from cabins. There was stirring about as people and dogs moved among the build-ings. I tried to wave, but I knew that was foolish. There was no way anyone could detect a hand waving in my small, frosted window. I put the last stick of wood on my fire and waited again. *Surely Wynn will soon be here,* I told Kip silently.

The fire burned out. I wrapped myself in blankets and hud-dled on the cot. Even that was cold. I began to fear for my hands and feet. I picked up the heavy fur rug from the floor and wrapped myself in that, too. It was bulky, but it did offer some protection. Kip whined to go out, but there was no way I could let him. I thought of trying to push him through the window, hoping that he might run down to the settlement and attract someone's attention concerning my plight. But the window was too small for Kip's nearly full-sized body.

Night was coming again. I bundled myself up as best I could and tried to go to sleep. I fell asleep praying.

I vaguely remember stirring once or twice during the night and feeling terribly cold. In my benumbed state, I couldn't sort out the reason for the cold. Kip stirred, too, and I pulled the blankets more tightly around myself and dozed off again, Kipp curled up on my feet. He felt heavy, but I did not make him move.

"Hallo. Hallo in there," a voice finally brought me to consciousness. I struggled out of my blanket covering and hurried to the door. It still would not open. "I can't open the door," I called as loudly as I could. I heard shovels then. Someone was digging us out. It was McLain and a couple of the Indian men. I was glad to see them, but I was disappointed that Wynn wasn't with them. When the door was finally cleared enough for them to enter the house, my first question was, "Have you heard from my husband?"

McLain paused for a moment and looked around. "Have you heard from Wynn?" I asked again.

"No, not yet, ma'am; but he'll be all right."

I took what comfort I could from his words. I wondered if McLain knew what he was talking about or if he was simply trying to put my mind at ease.

"How are you?" he asked me.

"I'm fine—I think," I answered, trying my arms and legs to make sure they still moved properly. "I was never so glad to see anyone in my life! Thank you."

"How long have you been without heat?"

"Just overnight."

"That's too long," the big man said, reaching for my hand. "How are your fingers?"

"Fine."

"Your feet?"

"Okay."

"Let's see them."

I started to protest, but he would have none of it. "Let's see your feet, Mrs. Delaney."

I went to my bedroom to remove my long stockings and padded out again in my bare feet. The cabin floor was ice cold. Mr. McLain sat me in a chair and looked at each foot in turn.

"You're a mighty lucky lady," he said at last. "I don't know how you kept them from freezing."

"Kip slept on them," I said, suddenly remembering.

"What?"

"Kip. My dog. He slept on them. I remember waking up in the night and I could feel the heaviness from his body on my feet."

"Well, I'll be," Mr. McLain said, and then he began to laugh. "Well, boy," he said, running a hand through Kip's fine fur, "I guess you're more'n just pretty."

One of the Indian men had been working on a fire in the fireplace. It was burning briskly now.

"We've gotta thaw this here place out," said McLain and crossed to the kitchen stove. "This here water in the pail is frozen solid."

It was. So was the basin, and so was, I discovered to my dismay, my china teapot. It had split right down the side from the force of the freezing tea. All of those days of enjoying tea with friends were behind me. I wanted to sit right down and cry, but the men were bustling all about, and I didn't want them to see my hurt. Besides, I was still worried about Wynn.

"Better get your feet dressed again," said Mr. McLain, and I realized I was still puttering about in my bare feet.

I obeyed, slipping into my nice warm moccasins and then I went to my kitchen to see what other damage had been done. A few tins of food were split from frost as well. The pail was okay. I guess the dipper sitting in it had given the ice an upward, rather than outward, thrust. The kettle I wasn't sure about. I would have to wait until it thawed before I would know if it would still hold water without leaking.

The basin was okay, too. It had slanted sides and the ice just seemed to move up them. There really hadn't been too much damage. And, thankfully, I still had all my fingers and toes.

"We didn't see any smoke from your chimney this morning. Gave us quite a scare," Mr. McLain was saying.

"I was scared, too," I admitted. "I didn't know when someone might come."

"The storm was tough on everyone. Nimmie has a whole Fort full of people that she's trying to get hot food into. A number of the families ran out of wood."

"Was anyone—?" I started to ask if any lives had been taken by the storm, but I couldn't finish the question. I was half-sick with worry about Wynn.

Mr. McLain surmised the question and hesitated for a moment, then answered slowly.

"We lost a few—mostly older ones. A little girl died, too. She was always sickly, and this cold was just too much for her. It's been hard on Nimmie. The girl was one of her special pets."

Poor Nimmie.

The fires were burning brightly now, and the room was losing some of its chill. It would be some time until it was really warm again. The two Indian men left. Mr. McLain brought in a good supply of wood from beside the door, and then he, too, turned to go.

"You should be just fine now," he assured me. "We'll keep a better lookout from now on. I don't think it's gonna blow tonight. Sky looks clear."

"Can I come with you?" I asked quickly. I knew that Nimmie needed my help. I was torn between going to her and waiting in the cabin in case Wynn came home. My conscience finally won over my heart and I reached for my heavy coat.

Kip moved to follow me, but I pushed him back.

"You wait here," I said to him. "I won't be long."

"I don't mind if you bring him, if you like," said Mr. McLain.

"He might get in a fight with a dog in town," I objected.

"He might."

"Well, I wouldn't want him hurt."

"Is that why you used to carry him?"

We had shut the door on the whining Kip and were making our way across the drifts of snow to the settlement.

My breath was blowing out before me in puffy white clouds. I didn't answer McLain; he was walking too briskly for me to maneuver my snowshoes, keep up, and talk all at the same time. I just nodded my head in assent.

"So you planning on shutting him in all the time now?"

I shook my head.

"What will you do then?"

"I'll walk him out there," I said, waving my arm at the vast emptiness in the opposite direction of the village.

"You won't be able to keep him away from dogs forever, you know."

I had thought about that.

"Appears to me," said the husky man, "that Kip would likely hold his own pretty good in a fight. You've been feeding him well, and he has several pounds on some of the village dogs that just forage for their food. He's had good exercise, so he's developed strong bones and muscles. He's right smart. I think he'd handle himself just fine up against another dog."

I wasn't sure just what the man was trying to tell me.

"Are you saying—?" I began, but Mr. McLain cut in, "I'm saying that, with a child or a dog, you've got to give them a chance to grow up—natural like. You can't pamper them forever, or you spoil them. They can never be what they were meant to be. Kip's a Husky. Sure, they are a scrappy bunch when the need arises. And the need will arise someday. Here in the North, it's bound to. I think you oughta give Kip the chance to prove himself before he gets up against an animal where his life depends upon his fighting skill."

I wanted to argue with this man—to tell him that Kip would never need to fight, that I would keep him away from such circumstances. But I knew Mr. McLain was probably right. Kip was a northern dog. He would have to be prepared to live in the North. I hated the thought, but it was true.

I walked on in silence, slowly turning over in my mind the words of the man beside me. I would have to let Kip grow up. I would have to expose him to the rigors of the village and the fangs of the other dogs.

First, I would talk to Wynn about it and see if he agreed with this man. Oh, if only Wynn would get home! He had been gone for three days. Surely his mission shouldn't have taken him this long.

I blinked back tears that made little icicles on my cheeks and hurried after Mr. McLain. Nimmie needed me.

Chapter Twenty-six

Aftermath

The situation at the Hudson's Bay Store was even worse than I had expected. People were crowded in everywhere. Nimmie, busy filling bowls from a steaming pot of thin soup, gave me a welcoming smile. Mrs. Sam was the only one in the group whom I recognized. A few of the children I had seen gathered around Nimmie for her storytelling.

Some of the people had bandages on hands or feet, and I assumed they were being treated for frostbite.

I crossed to Mrs. Sam. "Where's your husband?" I asked her. When she looked at me blankly, I said, "Sam? Where's Sam?"

"Trap," she answered, making a motion like a trap snapping shut with her hands.

"What about the others? Evening Star and Little Deer and Anna? Have you seen them?"

She shook her head.

We stared at each other, recognizing the questions and concern in the other's eyes. I didn't know if their husbands had been out on the traplines or not, not sure how much difference it would make to have them home or away.

Nimmie was relieved to see me. "I'm so glad you're all right," she said when she had finished serving the last bowl. "That was the worst storm I ever remember. I was afraid you wouldn't have enough wood."

Apparently Mr. McLain had not told Nimmie about the smokeless chimney, not wanting to alarm her until he had checked further. "Oh, I had plenty of wood," was all I said now. "What can I do to help?" I asked her.

"Those people over there—they still haven't had anything to eat. I've run out of bowls or cups. I don't know—"

"What about Miss McLain?" I asked. "Would she have some bowls we could use?"

"I hadn't thought of that—"

"I'll go see." I hurried out the door and around to the back of the building.

A call gave me permission to enter. I found Miss McLain in a warm room sitting before her fireplace, her feet on a block of wood to soak up the heat, and her hands folded in her lap.

I stood looking at her in bewilderment, wondering if she was totally oblivious to all that was going on just next door. I finally found my voice.

"I came because of Nimmie," I began. "She has two or three dozen people to feed and she has run out of dishes. We were wondering if we could borrow some."

She didn't even look at me. "Guess you can," she said flatly with no interest.

Her attitude made me cross, but I held my tongue.

I swallowed and then said evenly, "Where are they?"

"Now where do you suppose dishes would be?" she returned with exaggerated sarcasm.

"May I help myself?" I asked, still in check.

"I don't know who will if you don't," was her biting reply.

I took a deep breath, crossed to her cupboards and began to lift out dishes. I piled them in a dishpan sitting on a nearby shelf. When I had all I could find, I turned to go.

"Just make sure they're boiled when you're done with them," stated Miss McLain, her eyes not leaving the fire.

I swung around to face her. "Do you realize," I flung at her, "there are people just beyond that wall who are fighting for their lives? Do you know that some of them may well lose their fingers or their toes? Do you know that Nimmie has been up half the night taking care of them? And here you sit, all—all bundled up in your great self-pity—thinking only about yourself and your lost love! Well, do you want to know what I think? I think you were well rid of the man. If he thought no more of you than to—to desert you because of a whining, accusing sister, then he wasn't much of a man.

"And do you know what else I think?" I was pretty sure Miss McLain wasn't one bit interested in what I thought, but I went on anyway. "I think that if after twenty years, you are still sitting by your fire and tending your little hurt while people out there are suffering with cold and hunger, then you're not much of a woman either. And maybe—maybe the doctor's wife was right. Maybe poor little John is better off without you."

I left the room, slamming the door behind me. I was halfway back to the store before what I had just done fully hit me. I bit my lip and the tears started to flow. I had been praying so diligently for this woman. I had been trying so hard to show her real love and compassion. Nimmie had been trying to break down the barriers for so many years—and I had just wiped out any faint possibilities of progress in a moment of anger. I would have to apologize. I didn't expect her to accept my apology. I would never be able to repair the damage I had done.

"Oh, God, forgive me," I wailed in remorse. "I should never have said that."

The apology would have to wait. Nimmie needed me and needed me now.

We worked all forenoon. The people were fed and looked after to the best of our ability. Mr. McLain and some of the men made an inspection tour to all the village houses. It was even worse than we had thought. Besides the little girl, the storm had claimed five other victims: an older man and his equally old wife living in a cabin alone at the edge of the village; a grandmother in the household of our erstwhile driver on the trip to the settlement, and an elderly gentleman who had been very sick before the storm struck. The general opinion was that he would have died regardless because of his weakened condition. Also dead was a middle-aged woman who had attempted to gather more wood and lost her way in the storm. Because of the heavy snow and the cold weather, digging of graves was impossible, so the bodies were all to be bundled up in blankets and tied up in the branches of the trees to await springtime. The Indian people had a special stand of trees which served that purpose—the "burying trees," Mr. McLain called them. But before the bodies could be prepared for the burying trees, they had to be examined by the Royal North West Police and permission given. So they were lined up in a vacant cabin to await Wynn's return.

Caring for the needs of the people in the village helped to some extent to take my mind off Wynn, though I wasn't able to ignore his absence completely. Throughout the day Nimmie and I had our hands full taking care of all those who needed our help. By early afternoon the store was beginning to empty. Many had now gathered fuel for their fires and returned to their own cabins. Those who remained behind needed to be fed again; and so I worked over the stew pot, getting another all-too-scanty meal ready for them.

Nimmie had just finished checking a swollen hand when I heard her exclamation, "Katherine! Are you all right?"

I swung around and, sure enough, there stood Miss McLain. I knew my apology was overdue and that it shouldn't be put off, but this hardly seemed the time or the place. I wasn't sure what to do.

Miss McLain said nothing, so Nimmie went on, "Did you want something?"

"Yes," said Miss McLain matter of factly. "I want to help."

I don't know who was more astounded—Nimmie or I. We both looked at Miss McLain with our mouths open. Her eyes were red and swollen, and I could tell she had been weeping.

"I want to help," she repeated. "Would you tell me what I can do?"

"Well, uh, well—we are fixing something to eat again. Some of these people have just come in and they haven't had anything to eat for a couple of days. Elizabeth is making stew."

"What can I do?" asked Miss McLain one more time.

"Well, we'll—we'll need the dishes. We haven't had time to wash the dishes yet." Nimmie motioned toward the dishpan filled with dirty dishes still sitting on the back of the big stove. Without a word, Miss McLain moved to the dishpan, rolled up her sleeves, and set to work.

Nimmie looked at me and I just shrugged my shoulders helplessly. I had no idea what had brought about the change. And I wasn't about to ask—here.

By mid-afternoon we had done all we could for the village people. All had now returned to their homes. Smoke rose from the cabins circling the town clearing. Nimmie suggested we sit down and have a cup of tea, but I said I would rather get back home. Kip was still in and unattended, and I was sure Wynn would soon be home. And by now the fire would have burned out, leaving the cabin cold again. With all these reasons, Nimmie let me go.

Kip was glad to see me, fairly knocking me over with his enthusiasm. I let him out for a run while I rebuilt the fires. It took awhile for the rooms to warm up and for the teakettle to begin to sing. It leaked a bit around the spout, but was still usable. I lamented again over the loss of my teapot. I wanted a cup of hot tea now. I finally dug out a small pot and made the tea in that. Maybe I imagined it, but for some reason, it didn't taste quite the same.

When darkness came, the cabin was quite warm and cozy, but I still felt chills pass through me. Where was Wynn? How long did it take to find a lost trapper? I sat before my fire, reading and praying. Finally I laid aside my Bible and began to pace the floor, letting the tears stream unchecked down my face.

Finally I banked the fire, bundled up in blankets and curled up on the cot again. Kip climbed up to lie on my feet. This time I didn't scold him for being on the cot. I remembered the night before and the fact that Kip might have saved my toes.

There was a full moon and the rays of it streamed through the little frosted window. It seemed ever so bright, reflecting off the freshly blown snow. I was trying to pray again when there was a commotion at the door; and, before I could even worm my way out of the blankets, Wynn was there.

I didn't even jump up and run to him; I just buried my face in my hands and began to sob until my whole being shook. I was so relieved, so thankful, to see him safely home. He walked over and took me in his arms. As I clung to him, he held me for a long time, stroking my hair and patting my back. "There, there, Elizabeth," he murmured as to a small child.

We didn't try to talk. We really didn't need to. Later we would hear from one another all the details of the four miserable days of separation. For now it was enough just to be together again.

Wynn had a busy and rather unpleasant day following his

return. Besides the bodies awaiting his investigation, he had also brought one back with him on the dog sled. He had found the man in question, but not in time to prevent his death.

It looked as if the fellow had accidentally stepped into one of his own traps. He had managed to free himself; but, with the mangled leg, he was unable to get to his cabin or to find help. Wynn had discovered the body beside the trail.

I asked if he had a wife and family. "No," Wynn said, "his wife died in childbirth three years ago."

It was a sad time for all of us. After the bodies had been inspected and Wynn had filed the necessary reports, the Indian people were given permission to bury their dead.

It was a solemn assembly that filed, single form, out of the village that afternoon and made their way to the burying trees. Wynn and I joined the somber procession. The sound of mourning sent chills up and down my spine. I had never heard anything like it before. Not the sound of weeping, it was a cry, a whine, a deep guttural lament that rose and fell as the column moved along. It tore at my soul, and I wept quietly with the mourners.

At home again as twilight came, the drums took up their steady beat. As they echoed through the settlement, thumping out their message of death, even Kip stirred and whined.

"Will they keep on all night?" I asked Wynn, feeling restless and edgy with the intensity of the beating.

"Oh, no. They should be stopping any time now."

Out the window, I could see in the settlement below us open bonfires in the central area. Around the fires, Indians moved in a dance pattern. The drummers sat in the firelight beating the drums with their hands and chanting a monotone tune that rose and fell on the night air.

Wynn was right. The drumming stopped as abruptly as it had begun. I looked out the window again and saw the silhouettes of figures disappearing into the shadows of the buildings. The fires had died down to a dim glow. The dead had had a proper and respectable burial.

Chapter Twenty-seven

Village Life

January passed into February. We had more storms but none with the violence of the mid-January blizzard. For the most part, life seemed to slip into some sort of a daily routine. We still continued our Bible studies, and Miss McLain never missed a study. Though she was still difficult at times, her attitude had changed from the inside out. I never did apologize for my outburst—not that I wasn't willing to do so. It just didn't seem like the appropriate thing to do under the circumstances. *Thank you, Lord,* I prayed, *for turning something bad into something good.*

When new babies were added to the village families, the Indian midwives did the delivering. Four were born between the first of October and mid-January. And so far, in spite of the cold winter, we had lost no children except for the one little girl. It was a shock to me when I first heard Nimmie and Miss McLain gratefully discussing this fact.

You mean you expect to lose children? I wanted to ask. But their conversation told me very plainly that in the North death was nearly as accepted as life. Because of the severe weather, the lack of medical care and the poor nutrition, they did indeed lose children regularly. I was appalled. Especially when I knew that medicines and doctors could have saved a good number of them.

Wynn kept a close eye on the Mary-versus-Smith situation. He had been out to see Mary many times. She was again working her traplines. How she managed it, Wynn did not know. The stamina of that little lady was remarkable. She had lost some toes from her severe frostbite, but she hobbled along, checking and resetting her traps and skinning out her furs. She was getting quite a pile, Wynn said. He also said that all the evidence supported Smith's assessment: Mary was crowding his territory.

"There must be some mistake," I argued. "If she is cutting into someone else's territory, she must not realize it. I'm sure she wouldn't do that on purpose."

Wynn just smiled.

Kip was a beautiful dog. I discussed with Wynn what Mr. McLain had said, that I had to allow Kip to find his own place in the dog community of our settlement.

"Do you think he's right?" I asked reluctantly, fearing that Wynn might agree with Mr. McLain.

"I'm afraid so, Elizabeth," he said. "It will come sooner or later, whether you want it to or not. Kip will be challenged, and he will either need to meet the challenge or run."

I couldn't imagine Kip running. I wasn't sure I even wanted him to run. But to fight? I didn't want that either.

"Do you think he's ready now?" I asked, a tremble in my voice.

I looked at Kip's beautiful, silver-tipped fur and the lovely curve of his tail. I shuddered to think of him with torn bleeding ears and ragged scars.

"Don't rush things," said Wynn and squeezed my hand. "There's plenty of time."

Wynn spent many hours training his new dogs. They were getting big like their brother Kip, but Wynn did not want to put them in harness for several months, waiting for their bones and muscles to be fully developed. He had chosen another two pups from the second litter Smith had spoken about at the time of our visit. Wynn was very pleased with the new dogs. They were smart and strong and learned very quickly. So far there was no evidence of a mean streak. Wynn had trained them with firmness and kindness rather than harshness. They responded to him with respect and devotion.

My friends from the village were much too busy keeping the fires going and their families fed to have much time for tea. Occasionally, one or two did appear for a few minutes. The women I had joined in the berry patch sometimes brought new neighbors for me to meet. We still couldn't speak much to one another. Many of the ladies knew some English words, but most often they were words needed for trading at the post, not words that might be used for a chat over a cup of tea. With all of us combining our knowledge, and by using our hands extensively, we did manage to converse some; but often we sat for a period of time without saying anything, just enjoying companionship. It was a new experience for me. I had been used to chatter. To sit quietly did not come easy. However, with time and patience, I was learning.

Evening Star was expecting another baby. I had been waiting daily for the good news, praying that all would go well and that she, too, would deliver a healthy child.

She was a bit vague about the expected time of arrival. When I asked her about it, she just shrugged off my question. I thought she must not understand me, so I put the question another way. Again she shrugged, answering only, "Come when ready," which was Anna's translation.

We were awakened in the dead of night by someone opening our door and calling Wynn's name. Both of us sat bolt upright in bed, and then Wynn reached in the darkness for his clothes and hurried into them.

My heart was in my throat as I listened to the anxious voices coming from the other room. Soon Wynn was back to the bedside, lamp in hand. "It's Evening Star," he said. "She's having trouble delivering."

Wynn completed his dressing and then turned to place a kiss on my forehead.

"Try not to worry," he said. "I'll be back as soon as I can."

I tried not to worry but I wasn't doing very well at it. If the experienced midwives were unable to help Evening Star, what could Wynn do?

I finally got out of bed and went out to put more wood on the fire. I placed the lamp on the little table, wrapped myself in a blanket, and picked up my Bible. I paged through the Psalms, snatching underlined verses here and there of promise and assurance. It was one of those times when I couldn't really concentrate on my reading. Finally I closed my eyes and began to pray. For Evening Star and the unborn little one. For Wynn, that he would have wisdom and guidance. For myself, that God would still my trembling spirit enough for me to be able to concentrate on His Word.

After some minutes, I went back to the Bible. Again my eyes skimmed the pages. My spirit was calm now. My trembling had ceased. I read passage after passage until I came to Psalm 27:14. I stopped and read it through again. "Wait on the Lord: be of good courage, and he shall strengthen thine heart; wait, I say, on the Lord."

Yes, Lord, I prayed. *All I can do is wait.* I picked up the knitted sweater I had nearly completed for the new baby and worked while I waited.

It was almost daylight when Wynn returned. He was weary but his eyes smiled at me the moment he came in the door, and I knew he brought good news.

"She's all right?" I said.

"And so is her boy," Wynn answered me.

I shut my eyes for a moment of thanks, the tears squeezing out under my eyelids. Then I looked back up at Wynn, smiling.

"You must be very tired," I commented. "Would you like a cup of coffee before you go back to bed?"

"Back to bed?" laughed Wynn. "My darling, I do not intend to go back to bed. It's time to start another day."

So I fixed breakfast while Wynn shaved; and then, after eating and having our time of family prayer together, he did indeed go out to start another day—or continue the one he'd already started.

When chopping frozen logs for firewood, one of the children had an accident with an axe. They brought him to Wynn who, fortunately, was at home at the time. One look at the injured leg, and I felt as if I would lose my dinner. We removed the pillows from our cot, and Wynn stretched the boy out on the thin mattress.

His pantleg was ragged and torn and covered with blood. The first thing Wynn had to do was to clean up the area so he could see how bad the wound was. He asked for my scissors to cut off the ragged pantleg and then for hot water in the basin and his medical supply kit.

The Indian youths who had brought the boy stood around helplessly. They understood very little English and they didn't look much less queezy than I.

Somehow I managed to follow all of Wynn's orders—bringing the water and the sponge cloths, boiling the instruments in a pan on the stove, and handing Wynn whatever it was he needed.

Wynn cleaned the wound thoroughly, managing to stop the bleeding, and then put in several sutures. The boy's only indication of the pain he must have been suffering was a pale face and clenched jaw. I looked only when I had to. Most of the time, I was able to keep my eyes off the leg and look at my hands or the floor or Wynn's face. It seemed to take forever but, in actuality, it was all taken care of rather promptly. I sighed when Wynn said, "That's it." Now I could collapse.

But I didn't. Somehow I managed to stay on my feet. The two Indians moved forward to pick up the brave boy; he was pale and exhausted from the ordeal. I stepped forward, too.

"Perhaps he should stay here for a while," I suggested to Wynn. "He's too weak to move now, and I'll care for him."

Wynn, surprised, turned and spoke to the Indian boys who had carried in their friend. After a brief exchange, they nodded and left. Wynn made sure the young lad was comfortable and then picked up his hat.

"I'd better go see his mother," he said. "I want her to know exactly what's happening."

In about fifteen minutes Wynn was back with a worried-looking woman.

She crossed to her son and spoke some words softly to him. His eyes fluttered open and he answered her. She spoke again, nodded her head to us, and left the room.

The young boy's name was Nanook. He stayed with us for five days before he hobbled home on two clumsy sticks. I had enjoyed having him. He could not speak to me, but he could laugh. And he could eat—my, how that boy could eat! His leg didn't become infected, for which we were thankful. Wynn watched it very carefully, dressing it morning and night. By the time Nanook left us, it was beginning to heal nicely.

Before he left, I gave him a loaf of fresh bread to take with him. He tucked it inside his coat, his eyes twinkling. Then he patted Kip, whom he had grown to love, and hobbled out the door.

Chapter Twenty-eight

March

When March came, I began to think *spring,* but Wynn warned me that this was much too premature. No one else in the whole village was looking for spring at this early date. I chafed. Winter had been upon us for—for *years,* it seemed to me.

I was restless and I was lonely. My Indian friends had been too busy to come for tea for quite a while. Nimmie had been down with the flu, so our Bible study together had been missed. I still didn't feel very much at ease with Miss McLain, though I had now been given permission to call her Katherine. I could have talked myself into visiting her, but she was busy nursing Nimmie. I would have liked to have been Nimmie's nurse myself, but I knew it was important to Katherine to be able to do this. So I stayed home.

There was no sewing to be done, my mending was all caught up. I had read all my books over and over. It seemed that the extent of my day's requirements was to get three meals and do the dishes.

I was tired of the meals as well. It seemed as if I just fixed the same things over and over—from tins. Tinned this and tinned that. We did have fresh fish and fresh wild meat. But I was tired of them also. I really didn't enjoy the wild meat and craved even one taste of beefsteak or baked ham.

I longed for spring. But in the North, spring is slow in coming.

I decided to take a walk to the store. Maybe I would find some food item on the shelves that wouldn't be too expensive and would be a delightful change for our daily menu.

I bundled up and pulled on my mittens. Kip was already

waiting by the door, his tail wagging in anticipation.

"You want to go for a walk?" I asked him, an unnecessary question. I struggled into my snowshoes and started out. It was a bright sunny day and I dared to hope that maybe this once Wynn was wrong. Maybe spring really was coming.

We walked through the morning sunshine, Kip frolicking ahead or running off to the side to check out something that only dogs knew or cared about. I was feeling good about the world again.

I had not given even fleeting thought to the village dogs, so intent was I in getting out for a walk again. Had I thought about it, I might not have proceeded any differently. I had finally made up my mind that Mr. McLain and Wynn were right: I could not go on protecting Kip against real life.

Mr. McLain greeted me heartily about halfway into the village. I asked how Nimmie was, and he seemed relieved and said she was coming along very well now.

We were walking toward the trading post together when there was a rush and a blur at my side as a dog ran past me. I jumped slightly with the suddenness of it; then a yip to my left whirled me around.

Kip had been busy poking his nose into a rabbit burrow, and this dog from the village was heading right for him. I gasped, my hand at my throat.

Surprisingly, the dog stopped a few feet from Kip and braced himself. From where we stood, we could hear the angry growl coming from his throat. Kip stood rooted, unsure as to what this was all about. Mr. McLain reached out a hand and placed it on my arm.

"They're going to fight, aren't they?" I said in a tight voice.

"We'll see," said McLain. "Kip might be wise enough not to take the challenge."

"Wise enough? But you said he'd *have* to fight."

"Not this one. Not Lavoie's Buck."

I swung around to look at McLain. "What do you mean?" I threw at him in alarm.

"He's boss here, Miz Delaney. He's licked every dog in the settlement."

I looked wildly about me in search of a club or a rock or

anything that might stop the fight. There was nothing. "We've got to stop them!" I cried. "Kip might be killed!" I took a step forward, but McLain stopped me.

"You can't go in there. If there's a fight, you could get all chewed up."

The Lavoie dog was circling Kip now, fangs bared, his throat rumbling. Round and round he went, and I think he must have said some very nasty words in dog language. Kip looked insulted—angry. I expected at any moment the dogs to be at each other's throats.

And then a very strange thing happened. Kip's tail lowered and began to swish mildly back and forth. He whined gently as though to apologize for being on the other dog's territory. The big dog still bristled. He moved forward and gave Kip a sharp nip. Kip did not retaliate. The Lavoie dog gave Kip one last look of contempt, circled him once more, and—still bristling and snarling—loped back toward the village houses.

I didn't know whether to be relieved or ashamed.

Mr. McLain just grinned. "One smart dog," he said. "But ol' Buck better watch out in a month or two."

I didn't know what Mr. McLain meant, but I started to breathe again and hurried on to the village. The day didn't look nearly as sunshiny as it had previously, and I was rather anxious to make my purchases and go home.

Finally Anna and Mrs. Sam came for tea. I was especially glad to have Anna, because it meant that I could catch up on some of the village news. We talked now of the families and how they were faring. The life in the village seemed to be made up getting through the winter and coasting through the summer; and the summers were all too short.

Evening Star and her baby were both doing fine. I had not seen them since I had taken over the new sweater and a container of soup soon after the baby had safely arrived. He was a nice little fellow and Evening Star was justifiably proud.

We had had another death. An Indian woman in her forties had died from the flu. She had not been well for some years. She had given birth to fifteen children, and each time another child was born she seemed to weaken further. Of her fifteen, only seven were now living. Her body, also, had been blanketed and left in the burying trees. The ritual drums had thumped out the message, and the open fires had gleamed in the night.

Another baby had been born, too. This time the midwives did not need help from Wynn.

There had been some sickness, but no major epidemics. Everyone seemed to hold his breath and speak softly when the possibility of an epidemic was mentioned. The people lived in fear of a dreadful disease sweeping through the camp while they sat helplessly by, with no doctors, hospitals, and very little medications.

Our conversation turned to brighter things. I talked about my longing for springtime. Of learning from the women about finding edible herbs and plants in the forests. Of planting my own garden. Of finding the berry patches. We all looked forward to the days of sunshine and rainshowers. Even the dreaded mosquitoes would be endured when spring came.

"How is Nanook doing?" I asked.

"He runs," said Anna, her eyes lighting up.

"That's wonderful. Good. That's good."

"I often wonder about poor Mary," I went on. "I don't know how she ever manages to care for her trapline with some of her toes missing."

"She crazy," muttered Anna, slurping her tea.

I wanted to argue but instead I said, "I feel sorry for her. First she lost all her children, and then her husband died. Poor thing."

But Anna only said, very calmly, "Husband not die."

I looked at her. Surely she knew better. She lived right here and had for years.

"Are you sure? We were told that her husband was dead."

"Dead. But he not die."

I didn't understand. Anna finished her tea and stood to go. Mrs. Sam Lavoie stood also and began to shuffle toward the door. Anna followed and I followed Anna. When we got to the door, she turned to me.

"She kill him," she said deliberately and simply. "She kill him for the traps. My Joe see." And she was gone.

I could hardly wait for Wynn to get home so I might tell him

what Anna had said. She certainly must be wrong. Surely poor
Mary had not done such a thing. If she had, and Joe had seen
her, he would have reported it. Something was all wrong here.

When Wynn did arrive home, he had news for me instead.
Mary was now locked up in the settlement's makeshift jail.
Wynn had to bring her in. She would need to be escorted out
for trial and sentencing. Not only had she moved her traps onto
Smith's territory, but Wynn had found her in the very act of
robbing from Smith's traps as well. It was a serious offense and
Mary had to answer for it.

I felt sick. "Where is she?" I asked.

"There's a little room at the back of McLain's store. He uses
it for skin storage when it's not needed otherwise."

And now it was needed otherwise. It was occupied by Mary.

"Can I see her?" I asked.

Wynn looked surprised; then he answered. "Certainly. If you
wish to."

I did wish to. I went the next day, taking fresh bread and
stew with me. Mary took the food but did not even look at me.
I spoke to her, but she ignored me completely. I could see she
really didn't need my food. Mr. McLain or Nimmie had looked
after her well.

I tried to talk to her. She still would not look at me.

"I want to help you," I said. "Is there anything I could get
you or do for you?" She turned from me and went back to curl
up with a blanket on the cot in the corner.

I came home feeling even sicker than I had before I went. I
decided to discuss it with Wynn. Surely there was some other
way to deal with the situation.

"Do you really have to do it this way?" I asked him.

"I'm afraid so, Elizabeth. There is no masking the evidence.
I caught her red-handed. She was stealing from Smith's traps."

"But couldn't she be—be—scolded and given another
chance?" I continued.

"She isn't some naughty schoolgirl. She knows the seriousness of her offense."

"But surely if she knows that you are on to her, she won't
do it again," I insisted.

"Elizabeth, if I let Mary go, none of the people will have

respect for the law. Besides, Crazy Mary would try it again—oh, maybe not right away, but she would try it again, sure. She has an inner drive to accumulate pelts, and she will stop at nothing to get them."

I thought of Anna and her words. I had not passed them on to Wynn yet. I remembered them now with a sick heart.

Wynn went on. "She will get a fair trial," he assured me. "They will take into consideration her mental state. She will be cared for better than she would be out on her own on the trapline."

"But it will kill her," I blurted out. "She couldn't stand to be confined. She couldn't even stay here with us!"

There was sadness in Wynn's eyes. To lock Mary up, even with tender care, would not be good for Mary's emotional state. She needed freedom. Without it, she might not be able to survive.

"There is another thing to think about, Elizabeth," said Wynn. "If I didn't handle this properly and carry out the demands of the law, Smith or someone else would handle it in his own way, according to his own laws. Mary could be killed or beaten so severely that she would be left too helpless to work her trapline or even to care for herself. Either way it could mean death."

I hadn't thought about that.

Wynn dismissed further discussion. "I was sent up north to uphold the law, Elizabeth. To the best of my ability, I intend to do just that, God helping me."

I knew Wynn would follow the dictates of the law, not his own feelings.

Mary was not sent away for trial and sentencing. Two mornings later, Nimmie found her dead on the cot in the corner, where she had died in her sleep.

Chapter Twenty-nine

Nimmie

March had crawled by slowly on weak and tottering limbs. I ached for spring to come dancing in with vitality and freshness. I think all the village people ached for it as well.

For some of the women of the settlement it would mean reuniting with husbands for the first time in many months. Some of the traplines were a great distance from the village, and once the men had left in the fall, they did not return again until the winter snows were melting.

The men who worked the traplines nearer home came and went, spending some time with their families and some time in the bush.

Nimmie was well again, so we resumed our Bible studies. Each time we met together, she taught me some lesson. She was a patient, beautiful person with a heart of love and an open mind to truth.

I talked to Wynn about her one night as we were stretched out before our open fire.

"I've learned to love Nimmie," I said. "She's a beautiful person. It's strange—when I first saw her, I was so disappointed. I didn't tell you that before, did I?"

Wynn shook his head, his eyes studying mine.

"I guess I didn't because I was ashamed of myself. I was prejudiced, you know. I didn't realize I was. I love the Indian people, but I had wanted someone—someone to share things with. And I—I thought—that—well that—the person needed to be like me—white. Well, I was wrong. I was wanting a white woman, and instead I found a friend, a very special friend, in Nimmie."

Wynn reached out to take my hand. I think he understood what I was trying to say.

As the days went by, Nimmie and I shared more intimately our thoughts and feelings, our understanding of Scripture.

One day Nimmie came to see me alone. It was not our Bible study day, and I was a bit surprised.

"Do you have time to talk for a while?" she asked me. Now, time was one thing I did have—in abundance. So I asked Nimmie in.

She laid aside her coat and took a chair at the kitchen table.

I pushed the kettle forward on the stove, added another stick of wood, and waited for her to begin.

"I've been thinking about that verse we studied yesterday," she started, "the one about Christ dying for the ungodly."

I nodded, remembering.

"I'm ungodly," Nimmie continued softly.

"Yes, all of us are without God," I agreed in a near whisper.

Nimmie's eyes flew open. "You too?"

"Oh, yes. Me, too."

"But—?" began Nimmie, but she didn't go on.

"The Bible says, 'All have sinned,' remember? It was one of the verses we studied a couple of weeks ago."

"I remember," said Nimmie. "I just didn't think of it at the time, I guess."

"Well, it's true. The Bible also says that 'there is none righteous, no not one.' "

Nimmie sat silently. "I remember that, too," she finally stated.

"It also says that 'while we were yet sinners,' He loved us."

"That is the part that is so hard for me to understand," Nimmie blurted out. "I can't imagine someone dying for—" Nimmie stopped again.

"Elizabeth," she said, looking full into my face, "I am a terribly wicked person."

I wanted to protest, but Nimmie went on, "You don't know me, Elizabeth. You don't know what I almost did."

She did not weep. Weeping was not the way of her people, but her head dropped in utter self-contempt and her eyes refused to look into mine.

"Do you want to tell me about it?" I finally asked, realizing that Nimmie was deeply troubled.

"I took care of Crazy Mary. I brought her all her meals and the basin to wash her hands. I bandaged her infected toe that still refused to heal from the freezing. Each time I went we spoke together. I tried to encourage her—to tell her that things would work out. But each time I went she begged me for just one thing. She pleaded with me to bring it to her. Each time, I refused. She wanted her hunting knife."

I could not understand Nimmie's words. There was silence as I puzzled over them. Why was she wicked for taking such special care of Mary? Nimmie's head came up. "I knew why she wanted her knife. She could not bear to be shut up—caged like—like a chicken."

I understood then. Crazy Mary had intended to take her own life.

"Well, I kept saying no, no. And then the other morning I couldn't stand it anymore. She was going wild in the little room, and soon she would be taken far away from her land and her people and locked in another room—forever. It would kill her. It would kill her slowly. Wouldn't it be more merciful to let her die all at once?

"And so I found her knife and tucked it in my dress and took it to her when I went to bring her breakfast. Only when I got there, Crazy Mary was—was—"

Yes, I knew. Mary, mercifully, was already gone.

My mind was whirling, my heart thumping. What could I say to the anguished Nimmie?

Did she truly realize the seriousness of her near-crime? Wynn would have needed to arrest her. *She* would have been locked up in the little room at the back of her husband's store. She would have been sent out for trial and sentencing. She would have been implicated in a terrible crime.

The horror of the whole thing washed through me, making me tremble; but Nimmie was continuing.

"I am very *unjust*," went on Nimmie. "I am a sinner. I thought before when I heard those verses that it was speaking of someone else. Now I know that it speaks of me. My heart is very heavy, Elizabeth. I could not sleep last night. I love Him, this

Jesus. But I have hurt Him with my sin."

I could not have told Nimmie that what she had done was not wrong; I believed it was. It would have been a terrible thing if she had been party to Mary's suicide. But God had kept her from that. I thanked God for His intervention and mercy. I said nothing about the act that Nimmie had *almost* committed. Instead, I talked about what now must be done about it.

"Nimmie, when I realized that I was a sinner, that I could do nothing myself to atone for my sins, I did the only thing one can do—that is necessary to do. I accepted what God has provided for all of mankind—His forgiveness. His forgiveness through the death of His Son, Jesus. He died for our sins so that we need not die for our own. I don't understand that kind of love either, Nimmie. But I know that it's real, for I have felt it. When I prayed to God and asked for His forgiveness and took His Son as my Savior, that love filled my whole person. Where I had had misery and fear before, now I have peace and joy."

"And He would do that for me?"

"He wants to. He aches to. That's why He came—and died. He loves you so much, Nimmie."

Even though Nimmie's eyes remained dry, mine were filled with tears.

We bowed our heads together, and I prayed and then Nimmie prayed. Hers was a beautiful, simple prayer, beginning in faith and repentance and ending with joy and praise.

I reached over and held Nimmie for a moment when we had finished praying. Even Nimmie's eyes were wet now. We spent some time looking at God's wonderful words of assurance and promise from the Bible, and then Nimmie rushed home to share her good news with Ian.

As she left the house that day, my heart was singing. Nimmie was even more than a very special friend. She was a beloved *sister* as well.

We had no idea how quickly Nimmie's newfound faith would be tested. Less than a week after Nimmie and I had spent our time in prayer, disaster struck. The whole settlement was to suffer the consequences, but Nimmie and her husband would be hurt most of all.

It was about two o'clock in the morning when voices—loud and excited—reached our cabin. We both scrambled out of bed and hurried to the window. The whole world was lit up with an angry red glow.

"Fire!" cried Wynn before he even reached the window.

"Oh, dear God, no!" I prayed out loud.

But it was. It looked for a moment as if the whole village were going up in smoke. Wynn was dressed in the time it took me to understand the scene before me.

"Stay here, Elizabeth," he said. "I'll send people to you if they need your help. You know where all the medical supplies are kept. Get them out and ready in case they are needed."

Wynn was gone before I could even speak to him.

I dressed hurriedly, afraid I might be needed even before I could carry out Wynn's orders. The noise outside grew louder. I could hear the crackling of the flames now as well. Kip whined and moved toward the door. His instincts told him that there was danger.

"It's all right, Kip," I spoke soothingly to him. "You are safe here." I still didn't know what it was that was burning.

After I had followed all of Wynn's instructions and laid out the medical supplies, the bandages, and the burn ointments I had found, I put more wood in the fire and set a full kettle of water on to boil in case it was needed.

Smoke was in the air now, seeping through every air space into our cabin. The smell sickened me, for it meant pain and loss and even possible death. I went to the window to see if I could tell just how much of our small settlement was being taken by the fire. It was the Hudson's Bay Store that was burning. Wild flames leaped skyward. Men milled around the building, but there was really little they could do. There was no firefighting equipment in the village—only buckets and snow-drifts; and against such a fire, these had very little effect.

One cabin, close to the store, was also burning, and I prayed for the occupants' safety. I began to pick out figures then. There were men on roofs of other buildings. There were bucket brigades feeding them pails of snow. Women and children milled around or huddled helplessly in groups. The whole scene was one of despair and horror.

A noise at the door brought me from the window. Three women stood together against the night. One held a baby in her arms, and one of the others held a child by the hand.

I had seen them before at the trading post where Nimmie and I had dished out soup to the storm-chilled. I did not know them by name.

"Come in," I said. "How is Nimmie? Have you seen Nimmie?"

One lady shook her head. The others looked blank.

They pushed the little girl forward. Her face was streaked with soot and wet from tears. She had an ugly burn across her hand. I took off her coat and knelt before her.

I had no training in treating burns. I grabbed a jar of ointment and read the label. It didn't tell me as much as I needed to know. I felt I should cleanse the wound somehow, but how? I got a basin of water and warmed it to my touch. I did not want to damage the burned tissue further. With a cloth, I wiped away most of the dirt and grime, trying hard not to hurt the child. Then I generously applied the ointment and bound the wound with a clean bandage.

As soon as I had finished, the mother with the baby held him out to me. She coughed to show that the baby had a problem. She pointed out the window at the fire and coughed again. "Smoke," she said, knowing that word.

"He choked on the smoke?" I asked her.

"Smoke," she said again.

Smoke inhalation. What could I do about that? I had no idea how it was treated and, if I had known, I was almost sure I wouldn't have what was necessary to treat it anyway.

I took the baby. To put their minds at ease I had to do something. *What, God? What do they do to make breathing easier?* The only thing I had ever heard of to ease breathing was steam, and it might be the very worst thing I could do. I didn't know.

I unbundled the baby and laid him on the cot. Then I dug through Wynn's medical supply looking for something, anything, that might help the infant. I could find nothing that was labeled for smoke inhalation. I finally took some ointment that said that it was good for chest congestion and rubbed a small amount on the wee chest.

I had not finished with the small baby when the door opened again. More women and children entered our small cabin, more from fright than from injuries. A few of them did have a small burn or two but, thankfully, nothing major. The smell of smoke was on their clothing and the fear of fire in their faces.

Whenever a new group joined us, I asked the same question. "Nimmie? Have you seen Nimmie? The McLains? Are they all right?"

I got shrugs and blank looks in return.

The morning sun was pulling itself to a sitting position when Wynn came in carrying a young man who had badly burned a foot.

I was glad to see Wynn and sorry for the young man. "Nimmie?" I asked again. "What about the McLains?"

"They're fine," Wynn responded. "All three of them."

I was greatly relieved.

Then Wynn began to give instructions as to what he would need to care for the foot, and I carried them out to the best of my ability. After the young man was given some medication to dull the pain, Wynn did what he could for the ugly burn. Then he bandaged the foot lightly and, leaving the young man on our cot, went back again to help fight the fire.

Before he left he pulled me close, though he did not hold me long; there were a number of eyes fixed upon us.

"I think we'll be able to save the other homes. The fire has passed its worst. It shouldn't be long before you can start sending them home." Then he was gone.

I looked around at the still-frightened faces. "Sergeant Delaney says that the fire will soon be over," I informed them, gesturing with my hands as well, "and then you will all be able to return to your cabins. The rest of your homes are quite safe. You'll be able to go back to them."

I wasn't sure how many of them understood my words. I still knew only a few words in their tongue and none of them dealt with fire.

"But first," I said, "we'll have some tea."

It took a lot of tea that morning, and we had to take turns with the cups. Even so, it seemed to lift the spirit of gloom from the room. Some of the ladies even began to chat. It was a great relief to me.

I checked on the young man with the bad burn. He seemed to be resting as comfortably as possible under the circumstances. I asked him if he would like some tea, but he shook his head.

As the morning progressed, the fire died to a smolder of rubble, and two-by-two or in huddled little groups, the ladies and children left our cabin.

The young man had fallen asleep, whether from medication or exhaustion I did not know.

I set about doing up the dishes and tidying the small room.

By the time Wynn came, the young man had awakened and was asking me questions I could not understand nor answer. I was glad to see Wynn, for he would know what the fellow wanted.

I met Wynn at the door. After a quick look to assure myself that he was all right, I indicated the man on the cot.

"He's been trying to ask me something," I told Wynn. "I have no idea what he is saying."

Wynn crossed to the young man and knelt beside him. He spoke to him in the soft flowing sounds of his native tongue. Wynn spoke again and then, with a nod of his head, he rose and lifted the young man to his feet.

"I'm taking him home," Wynn said to me.

The young man seemed about to topple over.

"Shouldn't you—shouldn't you carry him?" I asked anxiously.

"I would," said Wynn, "gladly. But it would shame him to be carried through his village."

I looked at the proud young man. His face was twisted with pain, and still he was determined to walk rather than to be carried.

I nodded my head. "I hope he makes it," I said fervently.

"I'll see that he does," spoke Wynn softly, and they went out together.

When Wynn returned, he brought the McLains with him.

"Do you have enough food for five hungry people?" he asked me. I looked toward my stove. It was almost noon and no one had had anything to eat.

"I'll find it," I said without hesitation. But before I went to my cupboards and stove, I had to assure myself that Nimmie and Katherine were truly okay.

They clustered around our door, taking off soiled coats and kicking snow from their boots. Their faces were soot covered and streaked with tears, whether from weeping or the sting of the acrid smoke in their eyes I did not know nor ask. Their shoulders slumped with fatigue. It had been a long, hard, disheartening night. Their home was gone. Their livelihood was gone. In one night they lost their past, their present, and their future.

I crossed to them, unable to find words to express my feelings. I looked into Nimmie's eyes. My question was not voiced but she answered it. With just a quick little nod, she assured me she'd be all right.

I turned then to Katherine and put out my hand. "Are you all right?" I asked her.

Her answer was more as I would have expected. "I have no burns or outer injuries."

She was telling me that where she really hurt was on the inside. It would heal, now that she had found the secret to healing. But it would take time.

I turned back to Mr. McLain. "I'm sorry," I whispered falteringly, "truly sorry."

Mr. McLain was able to give me a crooked smile. "We're tough, Miz Delaney," he said. "Survivors. We'll bounce back."

I answered his smile and went to get them something to eat.

After we had finished our meal, we sat around the fireplace talking in quiet tones.

"What are your plans, Ian? Is there anything we can do?" asked Wynn.

Mr. McLain shrugged his shoulders. "I haven't sorted it out yet."

"You are welcome to stay here until you find other accommodations," went on Wynn.

"Katherine can have the cot," I hurried to add. "Is there somewhere we can find another bed?"

Nimmie shook her head. "There are no beds in the village,"

she said. "But don't worry. I can make all the bed that Ian and I need."

I looked puzzled.

"Spruce boughs and furs," explained Nimmie. "I know how to make a bed that even the richest white people of the world would envy!"

I admired Nimmie's attempt to lighten the situation and bring to us a little humor.

"It's not really *us* that I am worried about," McLain continued, his shoulders sagging in spite of his effort to keep up his spirits.

"You know what it's like this time of year," he went on, directing his conversation to Wynn. "It's been a long, hard winter. Most of the families are almost out of supplies. They were depending on the store to get them through the rest of the winter until the new growth brought fresh food again. Why, I'll wager that most of them have less than five cups of flour in the cabin. How they gonna make their bannock without flour? What about salt and tea and—?"

But Wynn stopped him.

"We'll all band together to look after them. They're hardy people. They'll make it."

There was silence for a few minutes. Mr. McLain broke it. "What about supplies for the two of you? What do you have here?"

Wynn shook his head. "Not enough for a whole village, that's for sure. We'll have to ration very carefully to get through until spring."

McLain nodded. "Right—that's a good idea," he said a little wistfully. "Don't be divying out what little you have. That way it won't do anyone any good. Someone has to stay healthy and on his feet, and seems to me you're elected, Sarge."

The full impact of our situation began to hit me. *Oh, God,* I prayed silently, *please don't let it come to the place where I have to turn hungry people away from my door. I would rather give away my last crumb of food and suffer with them.* Was McLain right? Would things become so desperate that we would be forced to withold our own in order to have the strength to minister to the community's needs? I prayed not.

"Well, I think the first thing that needs to be done is a little survey," Wynn said. "We'll go through the village family by family and find out what the situation is. I'll get you a little book, McLain, if you are up to coming with me; and you can record as we go along."

McLain nodded and rose to his feet, reaching for his heavy, soot-covered coat and his beaver hat, and prepared to follow Wynn.

Wynn turned to me then. "I would like you to do the same here, Elizabeth, as you find time. It's important to know exactly what we have to work with."

I nodded. It all seemed so serious.

After the menfolk had left, I turned to Nimmie and Katherine. "Why don't you try to get a little sleep?" I asked them. "You both really look all in."

"I'll help you with your inventory," offered Nimmie.

"No. No—it won't take me long. There really isn't that much to count. You get some rest."

Nimmie was still hesitant, but I insisted. Finally she was persuaded, and she and Katherine went to our bedroom, removed their soiled outer garments and soon were fast asleep.

I did up the dishes and straightened the small room again; and then, notebook and pencil in hand, I began to do as Wynn had suggested.

I counted everything—each cupful of flour, each tablespoon of tea. I sorted and counted every can of tinned food. I measured the salt and the sugar, the coffee, and the beans and rice. Every bit of my kitchen supply and then my storeroom was measured and recorded.

At first it seemed to me to be quite a lot; and then I began to think of the number of days until the supplies could be replenished, and I realized it was not very much. Mr. McLain was right. We were going to be awfully short of food supplies before this winter was over.

With a sinking heart, I returned to the kitchen. It would take very careful planning to make things stretch.

Now late afternoon, Wynn and Mr. McLain had been gone for a number of hours. I looked out the window nervously, willing them to return.

Nimmie came out of the bedroom looking rested. "Elizabeth," she said, "may I borrow your snowshoes?"

"Of course, but are you sure you are ready—?"

"I'm ready," she said with a soft smile. "I will even welcome the exercise and the healing of nature's breath."

"They are right outside the door," I told her. *I could use some of nature's restoring breath myself,* I noted in understanding.

Wynn and Mr. McLain returned before Nimmie. They did not have good news. The tabulation of food in the village was listed on two short pages. The Indians had come to rely more and more heavily on the trading post and did not store food ahead except for the roots and herbs they carried in and the berries they dried. By now, these too were in short supply.

The future looked even more bleak than it had before the survey. *Lord, please send an early spring.*

When it was dark and Nimmie had still not returned, I was becoming concerned. I didn't like to mention my fear because I knew Mr. McLain and Wynn already had enough on their minds. Stealthily I watched out the window. I wished I had suggested she take Kip with her.

Mr. McLain stopped what he was saying to Wynn in mid-sentence and turned to me. "If you are worried about Nimmie," he said, having caught me glancing out of the window again, "don't be. Nimmie is as at home in those woods as she was in her kitchen. Whether it's dark or light, Nimmie is in no danger."

I flushed slightly. "I do wish she'd come," I said rather apologetically.

Katherine came from the bedroom, also looking much better after her nap.

"I've nearly slept the day away," she confessed. "I'm sorry. I meant to be up to help you much sooner, but I just didn't wake up. You should have called me."

"I didn't have anything I needed help with," I assured her. "And, besides, you needed the sleep."

We prepared a meal. Katherine set out the plates and cutlery on the table. Because our table was small and we had only two chairs, we would fill our plates and sit about the room.

We were almost ready to eat when we heard Nimmie. I heaved a sigh of relief. When we opened the door to her, she entered the room almost hidden under spruce branches. How she had ever managed to load herself down so was beyond me. She smiled out from under the load, and Mr. McLain helped her to lay aside her bundles.

We ate together and then Nimmie disappeared again. When she returned, she had managed to get some furs from somewhere. With these at hand, she began to make a bed at one end of the room Wynn used for his office.

Wynn led our little group in prayer, and we all retired early. It had been a long, exhausting day, and there didn't seem to be anything more we could do to improve the situation at present. We would have to take our future one day at a time.

Chapter Thirty

Making Do

During the next few days, Wynn called for a meeting of all the people. They gathered together in front of the pile of rubble that had so recently been the source for the lifeblood of the settlement, anxious eyes surveying the pile of debris. Even the litter, as it had been poked and raked following the fire, had brought forth very little of use in the settlement.

Wynn stood before the people and spoke to them in their language. Nimmie, standing beside me with her head held high, whispered the translation.

"We meet together because we are one. We must care for one another. We have lost the trading post and the food it supplied. Now we must find our own way. It is not a new way. It has been done for many moons by our fathers. But it is a hard way. It will take us all working together.

"You have some flour and salt for bannock. You should watch your supply closely and use only a little every day. It can last for many days if you use it sparingly.

"We have the forests and the streams. They will not forsake us. They have meat for the taking. We will hunt together and share what we find.

"We have plants that can be gathered from under the snow. You know them well. We will send out groups to gather them. Those who stay behind will care for the fires.

"We have traps and snares if we run out of ammunition for our guns, so we will not starve.

"We have medicines if we become sick, so do not be afraid.

"And, most importantly, we have a God who sees us and knows that we are in need. He has promised to care for His children.

"We will live, and we will make it to the time of the flowing of the rivers, and the stirring of the new leaf upon the tree and the gathering of the wild greens."

I felt like we all should have cheered such a speech; but when Wynn had finished speaking, the people of the village filed away—silently. Yet their shoulders had lifted a little and the look of despair upon their faces had been replaced with silent acceptance and even a glimmer of hope.

Now, Wynn was hardly ever home. He organized hunting parties, carefully distributing counted shells to the sharpest marksmen. He sent out fishing parties to cut holes in the ice and spend silent, long, cold hours at the task of bringing home fish. He sent older women, bundled against the cold, into the forests with baskets to dig for edibles among the roots of trees, while the younger women were assigned neighbor's fires to tend besides their own. Children took on new responsibilities as baby tenders and firewood gatherers. All the village was called upon to work together. Even the ones who were too old and feeble to be actively engaged had a part. They stirred the pots and kept the home fires fed while others were busy with their tasks.

A previously empty cabin was repaired sufficiently for the family who had lost their home in the fire, and life in the village went on.

Some of the outlying trappers, who had seen the terrifying red glow in the sky on the night of the fire, came home to check on family. They stood with heads lowered as they realized what the disaster meant to the entire population of the village. I think they too must have been praying, in their own way, for an early spring.

Nimmie and I were alone a few days later. I knew she must be very sorrowful about losing her lovely home with all the beautiful handwork from her past. She admitted that it "made her heart sore," but she was able to smile in spite of it all.

"I still have Ian," she said with great feeling. "If I had lost him, then all would have been lost."

I thought of Wynn, and I understood what Nimmie was saying.

"I've been doing a lot of thinking," said Nimmie slowly. "Maybe this was God's punishment for my sin."

I wanted to protest, but I wasn't sure what to say.

Nimmie went on. "And then I thought, 'No, I think not.' You see, I was a sinner long before I brought the knife to Crazy Mary. I understand something now that I didn't understand before. I did not become sinful because I took in the knife, but rather I consented to take the knife because I was sinful. Do you understand me, Elizabeth?"

I nodded slowly. I did understand and I agreed.

"I have been a sinner for a long time. I just did not know about it. Oh, I knew that I had an unhappiness, a pain in my heart that twisted at times and brought me grief and shame, but I didn't know why or what it was.

"The pain is gone now. Even after the fire, I have peace. If God had been punishing me, then I wouldn't feel Him with me as I do now, as I did as I watched the fire burn away everything that had ever been mine. No, He was not punishing; but perhaps He is putting me through the testing ritual to see if I am going to be strong."

I nodded again. It seemed that Nimmie had it all sorted out. Tears filled my eyes. She was strong, our Nimmie.

"Ian and I talked long last night," Nimmie paused. "We are going to go away."

My mouth opened to protest and I reached a hand for her arm.

"We will be back," Nimmie informed me quickly. "We will be back as soon as the crows are back. We will build the trading post again as soon as wood can be hauled from the forest. And we will bring supplies back to the people."

Relieved to hear that they would be back, I still didn't understand why they felt they should go.

"Ian has much to do, to make plans for the new building," Nimmie explained. "He has to arrange for supplies to be shipped in as soon as the rivers are free of ice. We will be very busy. The time will go quickly. Ian is even going to show me the big cities that I have read about." Nimmie's face took on a glow. For a moment, I wished I could go with her; and then I quickly thought of Wynn, and any desire to leave Beaver River left me.

"Besides," said Nimmie matter-of-factly, "the supplies are low—even the supplies in *your* home. If we go soon, that will mean less people to feed and more life for the village."

"What about Katherine?"

"Ian is going to ask her what she wishes. We are sure that she will go with us."

There just seemed to be one question left to ask. "When will you go?"

"Tomorrow. Tomorrow as soon as the sun is in the sky."

Katherine did choose to go with them. They had very little to take. Mr. McLain still had his good team of sled dogs and his sled. They had no clothing to pack and no provisions except what they were given. Wynn made sure they had a good rifle and some shells. Villagers came shyly forward as the McLains prepared for travel and offered love gifts of food or clothing or traps. I knew that the people desperately needed the things they were giving away, yet so did the McLains. The gifts were not refused because it would have caused offense to the givers. They were given in love, and they were accepted in love.

At last the sled was loaded, the team harnessed, and the travelers were ready for the trail.

At the last minute, Nimmie drew me aside. I wasn't sure I would be able to talk to her without weeping.

"I have a wonderful secret," she said, her eyes shining, "and I wanted to share it with you before leaving.

"I am going to have a baby. Just think—after ten years of marriage, I am going to have a baby!"

"Oh, Nimmie," was all I could say, and I took her in my arms and cried all over her fur parka.

I was the only one in tears, for the Indian people expressed themselves in other ways. I knew their hearts were heavy, too. It was hard to see our friends go. It was hard to turn them over to the elements and the winter. I prayed that they would arrive safely. If anyone knew how to handle the rigors of the trail, it was the McLains. Nimmie had come from the forest, and Mr. McLain himself had spent many years working a trapline before becoming manager of the store. They would know what to do in all circumstances.

It would be hard for Katherine. She had not trained herself for the ways of the North. The trip would be long and difficult and very taxing. I prayed that God would help her.

And Nimmie. The little mother-to-be. The excited little mother. I prayed with all of my heart that things would go well for her and God would protect her unborn child.

I stood and watched them disappear over the whiteness of the hill outside our settlement, a final wave to us, our last glimpse of them. And then I placed a hand on Kip's furry head and started back to the cabin, the tears blurring my vision. I knew Wynn was watching me, making sure I would be all right.

Chapter Thirty-one

A Watchful Eye

"Isn't there any way I can help?" I asked Wynn.

He had been working almost day and night ever since the fire in order to make sure the settlement had food. I had been doing nothing—except ache for Nimmie.

"There is, Elizabeth. A very important way," Wynn informed me. "I would like you to keep a sharp eye on all the families for sickness. I think we'll pull through this winter just fine if we don't run into some kind of epidemic. The only way I see to prevent that from happening is to detect early anyone with symptoms and try to isolate them from the rest."

"So what do you want me to do?" I questioned. I certainly wasn't a nurse, nor did I have medical knowledge of any kind.

"Just visit the homes. Go around as much as you find the time to do so. Keep your eyes and ears open for any coughs or fevers or symptoms of any kind. Note the cabin and I will take it from there."

That didn't sound too difficult.

"How is it going, Wynn? I mean *really*?" I asked him.

He looked at me, and I knew I was going to get an honest answer. "It isn't good. We are managing so far to keep food in the cabins, but the real value of a little meat boiled with a few roots leaves much to be desired. Still, we will make it if we can just keep sickness away. Everyone is cooperating well, so far. If we can keep up the morale and keep them from giving up, we'll be all right."

"Surely it won't be much longer," I said hopefully.

"Until the snow goes—no. Maybe not. But, when the snow goes, the rest of the men will be back. True, that will be more men to hunt and fish, but it will also be more mouths to feed.

And it will still be several weeks after that before the forests and fields start to bear fruit."

Wynn drew me close and held me for several minutes before he left to resume his duties of another exhausting, long day.

I went to work on the dishes and cleanup. Since the fire, I no longer threw out tea leaves or coffee grounds after one use. Instead, I dried them and put them in a container to be used again. I saved any leftovers of our food as well, no matter how small the portion. It could be used in some way. Our meals were skimpy enough and were carefully portioned out. Meat had become our main staple as well, with only small servings of any tinned vegetables to complement it. Desserts were now only a dim memory. The nearest we came was to sprinkle a small amount of sugar on an occasional slice of bread. The bread was rationed as well. We allowed ourselves only one slice per day, and sometimes I cut those very sparingly, though I tried to make Wynn's a little thicker than mine—not too much different or he would notice and gently scold me.

I had been so happy for Nimmie when she told me of her coming baby. I had been longing for a baby of our own. Wynn and I had talked about it many times. Each month I had hoped with all my heart that God might decide to bless us; but now I found myself thanking God that I was not carrying a child. Our diet simply was not good enough to be nourishing a coming baby.

I'll wait, God, I prayed now. *I'll wait.*

As soon as my tasks were completed, I donned my coat and mittens and went out. We were now in April. Surely I wouldn't need heavy clothing much longer.

I visited several of the homes that morning. At each home I had to insist to the hostess, "No tea. No tea," and rub my stomach as though the tea would not agree with me. I did not want them to use any of their meager supply each time I came to call in the days ahead.

Many of these women I knew by name. They had learned to trust me, though they must have been wondering why I had nothing better to do than to wander around the settlement while everybody else was busy working. I kept close watch for anything that looked like potential trouble. At first, there was nothing more than one or two runny noses. I mentally noted them, just in case Wynn would want to check them out.

In the Arbus cabin, one of the children was coughing, a nasty sounding one that brought fear to my heart. *Please, not whooping cough,* I prayed silently and told Anna to be sure to keep him in and away from other children until Wynn saw him.

"But he get wood," said Anna. "His job."

"Not today. I will help with wood today. You keep him in by the fire."

Anna was surprised at what I said and the conviction with which I said it, but she did not argue further. I was *Mrs. Sergeant* and should be listened to.

I went for wood as I had promised. It was not an easy job. The snow was deep and the axes dull. It was hard for me to walk in snowshoes and carry wood on my back. I was not nearly as skilled as the Indian children. I had to make extra trips to get a pile as high as the others, and by the time I was finished, it was getting dark and I knew Wynn would soon be home. I had not made the full rounds of the cabins, but I would finish the rest the next day.

When Wynn returned home, I reported what I had found. "Good work," he said. "I'd better check them out."

"Why don't you wait until after you have eaten?" I suggested, "and I will go with you."

Wynn agreed and we ate our simple meal.

We walked over the crunching snow together in the moonlight, long shadows playing about us. From the cabins surrounding the little clearing, soft light flickered on the billowy banks of snow.

"It's pretty at night, isn't it?" I said to Wynn.

"But not pretty in the daytime?" Wynn prompted.

"Oh, I didn't mean that—not really. It's just—that—well, in the daytime all of the gloom and grime of the tragedy shows up, too. Some days," I went on, "I wish it would snow ten feet just to bury that terrible reminder heaped up there in the village."

"It's not a pretty sight, is it? But I thought you were very anxious for the snow to go."

"I am. I don't really mind the snow itself—it is pretty and I have enjoyed it—walking in it, looking at it. It's the wind I hate. I can't stand the wind. It just sends chills all through me. It seems so—so—vengeful somehow. I hate it!"

Wynn reached over to take my hand and pull me up against him as we continued to walk.

"I wish you could learn to appreciate the wind, Elizabeth. God made the wind, too. It has many purposes and it is part of our world. You will never be really at peace here until you have made friends with the wind. Try to understand it—to find beauty in it."

He pulled me to a stop. "Look, over there. See that snow-bank? Notice the way the top peaks and drops over in a curve—the velvet softness of the purple shadow created by the glow of the moon. See how beautiful it is."

Wynn was right.

He continued to point out other wind sculptures around the clearing. I laughed.

"All right," I assured him. "I will try to find beauty in the wind."

"Its greatest beauty is its song," Wynn continued. "I still haven't had the opportunity to take you out camping under the stars, but when spring comes we'll do that. We'll camp at a spot where we can lie at night and hear the windsong in the spruce trees. It's a delightful sound."

"I'll remember that promise," I told Wynn.

We were at the first cabin. Wynn looked carefully at the throat of the child and felt for fever. There didn't seem to be any cause for alarm here, but he did give the mother a little bit of medication, telling her to give one spoonful every morning. She nodded in agreement and we went on to the next cabin.

Again we found no cause for concern. Wynn didn't even leave medicine with the family. He told me to keep an eye on the child during the next few days.

When we reached the third cabin, we could hear the coughing even before we got to the door. Wynn stopped and listened carefully.

"You're right," he said. "I don't like the sound of that at all." Whooping cough was one of the dreaded killers of the North.

"Do we have medication?" I asked Wynn, counting on the worst.

"Not nearly enough if it turns out to be whooping cough," he said quietly.

We went in then and Wynn did a thorough examination of the throat, chest, and ears of the child, with the little equipment he had.

"How long has he been coughing?" he asked Anna.

"Two," she said.

"His cough is bad, Anna. I want you to keep him in. And keep the other children away from him if you can. Wash any of his dishes in hot, hot water. Let them sit in the water and steam. Give him this medicine—once when the sun comes up, once when it is high in the sky, and once when the sun goes down. You understand?"

"Understand," said Anna.

Wynn repeated all his directions in her native tongue to be sure Anna had fully understood.

"Understand," she said again.

"Mrs. Delaney will be back tomorrow to see how he is feeling."

"Beth come," she said with satisfaction. I felt a warm glow to hear her use my given name.

"Is there any way to get more medicine?" I asked Wynn on the way home.

"Not in time. We would have to send someone out and then have him bring it back. By that time half of the town could be infected."

"What will we do?"

"We'll just have to wait, Elizabeth, and hope that we are wrong. Wait—and pray."

Chapter Thirty-two

Traps

Now that my days were more than full, I had little time for Kip. I knew he needed his exercise, so I was forced to let him out to run on his own. I hated to do it, but he always returned home again before too much time elapsed.

One night he came in with marks on his fluffy long coat. I pulled him close and looked at him. There was a tuft of hair hanging from the corner of his lip. I pulled it out and looked at it, puzzling over what it meant.

"Looks like he's been in a little scrap," Wynn remarked as though it was of no consequence.

"Do you think so?" I asked in alarm, remembering the mean-looking Buck.

"He doesn't look much the worse for it," Wynn responded. "I'm guessing he came out top dog."

I brushed at Kip's coat. I could feel no injuries and he certainly didn't appear to be in any pain. In fact, he looked rather pleased about something.

"What will I do with him?" I asked Wynn.

"What do you mean?"

"Well, I don't have time to take him for his walks, and he can't be shut up in here all day."

"I think he will look after himself just fine."

"But what if he meets Buck? The last time, he submitted to Buck; but, if he's fighting other dogs now, he might try to fight Buck, too."

Wynn grinned. "Someone has to bring that big bully down to size."

"Oh, Wynn," I cried. "This isn't funny. He could be hurt!"

Wynn, more serious then, apologized. "I'm sorry. I didn't

mean to make fun of your concern. You're right. There is the possibility of Kip getting hurt. But it's more probable that he will come out the victor. Kip didn't meet Buck's challenge last time because he knew he wasn't ready. That's a smart dog. If he does decide to take him on, it will be because he thinks he is ready. Now no one knows whether he is or not. We just have to trust Kip's instincts, that's all.

"Kip has a number of advantages over Buck. He's a little heavier. He has had better nutrition. He is younger and more agile, and I believe that he's much smarter. If it should come to a fight, I think Kip has a good chance."

Well, a good chance wasn't good enough for me. I wanted to be sure. What I really wanted was for Kip to stay out of the ring completely, but it didn't look like I was going to be able to avoid it much longer.

"You behave yourself," I warned Kip, shaking my finger at him, "or I'll—I'll tie you up."

In making the rounds of the cabins, I found a few more sniffles but no more bad coughs. Anna's small boy was not getting any worse. In fact, the medicine seemed to be working. His cough was gradually getting better. Anna beamed. None of the other children had developed the cough. I was sure that she, too, had thought of the dreaded whooping cough—she likely knew the symptoms much better than I.

The sun's rays warmed the air a bit more each day. I found myself frequently pushing back my parka and even unbuttoning my coat. The drifts were getting smaller and the wind did not have the same chill. We were now into the middle of April. *Spring must be just around the corner!* I exulted.

"How would you like a day off?" Wynn surprised me one morning. I looked up from cutting the thin slices of bread.

"I'd love it. What do you have in mind?"

"I need to make a call on a cabin about two miles from the settlement. I thought that, seeing you have been doing such a good job at being camp nurse, you might like to come along."

"I'd love to!" was my enthusiastic response.

"The snow is getting a little thin in places. We won't be using the sled much more this year." That was good news too.

"When should I be ready?" I asked Wynn.

"In about half an hour."

"I'll be waiting. Can I bring Kip for a run as well?"

"Sure. Bring Kip. Just keep him away from the sled dogs. To them, Kip is a stranger and a threat."

I was sure I wouldn't have any trouble with that. Kip was obedient and heeled whenever he was told to do so.

I hummed as I went about getting ready to go. *It's so nice to have this kind of outing! A whole day with Wynn!* The sun was shining. Soon our winter would be over and our world would change again. Nimmie would be coming back. The new trading post would be built. Our people would have proper food and supplies again. The world seemed good.

"Thank you, God," I whispered. "Thank you for seeing us through."

Wynn was soon there with the sled. Calling Kip to heel, I went out to join him. It was a wonderful day as promised. Wynn made his call and checked the man who had been reported ill in his cabin. Wynn carried wood and water in and made sure he had the necessary supplies. He gave him medicine to take for a few days and told him he would be back to see him in a couple of days. The man didn't appear to be seriously ill, just down with the flu; so we left him and started our return trip.

We were about halfway home when a terrible cry rent the stillness of the sun-filled day. I stopped in my tracks, my skin prickling.

"What was it?" I asked Wynn, who had stopped the team and drawn up beside me.

"I'd better check," he said and reached for his rifle. The piercing cry came again.

"You wait here," said Wynn. "I won't be long. It must be an animal in a trap."

I sat down, my back to the direction Wynn was taking, trying to blot out the awful sound. I watched the sled dogs. They lay on the hard-packed snow, their heads on their paws or else licking the icy snow from between their toes. They seemed oblivious to the whole thing, only appreciative of the chance to rest.

I thought of Kip then. I momentarily had forgotten about Kip. I turned to look for him now.

He was disappearing just around the clump of trees where Wynn had gone. I thought of Wynn and his rifle. What if he had to shoot and didn't know that Kip was there and Kip got in the way?

"Kip!" I cried, springing up. "Kip, get back here!"

I ran after the dog, puffing my way through the snow. It was not far. I soon found Kip and I soon found Wynn.

And then I saw it. Lying on the ground, which was covered with blood, was a small furry animal. His foot was secured in the trap, his eyes were big and pleading, and his leg—his leg—. And Wynn was swinging the butt of his rifle.

I couldn't look. I gave a little cry and turned away. Wynn's head came up quickly and he came to me.

"Elizabeth," he said, taking me into his arms and turning my head away from the awful sight, "I asked you to stay—"

"But Kip—he ran. I didn't see him until—"

Wynn held me. I started to cry and to shake. "The poor little animal," I kept sobbing. "The poor little thing."

Wynn let me cry.

"Oh, Wynn," I wept, "it's so awful."

"Yes," he agreed, "it's awful."

"You killed him?"

"I had to, Elizabeth. You saw how badly hurt he was."

"Couldn't you have let him go?"

"He was in a man's trap. And even if he had gotten away, he would have died—"

"It's terrible." I began to cry again. "Can't you stop it, Wynn? Can't you tell them not to do it anymore? You're the law; they'll listen to you."

Wynn gave me a little shake to stop my hysteria and to bring some sense to my head. "I can't stop trapping. You know I can't. Trapping is their way of life. Their livelihood. If they didn't have furs, they wouldn't have anything. I know it's cruel. I hate it, too, but it's part of life. One that we just have to accept."

I knew Wynn was right. I tried to stop crying. I thought of

all the families back at the settlement. The furs for trading was the only way they had to buy their needed supplies.

I hated it, but I too would have to learn to live with it. *Yet surely, surely there must be a more humane way,* my heart told me.

I was sorry that our one day out together for so many long weeks had been spoiled. I tried to make it up to Wynn. I would not fuss further and I would not speak of it again. There wasn't any way I could prepare Wynn a special dinner, but at least I could be good company in the little time we had left. I planned a night before the fireplace, reading one of our favorite books.

When Wynn returned from settling the team, weary from the duties of the day, I told him about my plans. He grinned and lifted my face to kiss me on the nose.

"Sounds good to me."

We had just settled ourselves, and I was taking the first turn of reading aloud, while Wynn lay with his head in my lap. A commotion at the door made me jump and Wynn hollered. Fortunately, the book in his face had done no damage.

We answered our door to find one man with another man over his shoulder.

"Leg," he informed us and carried the man in and dumped him rather unceremoniously on the rug before the fire.

The injured man groaned in pain. Wynn knelt down beside him and began to feel the leg.

"It's broken," he said quietly. "We'll have to set it. At least the skin isn't broken. It's not too bad a break. No splinters or torn muscle or ligaments."

Wynn continued to feel the leg, and the man on the floor continued to groan.

"This isn't going to be nice," Wynn said to me. "Do you want to take a walk?"

"Do you need me?"

"I could use you—but I won't ask you to stay."

"I think—I think I can manage."

"Good girl." Then Wynn turned to the man who had carried the fellow in. "How did this happen?"

"Fall."

"How long ago?"

" 'Bout hour."

"Let's get him on the cot."

They lifted him together and Wynn went for his medical supplies. He poured some strong-smelling stuff on a small cloth and gave it to me.

"I want you to stand here and hold this to his nose and mouth. Like this. Wait until we are ready to set the leg. Don't hold it there for too long. I'll tell you when to let him breathe it and when to move it away."

I moved in by the man, the cloth in my hand, ready to follow Wynn's instructions. I didn't watch. I was too busy with the face before me and the cloth that I held. In spite of my ministration, the man still moaned and tried to throw himself off the cot. The other man was called over to hold him. At last the ordeal was over and Wynn tied the leg securely in a makeshift splint.

"Go get one of your friends," Wynn said to the trapper, "and you can take him to his cabin."

Wynn's forehead was wet with perspiration. He brushed back the wave of hair that had fallen forward. He moved to the man on the cot and reached down to him with a gentle hand.

"It'll be all right, Strong Buck," he said assuringly. "It's all over now. They will take you to your own bed. I will give you good medicine for the pain."

The man nodded. The worst of it was over. Wynn brought the tablet and the water and he swallowed it gratefully.

The men were soon back and carefully carried their companion to his own home to be welcomed by an anxious wife.

Wynn turned back to the fire and then looked at me and smiled.

"Where is that nice, quiet evening you had arranged, Elizabeth?" he asked me.

I crossed to him and put my arms around his neck.

"Is there *anything* you can't do?" I asked him with admiration in my voice. "You deliver babies, sew up ugly cuts, set broken bones, pull infected teeth, act as doctor to the sick, feed the whole village. Is there anything that you can't do?" I repeated.

Wynn kissed me. He smiled that slow, easy smile I had learned to love.

"Now, Elizabeth," he said teasingly. "Do you think I would be so silly as to confess?"

Chapter Thirty-three

Spring

Though we did not hear from the McLains, I began to watch for them. "As soon as the river thaws," or "as soon as the logs can be brought from the forests," was not too definite a time for their return. Well, the river was running again now and the forests were losing their snow quickly. I began to watch and to hope.

"I'll be back in time to plant my garden," Nimmie had said. "We will plant a garden together."

I was anxious for that garden. I was even more anxious for Nimmie. I thought, too, of Katherine. Would she be back too? Poor Katherine! She had faced so much in life, but she had lost so much of life by her own choosing. I was so glad she seemed finally able to start picking up the pieces again.

I wondered about Nimmie's coming baby. This was not a convenient time to be on the long, difficult trail out from Edmonton. I remembered the trip well. But then Nimmie was at home with the woods and the river. She no doubt would be a better traveler than I had been. I had watched for the first bluebird when at home in Toronto. I had watched for the first song of the robin. I had waited expectantly for the sight of the first spring crocus. I had relished the day when I saw my first dainty violet. But now I was watching and waiting for Nimmie. With Nimmie's arrival, I would know that it was really spring. With the coming of Nimmie and Ian, new life would be given to the dreary, winter-weary little settlement.

Heavy parkas were put away now. Children played out again in cotton dresses and flannel shirts. Women went to the woods with baskets on their arms, hoping to find some early spring greens. Men came back from traplines and turned their attention from trapping furs to tanning the furs. Smoke still lazily drifted from the fires in the cabins, but at times they were allowed to die out. Their warmth wasn't needed through all of the days.

There was a new feeling in the settlement, a feeling of being released after a long confinement. But still, I held apart, breathless, waiting.

Was it really spring, or might another biting north wind bring in the snow again? I hardly dared to hope.

And then it happened. A man rode excitedly into camp, his horse breathing heavily. He cried out in broken English, "They come. Many wagons."

Everyone came from their cabins.

"Where? Where?"

He began to talk to them in their own language then, and I was about to explode with my question.

I ran among the people until I found Wynn.

"Is it them?" I asked him.

"It's them," he assured me, grinning. "With many wagons of supplies."

"How far away are they?"

"About five miles."

Five miles. That still seemed too far. I could hardly wait. It would seem forever. "I'll go get them some supper," I said, about to bolt off.

Wynn caught my hand. "Hold it," he said, laughing. "They won't be here for an hour or so."

At my look of disappointment, he hurried on.

"I was wondering if you'd like to go out to meet them."

"Oh, yes!" I cried.

"Grab a sweater. It might be getting cool before we get back."

I ran for the sweater, my skirts whipping about my legs. I lifted them up so that I might run faster. *They're here!* Well, they were *almost* here. They were coming.

I hurried back to Wynn. "Let's go," I said, already out of breath.

He took my arm and slowed me down. "If we have a few miles to walk, you'd better slow down. You'll never make it at that pace."

He was right. I slowed down, and the people of the village began to fall into step behind us. They came, the mothers carrying babies and the fathers hoisting young ones on their shoulders. Even the old, who needed the assistance of a walking stick, tottered on at a slower pace. The whole village was going out to meet the trader and his Indian wife.

We walked along as swiftly as Wynn would allow. I breathed deeply of the fresh tangy air. It was still cool but it smelled of growing things, I thought. Or was it just my imagination?

"Do you think spring is really here?" I asked Wynn.

"I think so."

"What signs do you go by?" I persisted.

"The river is almost ice free."

I nodded my head in assent.

"The snow is almost all gone."

I nodded again.

"It's warmer," continued Wynn. "And I've seen several flocks of Canada geese pass over."

He waited. "Do you need more?"

I swatted at my cheek. "The mosquitoes are back," I said ruefully.

"There," said Wynn. "You have one more assurance. Spring is here all right." We laughed together.

Kip frolicked on ahead of us, sniffing at rabbit dens and barking at saucy squirrels. I laughed at him.

"I think he's excited, too," I said to Wynn.

Wynn took my hand.

"This winter has been hard for you, hasn't it, Elizabeth?"

"It's been hard for everyone," I answered honestly.

"But the rest—they are used to the hardships. You haven't been. Has it—has it been too much?"

"I admit I will be very glad for a fresh carrot. And I will admit I will be glad for a piece of cake. I will even admit that spinach, which I hate, might taste good. But I am not sorry that I came with you, Wynn."

Wynn stopped me and pushed back my hair and kissed me. He looked deeply into my eyes.

"I'm glad to hear you say that, Elizabeth. I have something to say, too. Something I maybe should have said long ago, but

I want to say now, with all my heart—with all my love. I'm proud of you, Elizabeth. Proud of your strength, your support, your ability to adjust to hard things. You've been my help, my support, my right arm, Elizabeth. I don't know what I ever would have done without you. You've more than proved me wrong—over and over. You belong here—with me."

Wynn kissed me again, and I brushed away happy tears and lifted my face again to his.

And then I heard the grinding of the wagon wheels. They were coming. Just over the hill was Nimmie. Just over the hill were the needed supplies—and hope. My heart gave a lurch in its happiness. I gave Wynn one more kiss with all my love wrapped up in it, and I turned to meet the oncoming wagon.

Spring had come.

JANETTE OKE
PRAIRIE LOVE STORIES